THE DIGITAL DETECTIVE: DARK WEB DESCENT

by

Tom Arnold

Illustrations by

Gary Trousdale

Cloud 10 Studios, LLC for young audiences

Las Vegas, NV and Dallas, TX

Summary: A couple of first-year 9th-graders discover an organized crime gang attacking students with sextortion and kidnapping for human trafficking. The plot and story are designed to help educate and raise awareness of young adults about the growing problems caused by deep fakes and online attacks. Enjoy.

Category: Young Adult Novel

Published by:

Cloud 10 Studios, LLC

ISBN: (ebook) 979-8-9954540-1-4

ISBN: (paperback) 979-8-9954540-2-1

Cover design by: Tracey Dispensa

Printed in United States of America

ABOUT THE AUTHOR

Tom Arnold is an American novelist, cybersecurity professional, digital forensics professor and former CTO (Chief Technology Officer) for technology companies PSC and CyberSource Corp.

Tom leverages his background in information technology and cybersecurity to create fictional stories with real-world examples of cybersecurity incidents. His current book series, The Digital Detective, is written for young adults to share compelling stories with relevant educational opportunities in hacking and digital scams.

Beyond the novels, Tom has been directly involved in investigating and resolving security breach cases involving unauthorized access to computer systems and cloud environments. He has been the lead investigator on large breaches where environments spanned over 7,000 servers and involved complex threat hunting to find the adversary. Tom has provided consulting to the US Secret Service, policy guidance to the US government and regulatory agencies, and is on the steering committee for the Las Vegas branch of the USSS/Cyber Fraud Task Force. He also delivered expert testimony to the US Senate and House of

Representatives on the proposed SAFE and Export
Administration Acts.

ABOUT THE ILLUSTRATOR

Gary Trousdale is an American animator, film director, screenwriter and storyboard artist. He is best known for directing films such as Disney's *Beauty and the Beast* (1991), *The Hunchback of Notre Dame* (1996), and *Atlantis: The Lost Empire* (2001).

In 2003, Gary moved to DreamWorks Animation where he went on to direct *The Madagascar Penguins in a Christmas Caper* (2005), *Shrek the Halls* (2007), and *Scared Shrekless* (2010) (the latter two being holiday TV specials for ABC), and a 12-minute short featuring Rocky and Bullwinkle (2014).

Currently, Gary is working for Cloud 10 Studios with DreamWorks alumni and founder, Tracey Dispensa. He is directing the upcoming projects: *The Greatest Gift* and *Surviving April*.

Gary continues to write and design stories for TV and feature animation and is now adding book illustrations to his repertoire.

DEDICATIONS

This book is dedicated to my wife and family who stood by and supported me during long hours writing. I must pay special thanks to Tracey Dispensa for her fabulous cover art; Gary Trousdale for his direction and excellent illustrations in each chapter; Alexis Scott for her editing and review of the story; Michael Baes for his guidance; and the wonderful people at Atlas Publishing. Lastly, there's a plethora of digital forensics and cybersecurity people, especially William Powell and Greg Moody. Lastly, a special shoutout to Victoria Kirchenberger for bringing light on the nasty subject of human trafficking.

1. FLIPPER PRINTS IN THE SAND

It's one of those gorgeous sunny mornings on a Caribbean island. A neighbor's rooster crowed at five AM, and I'm up. The damn birds wandered around and never seemed to sleep much. A pot of coffee was in order. I pushed the French press plunger down just as the rooster crowed again, and my shoulder and collarbone ached. Not bad enough for pain pills today, but maybe I'll swim in the warm waters just off my front door.

My name is Jason Palmer, and the constant throb and sling that I had to wear reminded me of the occurrence in Bulgaria that brought me here. I'm on forced leave from the National Security Agency. It's been almost a week since I last heard from my boss or anyone at the agency. The memory of my closest childhood friend, Reba, as she rescued me from the sealed basement where a gang had lashed me to a chair and beat me until my collarbone snapped. I remember vividly the image of Reba kicking through the door flanked by two-armed soldiers. She wore urban fatigues, a helmet and goggles. I knew it was her. Moments before she jammed a metal syringe into my thigh, I now remembered her whispering "Oh, JP, what have you gotten into now?" Then darkness.

Two weeks in an Army hospital in Germany, then I get a phone call from the boss I call "she who must be followed" telling me that I was on a forced leave. Even though I explained that the lead I had followed to

Bulgaria was solid and that real field agents should have been dispatched didn't matter to her. I was to remain entirely off-the-grid until I heard back from her or someone more senior. I asked to speak to Reba, but that request fell on deaf ears. She would not allow any contact. The Agency had all my evidence and the data that I'd derived from mobile communications. The Agency would handle everything now. Technical surveillance didn't matter, I thought.

My coffee was ready. Dark and strong Costa Rican Arabica that I'd imported as beans a month ago and kept in my cottage's freezer. It was a strong roast that I truly loved with hints of spice and probably apples that grew near the plantation. As I walked toward the door, my eyes strayed to a box containing all of my old case journals that I'd pulled from the rafters. My first-ever case journal sat on top of the box. This was where Reba and I had first encountered Lesta Andropov and the gang that I'd traced to

Bulgaria. I picked up the journal and set it back in the box as I saw a journal with the words "Dark Web" on the cover. I hadn't looked at this journal in many years. I didn't need to open the cover as it brought back real sour memories. I picked it out of the box. This was a journal worth reading while I recovered.

I stepped outside with my coffee, feeling the warm sun rising in the east. The sand between my toes was cool. In a few hours, it would be piping hot to touch. I walked to a close lounge chair and tossed the journal onto the seat then set my coffee cup down after stealing a sip. Swim first, I thought.

I stepped toward the lapping sound of the tiny waves slapping the beach. The waves here were much more what might be found on the banks of a lake, not the sea. The Cayman Islands sat on a large shelf surrounded by a barrier reef. The waves broke far beyond the shelf and the water striking the island was just six- or eight-inch waves that lapped instead of crashing.

As I stepped into the warm waters, I caught sight of footprints leaving the sea. These were actually flipper prints left in the wake of a scuba or skin diver emerging from the sea. Diving in the Caribbean just beyond the natural shelf was a huge attraction. Divers from all over the world traveled to the Island to swim among the largest population of sea creatures in the world. But rarely did they come ashore and not here, for sure.

There were more prints. I followed them up from the beach for a few meters until they transformed into about size-8 feet. The tracks led right up to the path toward my cottage. The trail picked up on the other side of the path and toward my kitchen window, where they stopped. The two final prints were deeper in the sand than the ones while walking. After an unknown amount of time, the trail led back to the water's edge and disappeared.

I don't even have my normal

smartphone. The Agency kept that. But I do have a throwaway Android phone that hasn't been updated since version 11. Careful not to disturb the trail, I returned to the house and dug into a kitchen drawer recovering the old Samsung phone. Charger, I need a charger. This phone was dead as a brick. I only hoped that its battery would still hold some kind of charge. I was relieved when the phone's red light came on a few moments after plugging in.

I wasn't too worried about the neighbors or others marching over the tracks in the sand. My cottage sat at the end of a small gravel drive and was concealed by heavy vegetation of trees and undergrowth that only a few big, blue iguanas navigated.

Slipping on a sturdy pair of Sketchers, I walked around the perimeter of the 900 square foot cottage, looking down and at each window to see if there was any more evidence left by an intruder.

Halfway around, the landscape became hard crushed shale. There wouldn't be any tracks to follow here. The branches on the trees were not bent or broken.

SWOOSH. My heart stopped and I jumped back just as a great blue iguana scampered into my route and stopped. The large lizard craned its head looking at me. Now I'm the intruder in his home. "Man, you scared me," I said to the lizard as I rubbed my chest. My shoulder ached again. I didn't want to move or challenge the nearly five-foot-long animal. They have sharp teeth, and I wasn't too thrilled by the thought of a doctor's visit. I took a step back, and big blue scampered into the brush. I carried on circling around to the gravel drive that stopped a few feet from the back of the cottage. Nothing. Then around the other side of the house. No lizards, no footprints, nothing unusual.

I avoided stepping on the trail as I returned to the kitchen where the Samsung was plugged in. There's just enough power that the device started. Passcode. Now, what was the passcode to this old phone. I tried a 6-digit number combination. Fail. Oh, crumcakes.

What is it? I tried another. Failed again. If only I had access to my password vault that was on my laptop smashed by Lesta Andropov back in Bulgaria.

"Relax, JP," I said. More coffee and think. This phone dated back many years. I got it when I was just a kid and used it to practice forensic extraction. There's a backup in the cloud, but I have no way to access that. What would I have set the passcode to back when Reba and I were running around setting the world right?

This wasn't an important device and wasn't even connected to a real cell net anymore. I would have done something memorable. Throw away passcodes were set to names or titles. Books. Authors.

"Authors, that's it." I keyed in 3-6-9-5-3. The phone opened. "Elementary my dear Watson." The author's last name.

I went outside and activated the camera, snapping orientation photos and close ups of the prints that led the whole way up to my cottage. Once I had everything, I grabbed a sturdy metal rake that I kept in the porch utility closet. Just as a good golfer might rake a bunker, I raked the sand, obliterating the trail. Wiping the sweat from my brow, I looked skyward. The sun was higher and getting much hotter. Admiring my work, I looked back out over the water. Just beyond the edge of the shelf in the distance, a small dive boat rested at anchor in the deep waters. The red flag with a diagonal white stripe flew from the boat's top mast signaling that divers were beneath it. I snapped a picture of the dive boat as well. That boat wasn't there when I first came out of the house, so I doubted it was related to the tracks on the beach. But why would someone approach my house and stand at a window for a while, then return to the water?

My shoulder throbbed, induced probably

by my panic that I was being watched. And watched by someone very closely.

Someone brave enough to approach my house risking detection and capture. I have my Samsung. Now all I needed was a wireless camera. I'd then network both the phone and camera to my cottage Wi-Fi to detect them should they return. That will be this afternoon's run to a store in town.

I dropped back in my lounge chair tilting the umbrella to block the sun from my head and picked up the journal. Just the title neatly penned on the cover brought back a host of memories again.

Reba, or Rebecca Ng, was my closest friend back when we were freshmen in high school. My parents had moved to the US from Bristol, England when I met her. We got into quite an adventure taking on Lesta Andropov back then, but nothing compared to the Dark Web encounter that followed.

2. THE AUCTION BOOK

Early February admission to Pine Grove Alpha Academy in Woodside, CA was hardly normal. After our experiences with Lesta and Anton Andropov, Reba and I were moved from our public high school to this private prep academy. Neither family could afford such a school, but the US Department of Justice had deep pockets when they wanted to keep someone close. Last Wednesday, our parents dropped us off at school. We'd be boarding here in the student dorms.

"This is highly irregular," Mr. Hannah the

school's headmaster said as he greeted us at his office door. "The school has agreed to this mid-term admission based on the recommendation by our attorney."

We stepped in and sat around a large oak conference table. The Ng family, minus older daughter CaCee, and my family around the opposite side. Hannah sat at the end of the table in a tall leather chair.

"You both have a lot of catching up to do since you've missed almost a month of class," he said.

"Well, we bought them the texts for the core classes and have made them read at least the first five chapters," my dad remarked.

"Yes" Mrs. Ng, Reba's mom said. "They are both bright children. I'm sure they won't be disappointed. Right, Reba?"

Reba nodded. "I'm ready."

"How 'bout you, young man?" Hannah said, pointing at me.

"I'm ready to go and versed in several of

these topics."

"We shall see," Hannah's voice drifted off. "Now, Reba, I'm informed that you're quite the athlete and skilled in soccer."

Reba smiled and nodded.

"Since the season's almost over, I got a special dispensation from the conference to make you a late add to the varsity team. If you perform well, you'll get to play in our remaining games. Otherwise, think of it as a red-shirt year."

"Red shirt?" Stafford, my dad asked.

"It's more of a college term that means a non-playing member of the team. Kind of the practice squad, if you will."

"My Reba will be the best," Mrs. Ng added.

A knock at the door interrupted the discussion. A portly woman weighing a few stones beyond the anthropometric scale. Her woolen dress draped over broad hips and was partially covered by a down jacket that she unzipped as she stepped into the room.

"Let me introduce you both to Mrs. Fadler. She and her husband Howard live here on campus. They're on the first floor of the dorms and manage the residences."

"I'm in charge of enforcing the rules, which you both will learn very quickly."

Hannah pushed back from the table and stood. "So, if there are no questions?" He hardly waited for a breath before continuing. "Both families will deposit luggage at the doors of the dorm. Say your goodbyes, and that's that."

"We can't see the rooms?" Mrs. Ng said.

"Sorry. Rules are rules. Only resident students and staff permitted inside the dorm building." He snapped a quick smile, more of a grin. Then he walked back toward his desk. "Mrs. Fadler will take over now."

We left the administration building following Mrs. Fadler toward a long two-story residence hall that had a red tile roof and deep brown siding that looked almost like redwood tree bark.

Fadler stopped on the first step and told our parents to fetch the luggage and leave them on the first step. Mrs. Ng and my mum hugged each other, tears sliding down their cheeks. It was my first experience at boarding school. Reba's too. Our dads brought two suitcases and then we all hugged each other. "I'll see you on weekends," mum whispered in my ear after she kissed my cheek. "You be good and don't get into any trouble."

I nodded.

"At least don't get into trouble until after you call your dad, okay?"

"Yup," I said. I wanted to cry as well. I glanced at Reba. She maintained her strong discipline and just smiled back.

A lanky man dressed in stressed coveralls stepped from the building and grabbed our suitcases as we followed Mrs. Fadler through the main double doors. I couldn't help but stare at the perfect bald circle atop his head surrounded by wispy gray hairs.

He'd look just like a Franciscan monk if he wore dark robes instead of coveralls.

"The students are all in class now. Howard," Mrs. Fadler said to him, "Just drop the bags here." She looked back at us. "This is my husband. He takes care of the grounds and helps with security."

I looked around. The entry hall was just as I'd expect in some posh private house with a double staircase flanking the entrance hall and curved up to the next floor.

"Pay attention now." Mrs. Fadler continued. "On the right side are all the boys' rooms. Left side girls." She pointed at two doors beneath each staircase. "Upper classmen and women are on the first floor. Neither of you will be found on the first floor. Ever." She smiled at both Reba and me. "Common area is upstairs adjoining the two sections. This is open until 9 pm each day. After that, girls in girl's rooms and boys in theirs." Now she looked straight at me. "For that matter, no girls in boy rooms, got it?"

I nodded.

Mr. Fadler set the luggage down beside us and walked off. I noticed that he had a few bay laurel leaves on his denim jacket. Nothing important but I wondered how they got there.

"Honey," she looked at Reba, "you take your luggage up to the common room and I'll be with you after I get Jason here settled in his room."

Reba grabbed her suitcase and climbed the left set of stairs while I followed Mrs. Fadler up the right staircase. My room was halfway down the hall on the right. I could see where a small brass plate had been removed from the door. Other rooms had last names engraved in the plate. The name "Maclean" was on the door next to mine. Inside, the room had a single bed, desk, and wardrobe.

She glanced at a pocket watch she caried in her sweater. "Get yourself settled in quick. You have class starting soon." She tossed a single key on a ring to me, which I promptly juggled from hand to hand and dropped it on the hardwood floor. "Don't lose that. It's the key to your room. Keep the door locked when you're not inside."

I retrieved the key and looked at it.

"If anything gets stolen from your room because the door's unlocked," she continued, "that's your problem. I'm going to help your friend." She walked out of the room.

I studied the key again. Schlage, four tumblers, a lock that keeps honest people honest. Oh, great.

Stuffing my suitcase in the closet, I retrieved my tablet PC and a small thread I spotted on the floor. Leaving the room, I carefully set the thread into the door jam and locked the door. If anyone entered while I was in class, I'd know.

The common room was large with a few sofas, game tables, and easy chairs. A overly full bookshelf lined one wall across from the expansive windows that overlooked a healthy oak woodland. A squirrel darted from branch to branch about the tree. My phone dinged. A text from dad told me to enjoy my new digs, and that he and mum were not far away if I needed anything. For now, there would be no more rides in his unmarked police car or evidence for me to help him with. I hoped he'd let me in on a case or two if he needed help. His department had a new policy for cost control.

Instead of the digital forensic lab analyzing evidence, the lab would only extract data from a device and then pass it to the requesting detective. It was the detective's job to analyze the data and find the bad things. Even though dad was sent to a 10-day class, I worried that he might not know all the intricacies of the artifacts or be able to find everything to make his cases.

I texted: "School's no problem. It should be fun. Just let me know if you need any technical help." Technology would answer all in criminal matters, I thought.

Mrs. Fadler and Reba stepped from the

opposite door. Reba's face was as sober as I can remember. Instead of her usual bubbly self, she looked like she was broken. Now I was worried.

"Both of you," Fadler said. "Straight out the front door. Classroom building is just to the left of the administration building through the traffic circle and courtyard. The building on the far right of the administration building is the dining commons. That's where you'll go for meals. Got it?"

We both nodded.

"Now, scoot. Get out of my hair until this evening."

Outside the dorm building stood a central courtyard and traffic circle for pick up and drop off of students. All four of the school's buildings faced this courtyard. In the very center, a tall multi-tiered fountain stood encircled by planters and flower beds. No flowers on this winter day, but spring should be full of glorias color. A stone drive connected on one side to the main road was inlaid with pavers that could easily twist an ankle.

The classroom building turned out to be the largest. A single-story complex with a couple of classroom halls, a library, and a large gym at the back that opened onto the sports field beyond. A trail led from the courtyard to the staff parking area. All intersected to a quarter-mile drive that led to the main highway and into the quaint village town of Woodside.

Groups of students passed in the halls all heading for their next classrooms. Reba and I found number three with no problem at all. We chose two seats near the back of the room just as the tardy bell rang.

A skinny, bespectacled teacher, Mr. Walker, stepped into the room. He stereotypically wore a tweed jacket that he slipped off, rolled up his white shirt sleeves, and adjusted the round metal framed glasses on his nose. His necktie had a dark stain that matched a stain on his shirt. The room was totally silent. You couldn't even hear the other students breathing.

"Class," Walker called. "I see we have a couple of new students today. This is your home room." He glanced at a sheet of paper on his desk facing the class. "Rebecca Ng. Jason Palmer. Please stand up."

We did.

"Introduce yourselves. Tell us why you're here."

We looked at each other.

"Ladies first," he said.

Reba cleared her throat. "I'm Rebecca. I was in Leigh High School until a few weeks ago when I got the opportunity to come to Pine Grove Academy."

"Pine Grove ALPHA Academy," Walker corrected. "Go on."

"I was an advanced placement student, and the opportunity to

come here just happened."

"Hmmm," Walker said. "Okay, class let's welcome Rebecca." His hands went up like an orchestral conductor and led the class in a hearty "Welcome Rebecca."

Reba sat down leaving me standing alone.

"I'm..." I spoke as the teacher showed the palm of his hand silencing me.

"Rebecca, I don't think you're telling us all, but we'll find out more as the year progresses. I see that you're going to be on the varsity soccer squad. Hopefully that team will do a bit better in the conference this year.
"

I saw a blonde girl with a single ponytail drop her head at that comment.

"Let me introduce you to Kayleen Masterson," Walker said as the girl's head rose. "Stand up Kayleen." A girl dressed in a very conservative skirt and blouse rose turning to look at Reba. "Kayleen is the captain of the lady's soccer team, and I think it appropriate that she be your guide for the next few days."

"Pleased to meet you, Rebecca," the words felt harsh from Kayleen. I couldn't turn to see Reba's face, but somehow, I knew what she might look like.

"The team has a match in a couple days and a practice this afternoon," Walker said. "Hope you're up to it and will bring a new spark to the squad."

Kayleen just grinned, and teacher motioned for her to sit down. My turn.

"I'm Jason Palmer," I just began wanting nothing more than this moment to end. The teacher gestured for me to carry on. "I too came from Leigh High School's advanced placement."

"So, you two are buds?" Walker asked.

"We're muckers."

A few students giggled at the term.

"I'm sensing a slight accent. Where were you from before Leigh High School?"

"Bristol, England. Family moved here about a year ago."

"Excellent." The conductor's arms rose again. "Let's welcome Jason to our school."

"Welcome JASON," the class said in

unison. Get me out of this, I thought.

"Well, Jason. I think your guide should be Mr. Robbie Maclean. Stand up Robbie."

A slight nerd-looking kid with brown skin like me and heavy black framed glasses stood from the front of the room and turned. He waved and smiled at me. Just the opposite of Kayleen. "I'll show you everything you need to know," Robbie said.

"Cool. I actually think we're neighbors in the dorm."

"Awesome. I'll meet up with you after class."

"Okay," teacher barked. "Enough pleasantries. The class is trigonometry. Let's go."

#

That evening in the dining commons, Reba and I filled our trays with sirloin steak, potatoes and mixed veggies, then sat at a table by ourselves. Robbie got his tray and stood at the end of the line looking around the room. His eyes lit up when he saw us and came over to sit next to me on the bench seat.

"So, what do you think?" Robbie said after swinging his legs around to sit.

"It's a bit overwhelming," I said. "Drinking from a fire hose."

He nodded and took a bite of potatoes. "You'll get used to it. It's not bad, and the school has an amazing placement record."

I nodded.

He continued before I could speak. "By the bye, I go by Bobby, not Robbie." He shook his head so the frothy curls in his hair wiggled.

"Okay, Bobby," I said. "I go by JP to my friends."

"Cool. So, we're already friends. That's cool."

"So, Bobby," Reba broke in -- thank goodness. "What's Kayleen's deal."

"You mean, Crystal," Bobby said. "She goes by Crystal. She's the social queen around here. Think she believes she embodies the characteristics of the character in Resident Evil: Afterlife."

"And does she?" I asked.

"Not even close. She's a blonde, mean girl."

No sooner than the words came from his mouth, Crystal and a boy approached the table. He was buff and athletic. "Hi, Rebecca," Crystal said as she wrapped her arm around his, and the boy grinned.

"Hi, Kayleen," Reba said.

"I prefer Crystal," she replied and continued not letting Reba speak. "I see you've found the dining commons. I think you know everything you need to know. You've seen the classroom, the headmaster's hovel, and the dorms. What more do you need?"

"The gym and locker room for the game on Friday might be helpful," Reba said.

"Oh, I think you can just change in your dorm room. No need to be early for warmups or coach's briefing, because you will be wearing a vest." Non-playing team members wear vests as a symbol of their status on the bench.

I sensed the anger steaming from under Reba's collar.

"Tootles, noob," Crystal turned to the boy she held close. "Let's go." She tugged at his arm.

"Hey, Bobs." The boy said as Crystal pulled him away. "Stop by after dinner. I need your nerd services."

"Ooooo," Reba spewed in their wake as they crossed the hall and sat with another group of girls.

"She's not worth it," I said trying to settle Reba down.

"As I told you," Bobby said. "She's a mean girl, nothing more."

"Right, she's the captain of the team," Reba said. "She's probably polluted my reputation with the coach."

"So, Bobby," I said breaking the tension. "Who's the dude?"

"Toby," Bobby said almost under his

breath. "Tobias Adams goes by Toby. They're actually a perfect, mean couple." The final statement was under Bobby's breath.

"Ok," I said. "So, what'd he mean when he said he wanted to see you later to do some 'nerd' stuff?"

Bobby smiled, a big teethy grin.

"Well?" Reba prompted.

"I think it's okay to keep people close that might hurt me."

"What?!" I said. "Have you been threatened?"

"No, no, no." Bobby took a last bite of his au gratin potatoes. "These are great. Did you try them."

"I get it," I said. "You don't want to tell us."

"Have you tried the steak? The mushrooms are great, too."

Reba smacked my shoulder. "I'm heading back. Coming?"

"Yup," I said. "Catch you later Bobby."

#

Friday came quickly. It was 2 PM, and school had let out so that the student body could attend the soccer match. As expected, Reba wore an off-yellow vest along with a couple other players. They were the non-playing squad that would run onto the field with four-packs of water bottles to water the players on the field. It seemed that Crystal kept focused on Reba as she ran onto the field, taking one of the bottles from Reba's rack. Crystal was animated talking to the other players. She took a drink and let go of the water bottle just as it was above the rack held by Reba, sending it to the turf with a thud. Reba picked it up under Crystal's proud stare.

With just under 5 minutes left before the half, the opposing team scored the first goal on a header from an inbounded corner kick.

The corner had been awarded after the ball bounced off Crystal's shin and over the end line. Right after the goal was scored, two things happened. Coach sent Reba out to run laps back and forth on the out of bounds area, and Agent Wilson from the FBI showed up sitting next to me on the bleachers.

Wilson was dressed in a gray suit with a very conservative white blouse and black-down jacket. "Jason," she said. "Good seeing you. How's the game going?"

I looked around. None of the parents, faculty or other students were seated near us. "We're losing," I said. A whistled and loud cheer from the other side of the field echoed.

"Now, it seems you're losing by a bit more," Wilson said. "Go figure."

"I won't stay long. I left something in your dorm room that I'd like you to examine with a fine-tooth comb if you don't mind."

"What is it?"

"You'll see. It's from a case that a colleague is working and the Lab doesn't have time for it."

"Okay."

"Good luck with the rest of the game."

Agent Wilson climbed down the bleachers in her 110 mm heals and out through a side exit from the field. No sooner had she disappeared than Bobby showed up and sat in her place.

"So, who's the hot babe?" Bobby asked.

"I don't like your tone, and it's absolutely none of your bees wax."

"Okay, okay. Just trying to make light talk."

Halftime and the two teams left the field. Music played over the loudspeakers. I guess private schools didn't have pep-bands for sporting events or cheer squads. At least this private school was small enough that the headmaster ran the PA and played the music. Heck, Reba didn't expect to play so she didn't even tell her parents or mine for that matter. Yet Agent Wilson knew exactly what was up and that I'd be here.

"I mean," Bobby said. "I was just curious and didn't mean anything by it."

"Look, let's play fair here. If you want to know something, then you have to offer something back, okay? I asked you a straight question last evening at dinner, and you clammed up. Now you want to learn more. So, give on my question first."

"Okay, okay. I'm sort of good with tech stuff, and Toby can be all thumbs, if you know what I mean."

"So, you do his homework for him?"

"No, nothing like that. I wouldn't," Bobby replied quickly. A bit too quick for me, kind of like he was trying to convince me.

"Then what?" I probed.

"He gets screwed up. New updates come in, his laptop or phone gets screwed up, and he can't remember how to fix them. Think of it as tech support. I can help you out too."

I shook my head. "I'm good."

The next half started with the teams at midfield. Crystal kicked the ball back to a halfback who launched a high shot just ahead of Crystal. She headed the ball forward into the feet of an opposing defender. The other team made several passes until they were deep in our end and punched a ball into our goalie's clutches. Our goalie dribbled the ball twice as the two teams spread across the field and kicked it. Target on Crystal. She ran to the ball and dribbled with her feet just as one of the other team members slid into her ankle knocking the ball away and sending Crystal to the ground writhing in pain.

"That's a yellow card!" I shouted, jumping to my feet.

The referee stopped play and signaled to the sideline that medical staff was needed. Two boys wearing white pullovers that said "stretcher" ran onto the field. One of them I recognized as Toby. The other was the team's trainer. He touched and worked on Crystal's ankle. She was clearly hurt but pushed the trainer away and tried to stand. She collapsed back down to the turf. She was loaded onto the stretcher as the two boys lifted her and walked toward the sideline.

Our team's coach was livid. She called the referee and insisted on a yellow card for the other team's player. The referee would have none of it. The coach called for a substitution, and the referee agreed. Coach turned and pointed at Reba. As the stretcher approached the sideline, the Coach stopped them and went to Crystal side. Coach spoke briefly then slid the captain's armband off Crystal and flipped it to Reba. Reba was now captain and slipped the band on as she ran onto the field. Crystal moved around in pain and her face was locked on Reba joining the team.

One of the other girls took the penalty kick, sending it directly to Reba who deked around another player and scrambled down the center of the field. As the other team's halfback chased Reba down, Reba tapped a hard pass to another player. Reba ran around one of the defenders as the other girl sent her back the ball. Reba dribbled around two other girls and took a shot at the corner of the other team's net. The goalie tipped it down, but Reba was not to be denied. She followed her shot and pounded the rebounding ball into the back of the net.

Bobby and everyone in the stands went nuts screaming and applauding. Not to be outdone, Reba ran toward the sideline and slid on her knees holding her arms in the air. The rest of the team crowded around her.

"Now, that's what I'm talking about," I shouted.

Bobby faced me, held up his hand and gave me a high-five. I watched Crystal lifted back up and sat on the bench while the trainer applied a large ice pack to her ankle and wiped the blood left behind when the other player's cleats slammed into her ankle.

That was the first of a perfect hat trick for Reba. The other team just couldn't stop her attack over the half. She kept passing to other players, defending well and tackling a couple of the other team's players. It was a magnificent 3 to 2 victory.

As the final whistle blew, Reba was drenched in bottles of water sprayed by teammates. She looked up and walked toward the stands. I joined her at the bottom of the bleachers but without Bobby.

"This is how the game's played," Reba said. "Let's head back." "Aren't you going to go to the locker room and get cleaned up."

Reba smiled. "I didn't want to aggravate the great Crystal, so I changed in the dorm as she instructed me."

"Wilson stopped by," I said as we walked.

"What's up?"

"She wants me to check out some data on a drive she put in my room."

"I'll meet you there."

#

I watched for Dorm Mom, my new tag for Mrs. Fadler. She was nowhere in sight. The thread I'd lodged in the door was gone. I'd had a visitor to be sure. Inside, stuffed under a magazine was a Samsung T5 SSD drive. Just for safety, I started a virtual machine that was isolated from the school's network.

The drive contained two E01 compressed images extracted from a subject machine. One was listed as 'S2501-laptop-logical.e01' and the other labeled as 'S2501-laptop-physical.e01'.

I fired up the Autopsy forensic investigative tool and loaded the physical image first. I selected and ran the hash lookup, file type, file mismatch, and archive extractor ingest modules.

This would take a bit of time to process so I used Hasher to calculate a SHA256 for the logical image. The drive left by the FBI had two text files that listed the SHA256 hashes from the initial acquisition. My hasher tool calculated an exact match, telling me that I could trust the logical.e01 image as being unaltered from when it was first collected. I mounted the logical image with Arsenal Image Mounter and read the volume information. The volume contained in the logical.e01 was connected in read-only mode as drives E on my system. There was a knock on the door. Reba slipped in, shut and locked the door behind her.

"Any sign of Dorm Mom out there?" I said.

"Who?"

"Mrs. Fadler. I tagged her as Dorm Mom after the frosty welcome the other day. You're in a boy's room, and I don't want to really mess with her. At least not yet."

"Cute. I think she's tending to Crystal's ankle in the infirmary. That's over in the administration building. What do you have?"

"Drive left by Agent Wilson. Two images onboard that were collected about 2 days ago. Pretty straight forward Windows 10 system from a Dell laptop. Autopsy's crunching away at the physical image, but she gave me a logical view that I might be able to inspect quickly. She said her local FBI Lab was swamped, and an agency took the laptop from a known Armenian gang member."

"Could be serious." She pulled up a chair and sat next to me.

"Could be anything or could be nothing." I launched KAPE once the logical drive was mounted as volumes on my machine. KAPE would extract some meaningful files and put them into what I liked to call a quick triage folder. I commanded KAPE to extract the Master File Table, prefetch files, and images. KAPE finished in just 3.25 seconds, extracting the files and copying them to a Cases folder I made on Wilson's drive.

"Why not just wait for your Autopsy tool to parse all the data on the physical drive?" Reba said.

"I'm impatient." Activating a KAPE module, it parsed the MFT into a timeline and processed all of the prefetch files. Another job that only took a few seconds. "Let's see what's been going on with this laptop for the past 5-days prior to the laptop being seized and imaged by police."

"Find anything?"

"Check this out." I pointed at the screen. "The MFT lists a file that was opened a few times over a couple days using a browser." I changed to the Autopsy window. Ingest modules were still running, but I could browse the files already parsed from the physical image.

The target file was a PDF. I opened it with a viewer. The file contained about 50 images and details. Each image had a starting price in EU dollars and a fairly long item number under each. It was an auction catalog. Large number strings beneath each item caught my eye. I went back to the MFT timeline and discovered 6 image files that were named with matching item numbers. Each of these files had an Alternate Data Stream value showing that they'd been downloaded from the Internet and the same URL reference where the auction catalog had been downloaded.

Prefetch data showed that each of the

JPG files had been opened by a decryption tool and then viewed in the Windows picture application. This all happened while the auction catalog was still open in a PDF reader.

Fast fingers Reba tapped on her cell phone. "Interesting," she said.

"Yes, it is."

"Not that. I just referenced the registration for the record locater where the file was downloaded. It's a Web site hosted in Romania."

Noting the file names, I searched for them in Autopsy on the physical image.

"The six files have been deleted. They're not on the usual user drives," I said. "The logical volume doesn't have any of the files either." I expanded the search to cover all the volumes on the drive and hit all 6 files mysteriously stored within the system reserved partition. The images that KAPE parsed file names from the artifacts didn't exist in usual places. "Seems the target files were moved into the reserved partition, a place that is usually used exclusively by the operating system. Someone's trying to hide something. The files are unallocated orphans. Their MFT records claim the files were accessed a few years ago, but the MFT File Name attributes show the real time was just days before the laptop was seized."

I recovered the file blocks and placed them in an extract folder. Although each file was tagged as a 'jpg' image, their contents were encrypted.

"What now?" Reba said. "How can we see them?"

"The catalog and all 6 of these file images were downloaded within a few minutes of each other. All except the PDF of the catalog were encrypted. If someone was trying to communicate with others, assuming the laptop is the receiver of the files, there must have been a way to send the encryption key."

"Mail?"

"Maybe, but a bit too obvious. Let's see

what else might have been downloaded from the machine in Romania."

Using Timeline Explorer, I ran a search on the alternate data stream column for the Romanian server's URL. It hit on one more image file that was named: 'Istanbul' with a numeric string and .JPG extension. I did a filename search on the physical drive for the file. The actual file was nowhere to be found on the drive. There was a link file pointing to a location where the file had existed, and the MFT timeline showed that the file had been accessed soon after the 6 encrypted image files were downloaded. After the image file was accessed, a prefetch record showed that an encryption tool was run, and after that, a wipe tool was run with an argument to remove the Istanbul JPG file.

"Looks like the Istanbul picture was wiped," I said.

"That destroys the picture?"

"Yup. The wipe tool writes garbage all over the clusters that made up the original file and then deletes it. The records in link files and the MFT would still show the file, but the file is totally gone. I think we need to find the Istanbul picture," I said. "Let's step back in time and cross our fingers that a system snapshot might get it."

Once again, back to Arsenal Image Mounter, except this time I mounted the full physical image as volume. I ran KAPE again on the mounted physical image instructing the tool to process any volume snapshots existing on the drive. Fortunately for me, Windows 10 kept a volume snapshot for quick recovery of the laptop. The 6 image files found as orphans in the document folder were intact and encrypted. The Istanbul image that didn't exist anymore on the live laptop was also in the Documents folder. I opened the file. It was a single nighttime photograph of the Blue Mosque in all its glory.

"Now, why would someone wipe this picture at about the same time the other encrypted images were opened?" I said.

"Could the decryption key be hidden in the image?" Reba said.

"That would be a sure way to exchange the key." I opened the mosque picture with a hex editor. "Well, well, what have we here?"

At the end of the file there were two seemingly encrypted strings, each 64 characters long. I copied the two strings to a text file and then opened a terminal shell in the Windows Subsystem for Linux on my virtual investigative platform. This made running an XOR command on the two strings really easy, leaving me with a single string. I copied this and instructed a crypto tool to decrypt the 6 image files. "Bingo, good call Reba," I said. "This may take some time."

"It's only 30-minutes 'till curfew." Reba glanced at her watch. "Text me if you find something."

#

The next morning, just 15 minutes before breakfast time, I heard a soft knock at the door. Reba came in. "Find anything?" she

said.

"The files only finished decrypting about half an hour ago. It was a real slow process." I still had the art auction catalog open on my screen as I opened the first of the images. It was a picture of a young, teen girl lying on a couch. Her eyes were closed and her arm dangled off the sofa. Her dress was pulled up around her waist showing her panties.

"Open the other pictures," Reba said.

Each of the other pictures were of girls or young boys either lying, passed out on a couch like the first, or standing facing the camera. The photos were all taken in nondescript rooms. One of the pictures was a young boy probably just a bit older than me.

"I think I get it," Reba said. "Each picture has a file name that is the same as the ID in the art auction catalog. The item in the catalog looks like crap but has a real high starting bid price in EU Dollars. I'll bet the item being auctioned is actually the kid in the pictures and the details in the catalog give the auction information."

"Human trafficking," I said.

"Of the worst kind. Two of the girls clearly look like they're unconscious. The other two girls are standing having a picture taken and wearing little summer dresses. The boy is seated; we can't see his arms or legs. Just chest and face. He could be bound to an armchair for all we know."

"Technology is everything, and I'm the best," I said. "I'll write up all that we did and arrange to get this back to Agent Wilson."

3. CASE OF THE BEARDLESS PIRATE

A dense biscuit, bacon, and runny scrambled eggs slopped on my tray. Oh, goody. Nothing healthy in this, I thought. I saw Reba and Bobby at one of the long tables by themselves. "Hey guys," I said as I swung my legs over the bench seat sitting across from Reba.

"Did you get that note off we talked about?" Reba said.

"Yup. On its way." I leaned close to Reba and whispered. "She wants to meet us for lunch at a place called Buck's. We just have to figure out how to get there."

Crystal, wearing a heavy ankle isolation boot, staggered toward their table with Toby in her wake. She didn't have her arm around him for support. "Hey, Rebecca," Crystal said. "Not that it was much, but that win got us into the conference playoffs. All the girls are talking about your hat trick, not the work I did in all the other games."

"Happy I could help," Reba said.

"Well, you better be up for the match next week."

"How's the ankle?" I asked.

"That's so sweet of your puppy dog to ask," Crystal said with a broad grin. "It's a grade 2 sprain with a couple of cleat cuts from where that shrew slid into me. Oh, and Rebecca, don't get used to wearing the captain's armband. Marcie is my number two."

"So, how long are you out having to wear the boot?" I asked seeing Reba's face changing colors.

"They say a few weeks, but I'll be back before then," she said. "Rebecca, be ready for a tough, full-on practice Monday afternoon."

"It's Saturday," I said. "Thought you'd be at home icing and putting your leg up."

"Home? Hah! Parents don't want me sitting around feeling sorry for myself. I'm here at this school because they don't want me around at all. Anyway, I have Toby darling here to fetch things for me."

Toby grinned.

"See you at practice, Rebecca." Crystal turned and hobbled off. Toby just shrugged his shoulders and followed.

"She's something else," Reba said. "If the other player hadn't slammed into her leg, I probably would have."

"That was fun," Bobby said. "I have to head over to Toby's room to do a bit of IT maintenance on his laptop."

Just as he stood, my phone echoed an alarm from my laptop. I read and silenced the message, but another came in right behind it.

"What's up?" Reba asked.

"It's Suricata. My system's still on and connected to the school network. Seems someone is trying to hack in."

We stood and bussed our trays just as another alert chimed.

"Sounds serious," Reba said as we left the commons heading toward the dorm.

"It's set up to do host intrusion detection. I was going to head home to be with the family tonight, but this may change everything. I really don't like that someone's attacking my machine."

#

Reba followed me into the room. I quickly kicked my dirty clothes under the bed. She doesn't need to share my mess.

I'd disconnected the drive from Agent Wilson and shutdown the investigative virtual machine so those were all safe. I left my Maingear laptop running a software update before heading to breakfast. Suricata auto starts on boot and monitors inbound network activity. The alert log showed that someone was probing my system for open ports.

"Network first," I said.

I logged in and didn't disconnect or shutdown the system. No need to tip off the attacker that I've discovered them. CapLoader, grabbed and parsed the network packets from my port so I could see what was going on. As the traffic scrolled across the screen, I saw that the probes were coming from within the school network. Randomly timed attacks hit the network interface. Each timed between 1 and 18 seconds apart.

"Whoever's doing this is smart," I commented. "The traffic is sequenced and coming from different IP addresses."

"Are different systems used in school?" Reba said.

"Hard to tell. Probably IP spoofing." I pointed at the CapLoader screen. "Look here. The probes are trying to enumerate vulnerabilities using a Metasploit signature. If anything, this is a somewhat lazy attacker trying to gain a foothold. Do me a favor, run get your laptop. Let's see if yours is suffering the same attack."

Reba returned with her lightweight Asus system. I booted it up and plugged in my response thumb drive. In a few moments, I had CapLoader running on her system as well. Reba was smart enough to have me set up her Windows Defender and firewall. Within a few moments, CapLoader displayed the same attack running against her system as well.

"You know, one thing really bothers me. The school has a firewall blocking everything from the Internet and even blocking us from opening encrypted connections like VPNs through it. There's a good chance this attack is coming from within the school network. Let's see if I can pull a switch-o-change-o now," I said. I launched a new virtual machine on my laptop, aptly named SweetHoney. This was a basic installation with only a program that would dump network packet captures and all possible system logs. Before connecting the virtual machine to the network, I gave it the same IP address as Reba's system. Time for the switch. I shut down Reba's real laptop and immediately activated the network connection on SweetHoney. As expected, the attack traffic ran against the virtual machine that was vulnerable to most attacks.

Within a moment, Metasploit cracked an RDP port and installed a payload on SweetHoney. Then, a Meterpreter session opened trying to escalate privileges from a normal user to full administrator. This began with a brute force attack and continued.

"It looks like they got in," Reba said pointing to one of the log records.

"That's the point," I said. "The objective is to let them finish the attack and see how they do it and what kind of tools they're using. It's also one of the only ways we can discover where they might be coming from." I pointed at the log records scrolling over one of the terminal windows. "They are really trying to escalate privileges so that they will own this system. If it follows a typical attack pattern, they should be aware they're in and waiting for a command-and-control beacon to start."

"And you're going to let them do it?"

I nodded. "I don't want to make it too easy for them, but yes. They will successfully brute force a 5-digit admin password. It may take a bit of time."

There was a soft knock at the door. Reba glanced at me, then moved toward it. As she reached for the knob, Bobby pushed open the door. "Hello," Reba said in a deadpan voice that I knew all too well.

"You guys left me alone in the Commons. Mind if I hang with you?" Bobby took a couple steps into the room as I popped open the Task View pane and switched to a clear desktop, hiding SweetHoney. Bobby plopped back on my bed as Reba pushed the door shut. "It's really kind of quiet around here on weekends. Most kids head home to their families."

"How about you?" Reba asked. "Are you heading home this weekend?"

"Naw, my dad's been in Nevada all week with my stepmom. They should be flying out to Colorado about now, so I'm here with Mrs. Fadler as my babysitter."

"Doesn't she ever take a day off?" Reba said. "Slide over. Don't hog the bed. I have to sit here, too."

Bobby slid toward the end, and Reba sat just below my pillows. "She'll go shopping for around 6 hours at about eleven-thirty. The cooks will prepare sandwiches and lay out fruit in the commons, then they'll all leave for the rest of the day."

"So, we'll be alone?" I said.

"Yeah, pretty much. Mr. Fadler will be out and about in the garden and the sports field. Sometimes a farmer comes in mowing the grass in the oak woodland that's adjacent to the driveway. He sometimes moves cattle to graze as well." Bobby referred to the nearly half-mile long driveway that ran from Woodside Road into the school through stands of oak trees and mixed shrubs. The long setback from the highway meant the school was shrouded from view and prying eyes. Not even the tile roofs of the buildings could be seen. At the junction, there was no sign or name post for the school, just two old stone columns and a steel anti-car gate, which Mr. Fadler managed. The gate was open on most days but closed and padlocked at the start of dinner hour. From then on, the Fadlers would prowl the grounds providing security and punishment for the resident students caught wandering about.

Bobby started playing with his phone.

"What is that?" Reba asks looking over his shoulder.

"Just a game."

"It looks gross. You run around shooting at people on the street."

"Yeah, but we have an arena set up for just students so all except the bystanders are students. Check this." Bobby held the phone so that she sees an image of a young, busty woman wearing daisy dukes and a tight shirt. "That's Crystal."

"What? Lemme see." Reba grabbed the phone from Bobby.

"Hey." He tried to grab it back but was no match as Reba smacked his hand away. "Be careful. She hides weapons and tries to get close to you."

"She stabbed me and the game has reset." Reba tossed the phone back to Bobby.

"I warned you." Bobby grabbed the phone as a message from Crystal popped up.

"So, wait," I said rolling my chair close to the other two and grabbed the phone. "Let me see that." Several chat messages scrolled across the screen extoling how stupid Bobby was for getting too close to Viper, Crystal's screen name. Once reset, the game went to a street scene. A bright yellow Ferrari was parked by the curb. I slid my finger up the screen moving a bit closer when Viper,

Crystal's avatar, moved and sat back against the car. She flicked a knife blade open and closed in her hand. Bobby stood and looked at the screen over my shoulder. Reba got up and looked over my other shoulder.

"I don't have any weapons yet, so stay back from her," Bobby said.

More messages scrolled across the screen. Crystal typed that she can't make any classes next week because she's in pain and very depressed. She posted that she blamed her injury because she was distracted by the new girl.

"Me?" Reba said. "I was on the bench and wasn't even watching her."

Another character that looked like a stuffed teddy bear approached Viper on the car just as a response from a player whose handle was 'Fluffy' posted: "I'll help. Do you want something to take the edge off?"

At that precise moment, Bobby's phone rang and switched showing a picture of a middle-aged man with full black hair, dark rim glasses, a soft white goatee, and smooth complexion.

"That's my dad calling," Bobby said grabbing the phone and heading toward the door. "Hello," he answered the phone as the door shut.

"That was kind of telling," I said.

"Yeah think?" Reba went back and sat on the bed. "This school is more screwed up than the public school."

"Who do you think was Fluffy, teddy bear character?"

"Ten will get you twenty that it's Toby."

Ding. Now Reba's phone chimed. "It's a WhatsApp message to the students." Reba opened the app and scrolled around. "It says there's new content on the file share for student entertainment. There's no link."

I opened the app on my phone. Sure enough there was a post from someone listed as Adda. "Let's check this out while SweetHoney is under siege."

I opened a File Explorer window and

connected to the school's file share where students could store papers, get research material and anything else. "Maybe it's the Share."

There were tons of files on the server and probably 40 or more directories alone. I sorted the folders by date modified. Two listed changes have been made over the past several hours. One of these, a folder named Protein, contained a collection of numbered subfolders. I went to the highest number and opened it. The folder contained some of the latest music and movie content from studios like Disney and Warner Bros. The mp4 files were some of the most recent releases.

"Adda is posting pirated content." I poked around some of the other folders then opened a WSL shell pointing to the same folder.

Running a 'ls -R | wc -l', I did a recursive count of all the files and folders in the subdirectories. The response was just under 3,000 objects. That's a lot of content. I then typed a 'find' command with arguments to examine only files and arguments to give me the types of files based on extension. Most of the 3,000 were movies or music, but there were a handful of jpg and png image files. "Pirated music and movies, but there's 24 image files. Let me extract these first." I started a process running to pull the 24 files into a local temp directory on my laptop.

"Do you know if these movies are actually pirated?" Reba said. Reba took the mouse and went to one of the image files named 'brought2Uby.jpg' and double clicked it. The image opened to a picture of an anime girl dressed as a swashbuckling pirate complete with long flowing black locks, an eye patch, frilly white shirt and distressed leather vest. Beneath the image, there is a single line of text. "With love, Adda Lovelace," Reba read aloud. "Who's Adda Lovelace?"

"I'd say that's the pirate."

Reba smacked my shoulder with her fist. "Well, duh."

"Ouch, I wish you wouldn't do that."

"Then don't say dumb things."

Back to Task View. I changed and brought the main screen for SweetHoney back up. Meterpreter hadn't yet completed credential exploitation and was still attacking.

"This may take a wee bit longer," I said.

"Aren't we supposed to meet Agent Wilson at noon?" Reba asked. "It's just after eleven. If Bobby's right, Dorm Mom's car should be gone, and she should be out for the next few hours."

Reba kicked-off Google maps on her phone and held the resulting route so that I could see it. "That's a hike. Mile and a half there and back. Wish we had our bikes here."

"Maybe we can borrow some?" I asked.

"Bobby might know," Reba said as she walked out of the room.

A moment later, Reba returned. Bobby was still on the phone but muted the call and told Reba that there were some bikes for student use near the gym.

#

The bikes leaned against the back wall of an equipment closet. They were nothing to write home about. There was one with big balloon tires and rusted chrome handlebars that curved upward. Two others had flat tires and then there was an old, rusted out Schwinn 3-speed bike. Reba grabbed the balloon bike. The bike was so large that she couldn't sit on the seat while touching the tips of both feet to the ground. I got the rusted out, dark red Schwinn.

"We may die going a half of a mile on these much less a mile and a half," I said.

"Can it, JP," Reba said. She stood on the pedals and took a couple of pumps. The chain skipped and she nearly lost control heading for the gym door. "Needs oil on the chain."

My bike was small and the seat was all the way down. As I pedaled the few strokes to get to the door, I felt that my knees were in my chest the whole time. The chain was good. I didn't try to flick or change the gears.

It was moving, and that was good enough for me.

Outside, Reba led the way standing over her seat and pedaling through the large courtyard connecting the buildings. Her chain skipped with every few cranks, but she did pretty well. I just rode along feeling every crack between the stone pavers. We pedaled by the staff parking lot, and sure enough, Mrs. Fadler's banged-up Toyota Corolla was nowhere in sight. The first parking space reserved for the Fadler's car was vacant.

Reba made a loop around the parking lot and came up behind me with some speed. "Let's roll," she said passing me by. With that, she turned onto the main drive and started the gentle climb out of the property. I cranked as hard as I could and stood on my pedals, forcing my body weight to help press the cranks down.

It took us nearly twenty minutes to get to the restaurant and lean our bikes against a side wall. My thighs burned, and my butt hurt from the weathered, old seat. The one thing we really hadn't tested was the brakes. When Reba back pedaled, her rear tire locked and skidded. As for me, the front and rear brake handles came all the way down and the bike screeched in agony. We're gonna die, I thought.

I was pleased to walk a few steps away from the bike. I loved my BMX at home, but this piece of junk was really scary. Inside, Agent Wilson was seated at a back booth and waved at us. She was not in her usual suit and wore a pair of baggy sweats and loose-fitting tee shirt. She looked like she was ready to take a run.

Reba and I sat across from her.

"How's school?" Wilson asked.

"It's okay. A bit weird, but okay," Reba said.

I pulled the hard drive from my pocket and slid it over to her.

"I ordered an iced tea," Wilson said. "Would you guys like something?"

"I'd love a hot tea with milk and sugar, please," I said.

"Just water for me," Reba said.

A waiter took the order and left. "All right," Wilson tapped her finger on the drive, "what did you uncover?"

Solutions first, I thought as I told her about the art catalog and link to the encrypted photos. "I hate to say it, but it seems like whoever seized this stumbled onto a human auction," I said.

Wilson quizzed us both about the findings. My tea arrived. Crap tea bag in a small pot with a bit of half and half, not milk and some sweetener. It was horrible on first sip, but I'd drank it anyway. "Did you set everything out on here?" Wilson tapped her manicured fingernail atop the drive again.

"There's a folder named cases. I've put a short report in there for you and organized all of the extracted evidence."

"When JP decrypted the pictures," Reba said, "we found a match between the number on the image file name and the item in the auction catalog. The auction catalog has pieces of art, but the prices listed seem to be way more expensive than what they'd be worth."

I nodded and pointed to the drive. "If you replace the item with the corresponding picture, the pricing and offers make sense."

"Some of the pictures of the girls look like they're passed out or asleep," Reba said.

Wilson sighed deeply. She sucked on the straw to her iced tea. "Well, this sheds a new light on things. Any links to the user of the laptop?"

"Yes," I said. "I built a small timeline showing when the user logged in and then opened the catalog. Then opened a picture of the Blue Mosque in Istanbul. The mosque picture hid two strings in excess data. The user then used a crypto tool to XOR the two strings, giving them the decryption key. They used the same tool over the encrypted image files, generating a new set of decrypted files that they saved in a temporary folder. Once decrypted, the user simply used the Windows picture tool to open each of the pictures, thus having the catalog and pictures all open. When the user was done, they closed the pictures and then used a PC cleaning tool to wipe the clusters that contained the decrypted image files."

"Impressive, both of you," Wilson said. "I think we have some more information to feed back to the law enforcement agency and that we should probably take this case over. Nice job. Sure you don't want something to eat?"

"Naw," Reba said. "We had food back at school."

"We're a bit AWOL," I added. "So, we better be getting back."

"One more thing," Wilson said. "Did any of the pictures have geo-coordinates suggesting where they were taken?"

"The EXIF data was gone," I said. "Possibly removed. Each picture was taken by a different model camera. That data was still there. But no geo-coordinates."

Wilson finished her iced tea as the waiter arrived with a plate of scrambled eggs, bacon and toast. It looked good and smelled better. Wilson's tea was refreshed.

"We gotta get back," Reba said. We downed our drinks and got up.

"Be seeing you," I said.

"And both of you," Wilson said.

Outside Buck's, our two broken-down rides leaned against the wall where we'd left them. Sadly, no one stole the bikes. Then again, who'd want these scrap heaps?

Reba and I made it back to school. For me the ride was better since it was slightly downhill. We coast down to the entrance, then swung by the stone pillars, flanking the school's entrance.

"She's still out," Reba said as we passed the staff parking lot.

No sign of Dorm Mom's car. We got to the gym building and walked the bikes down the hall back toward the supply room.

"HEY! You two," a booming male voice sent a shiver down my spine. It was Mr. Fadler, Dorm Dad, holding a long broom like a hockey stick.

"We just rode around campus to get a bit of exercise," Reba said as the hefty man approached us.

"Did you ask permission?"

"We're new. Didn't know we needed to ask," Reba said.

"You didn't leave campus, did ya?"

"No," I said. Reba shouldn't be the only liar. "Just rode along the campus drive."

"I should report you both. You need to get permission to use anything in there, especially those two broken bikes. Hey, wait a sec," he looked Reba in the face, "Aren't you that girl on the soccer team that scored a hattrick?"

"That's me."

"Well okay, then. I won't report you two this time. Just find me and ask if you want to use the bikes or other stuff. I mean, you two could have been hurt and nobody would know where to find you or even look. You could both be bleeding away in some ditch."

"Yes, sir. Next time we'll ask."

I nodded. Reba and I stored the bikes away.

4. THE PHILANTHROPIC, CIRCE

I'm reminded of a quote from Homer: "Be wary, mortal, for the gifts of a goddess are not always what they seem."

The rest of the boring weekend passed, and I still worked to try to find who was attacking my system in the room. I had a MAC address, the hardware address of the machine that was on the school network and source of the attacks. If only I could install a network tap to capture all of the school's traffic, I might have a chance of zeroing in on the source and whoever was masquerading as Adda Lovelace.

My ancient history class was a lot of fun. This was something new that I probably wouldn't get back in public school. The works of Homer in the Odyssey were fun to read. The poetic prose drew vivid images of the Greek gods, and I felt the adventures. We'd be reading from Ovid's Metamorphosis next, but I skimmed ahead to Book 4 and how Perseus took on the gorgon Medusa. To think that he never once looked the gorgon in the eyes and successfully took her head, creating one of the first weapons of mass destruction that he kept in a sack and exposed her face and eyes to adversaries.

Coming out of class, I was one of the first out the door carrying both of the thick books and my backpack. I struggled a bit as I left the classroom building and made it to the large fountain at the center of the main courtyard before dropping the books. I stopped and stuffed them in my rucksack. It was a glorious, warm day. The clouds from the night before were all gone and the air warmed in the midday sun. I sat back and rested on the wide bench that surrounded the fountain.

Dorm Dad, my nickname for Mr. Fadler, worked on a flowerbed adjacent to the dorm building entrance, carefully raking leaf litter from beneath the shrubs. Although it was still winter, it felt like spring was about to surge forth. A few students passed toward either the commons or the dorms. They were bundled up in winter garb and looked quite cold. For me, I slipped off my jacket and sat in shirt sleeves. It wasn't long before my mind wandered down from Mount Olympus and back to Adda Lovelace.

I opened my computer and tapped my access password on the machine. It logged into the campus-wide wireless network, but I didn't really care. The sun felt warm on my back as I opened up CapLoader and the captured network PCAP file from the other day. I filtered the traffic to only show me hosts that were unique IP addresses from the network. Adda, or whomever, had been smart randomizing the source of the network mapping used to find open ports on my system. There were thirty hosts. Each used randomly to launch recon packets at my system.

Opening another view of the packet captures, I quickly looked at the network flows and figured the only way I could identify the actual source system was to capture network traffic with a tap. I'd have to install the tap on the internal switch at the school, which wasn't without challenges. There are a lot of devices connected to the school network, and the amount of traffic might make it nearly impossible to collect the packets unless I could somehow connect directly to a switch span port. The span port would merge all traffic and allow me to capture everything. During the case involving the Andropovs, their home network was easy to span in a single tiny tap. This network would take at minimum a full gigabit Ethernet capture, which meant a computer.

As I studied the flow analysis and identified the primary switch, I didn't notice Bobby walking up to where I sat by the fountain. He set his bag next to me.

"Hey, JP," Bobby said. "Whatcha up to?"

"Just studying some network stuff. What are you doing?"

"Oh, man, I spent most of the night working on a computer to recover data that was lost."

"Your laptop?"

"Nah, that would have been easy. Hey, I seem to be the go-to IT guy for other students, especially the jocks. Damn, Mac was a nightmare to work on. I told the idiot to make regular backups, but no, he was too lazy."

I figured that the machine might belong to Toby, but Bobby was a bit too cagy and didn't let on.

At that moment, two large black Cadillac

SUVs swung off the drive and slowed to a stop in front of the administration building. The windows were all darkened. Bobby and I both stood to look at the vehicles and catch a glimpse of whom they were delivering. The drivers of both SUVs opened the back doors. From the first car, a lean olive-skinned man with a bald head stepped from the back. He wore a grey tailored suit and buttoned the jacket as he stood, then brushed off his coat. He had a white shirt and bright red tie, but what JP noticed was the small strand of dark prayer beads that he flipped in his hand.

"Must be VIPs," Bobby said.

Another man stepped around the vehicle from the passenger seat of the second SUV and took a position leaning against the back quarter of the vehicle. He had to be 6 feet tall, dark greased-back hair and broad shoulders. From his position, he had a direct view of not only Bobby and me but of anyone else that might approach the vehicle. He gave a single nod of his head to the driver that stood ready to open the back door.

The back door swung open and a very attractive woman in a sleek black and white ankle length dress slid from the vehicle. She slipped on a pair of almost face-covering dark glasses, then adjusted a broad black and white hat that would be suitable for a race day at Ascot. The broad brim flopped a bit in the slight spring breeze. Her long black stiletto heels clacked on the pavers as she led the lean man and larger escort around the vehicles toward the entrance of the administration building.

Bobby and I just had to pack up and move toward the dorm room to get a better view. Headmaster Hannah and Dorm Mom stepped out opening the double doors to the administrative offices and held them for the VIPs to pass through. Mr. Hannah whispered to Dorm Mom who walked toward the classroom building and then Hannah led the group inside the admin building.

"Wonder who that is?" Bobby asked as

the two drivers pulled the SUVs back toward the staff parking lot.

"Must be important not to share an SUV."

"That big guy looks like some kind a bodyguard."

"Who knows," I shouldered my pack. "Probably enrolling their kid or something. Hey, dude, I'll meet you later in the commons. I really got to get some stuff done in my room."

"Check you later." Bobby walked off back toward the classroom building.

I didn't have another class for an hour and a half and I really wanted to get back to my room and compare some of the network traffic.

In my room, I finished setting up my laptop and just sat down when there was a knock at the door. Couldn't be Reba, I thought, she'd just barge in. Probably Bobby wanted to whine a bit more. I opened the door. Dorm Mom stood and smiled waving a beckoning finger at me.

"Mr. Palmer," she said. "Come with me. You're wanted."

Oh great, I thought. I looked back at my machine. It had just finished starting and wasn't yet logged in. "Lead the way," I said.

We walked downstairs, out of the dorm building and around to the administration building. My mind immediately wandered to the image of the group arriving from the large black SUVs as we entered. In the hall outside the headmaster's office, Reba sat on a bench. She smiled at me as Dorm Mom directed me to sit next to her.

"Wait here with Ms. Ng," Dorm Mom said. "You'll be called in a moment. Dorm Mom left, and we were alone in the hallway. The walls of the office were heavily insulated, and we could hear nothing but the clock that made a click each time the minute hand moved. It was nearly 11 AM.

I looked around and whispered, "You too?"

"Dorm Mom just got me from the gym and told me to sit here until I'm called."

My mind rushed over the other day when Mr. Fadler caught us sneaking the bicycles back into the storage room. "The bikes?" I said.

"Who knows. Mr. Fadler said he wasn't going to report us.

Maybe someone saw us when we went into Buck's for the meeting with Wilson."

"We haven't been here long enough to get rewarded for being great. What could it be?"

Reba looked at me and smiled. "I love that you always have such a positive outlook on life. You haven't done anything great, but I got the team into the soccer playoffs."

"True. But why have me here then?"

"Sometimes you can be a bit careless when you're off your computer."

At that moment, the office door opened and Crystal hobbled out into the hall followed by the headmaster. "Thank you, Ms.

Masterson."

"My pleasure, Headmaster."

He turned looking at Reba and me. "I'll get to you two in a moment." Headmaster Hannah stepped back in the room and shut the door.

"Hi, Crystal," Reba said. "How's the ankle?"

Crystal just grinned, offering a polite snub to us. She turned and clomped with the large orthopedic boot out the main doors. "And to think she was supposed to be my mentor," Reba said once Crystal left.

"She really has serious attitude issues," I said.

"Yah think?" Reba's voice dropped to a whisper. "I have to really watch out for myself when I'm at practice. I don't know what that witch might do to my water bottle or anything. I really think she somehow blames me for her stupid sports injury."

"Me thinks you're paranoid."

"Yeah, rightfully so. Earlier, when we

were in the locker room my panties went missing. Crystal was standing just a few feet away, and I think she snatched them. Even my brat sister, CaCee wasn't that bold."

"Your underwear, really?"

Reba nodded. "When I couldn't find them, I was as polite as I could be to that witch. I didn't want to give her any satisfaction at all. Chúa only knows where they might turn up."

"Chúa?"

A blank stare at me, then a frown.

"I don't speak Vietnamese," I said.

"It means God, as in God knows where they might turn up. I'm sure she'll do some voodoo magic or something or stuff them somewhere really embarrassing."

Mr. Hannah's timing couldn't have been better. The door opened and he beckoned us to come into the office. Reba led the way, and I followed.

The woman who looked like she came out of the pages of a fashion magazine sat at the middle of the table. She'd taken the hat and glasses off, and I could see that she had a very full head of jet-black hair that flowed over her shoulders. Her bright blue eyes watched as the two of us entered the room and stood across from her. The lean man sat next to her, and the big bodyguard stood behind them.

"Ms. Solomon," Hannah pointed to Reba and me. "I'm very pleased to introduce you to Ms. Rebecca Ng and Mr. Jason Palmer. Two of our promising students."

Solomon smiled broadly and nodded her head at us. "Ms. Ng. Mr. Palmer. The honor is truly mine." She motioned to her right. "May I introduce you to my American business affairs manager, Mr. Sargis Petrosyan. He looks after my assets in the United States."

"Ms. Solomon comes to us from Istanbul, Turkey," Hannah said. "She has graciously decided to have her philanthropic trust make a substantial donation to the school."

"That's wonderful, Ms. Solomon," Reba

said. "Speaking for both of us, this is much appreciated."

"Be seated, both of you," Solomon pointed at the chairs opposite her. Mr. Hannah sat at the head of the table behind a small set of papers. "Comfortable?" She asked as we sat. "Water, coffee, tea?"

"No ma' am," Reba and I said at the same time.

"Well, Ms. Solomon," Headmaster Hannah said. "These two students came to us from a public high school down in San Jose. Rebecca here has already brought some fame to our school in only a couple of weeks. She's the one that scored a natural hattrick during her first soccer match and took us into the regional finals."

Solomon smiled broadly at Reba.

"Jason, here, or so I'm told by his teachers, is showing a great amount of academic prowess. In all, we're very proud to have them in our community."

"So, Jason," Solomon said. "How are

you enjoying it here?"

I nodded. "The teachers are very good and knowledgeable in their subjects. I'm being enlightened about this school, the other students, and the subjects. The classes are much better than the AP sections at our old high school."

"AP?"

"Advanced placement," Reba said. "I was in AP classes as well with Jason, and I agree with his assessment."

Solomon nodded and motioned to Petrosyan to take a note.

"That's very good," she said. "Let me tell you that the funds my foundation have promised to the school are specifically committed for this school to select and admit students whose parents may not be able to afford such an institution as this. I asked Headmaster Hannah to introduce me to students who might be representative of the, can I say, less fortunate to achieve this level of education."

I sensed the steam boiling from Reba as she shifted in her seat and clasped her hands in front of her.

"Rebecca, do tell me what your parents occupation is and what they think of you being here?"

"My family has a restaurant that they both work very hard to run. Dad was a geologist before coming to the United States. He always had a knack for fine French cooking. A loyal friend of his gave him the capital to open the restaurant."

"And do you miss your family since you're living here?"

Reba thought for a moment. "My mom. She always kept me charged up and working hard. But I'll see them on the weekend and during summer."

Solomon turned to me.

Given the questions, my brain was swimming with how to answer questions about my mum and dad.

"And Jason," Solomon smiled again. "Tell

me more about yourself and what sort of things interest you?"

Phew, I thought for a moment. "Math, science, and ancient history."

"Math and science. Those are broad fields. And ancient history. We have a large amount of history dating back before the Romans in Turkey. Couple math and science with history and you may end up in archaeology."

"Archaeology's interesting. I like solving puzzles." She nodded.

"And, Mr. Petrosyan, do you have any questions for our guests?"

Petrosyan sat back a bit and actually rubbed the top of his bald head. A clear nervous reaction to the question and a habit. "Just one," Petrosyan said, sitting forward and looking at Jason. "Tell us what you do in your spare time, Jason. You can't just study math and science all the time. We know that Rebecca is into sports. What are you into?"

"I read and I like bicycling when I can."

Not saying anything about drones or computer forensics or chasing hackers.

"What are you reading now?"

"I'm enjoying Ovid's Metamorphosis."

Petrosyan's eyes widened. "Greek mythology told in poetry. That's all?"

"I like mystery fiction when I have nothing else."

"What part of the Ovid do you enjoy?"

I couldn't help but look at Solomon's face then back to Petrosyan. "I'm really enjoying the story about the gorgon Medusa."

One of Petrosyan's bushy black eyebrows rose. "Interesting."

Solomon stared at me then pressed her hands on the table and stood. Headmaster Hannah immediately rose from his seat. Petrosyan remained seated. "It was very nice meeting you both," she smiled and reached across the table to shake my hand.

Reba and I both stood. We were clearly dismissed. I shook her hand firmly and was followed by Reba.

"A pleasure meeting you both as well," Reba said.

"Likewise," I said. "I think you'll find that any funds you offer to the school will be put to very good use."

"I'm sure," Solomon said and then looked to the headmaster. "We have a few more things to cover."

"Certainly," Hannah said rounding the table and guiding us toward the door. He didn't follow us out as he did with Crystal before us and just shut the door in our wake.

Reba gave me a wide-eyed quizzical glance as we both headed out the door. Once outside, Reba stopped halfway between the buildings. "That was interesting," she said.

"I wonder who really selected us to meet with them? The headmaster?"

"That's the first question we need to answer. You head back to the dorm. I'll meet you there in a bit." Reba ran back toward the administration building. I was left baffled by her action but headed up to my room.

I hadn't had a chance to leave the thread in the door jamb and couldn't tell if anyone cracked the lock and went into my room. Inside, everything looked in its place. Books stacked bedside. Computer's screensaver raced colored waves across the screen, just as it should. Tablet PC shut and beside the desk. There was one wrinkle in the blanket over my bed that troubled me. That was smooth and tight. A 25-cent piece could be dropped and bounced off the way I kept the blanket. I lifted the top mattress and looked to where my lock bag was stashed. This was an old cash deposit bag that required a 5-cylinder key to unzip it. It was metal lined and couldn't be cut open. Old technology to protect and store my portable solid-state drives. The bag was in its place and appeared untouched. It was still in between the barely visible wax lines I'd marked on the lower mattress. I unlocked the bag. All three drives were inside. I took a Samsung T7 drive out then secured the bag and slipped the bag back in its place between the top and bottom mattresses.

After plugging the drive in and loading my forensic station, I set about loading another set of network captures I'd taken from SweetHoney. There must be something that I missed when I first examined the network flows that could lead me to the actual source of this malicious online behavior. The Suricata alarms went off again as my system was now being probed again.

My room door swung wide open hitting the fiberboard armoire with a slap that made my heart sink. Reba held up her hand as she stepped inside and peeked back out in the hallway, then shut the door.

"JP," she said. "I got it." She dangled a brass key on a single ring with a tab.

#

"I still think you're nuts. If we get caught, we'll be in super big trouble," I said as we stood in the dark outside the administration building. Even though it's late, anyone looking out a dorm window might see us.

"Don't be a silly willy," Reba said as she pressed the key into the lock. The door moved as she inserted the key. It's not locked.

"Someone must be inside. Let's get out of here." She stepped through the door and pulled my arm. Inside the hall lights were on, but the office area for the receptionist was dark. We stood for a bit and just listened. No sounds.

"Come on," Reba said stepping behind the office counter. The headmaster's mailbox was stuffed full with correspondence. I took that on as Reba went to the desk and started looking through papers.

"This is just inbound mail and junk." I held up a stack of papers and ads that were in there. There was one envelope that looked like a bill for maintenance but was unopened.

"There's nothing here," Reba said. "Let's go to Mr. Hannah's office, maybe we can find something there."

We snuck around the counter and down the hall to the headmasters closed office door. My foot jammed into the bench seat that was in the hall. It screeched against the floor and slid a bit.

Reba turned and gave me that all too familiar mad look. She turned the doorknob slowly and opened the door just a crack. The office was dark inside. She pushed it open, stepped inside, and I followed. Reba carefully shut the door. I reached for the light switch.

"Wait, not yet," Reba said. She slipped her black jacket off and stuffed it under the door. "Now turn the lights on. We don't want anyone working in the hallway to see the light under the door."

The office area lights went on. Fortunately, the curtains were drawn and would block most of the light from the windows on the backside of the admin building. The building backed up to the sports field and there shouldn't be anyone out there at this hour of night.

I went behind the desk and touched the mouse of the headmaster's desktop. The screen lit up. No passcode required. The system was left logged in. I love it when people help me do my job. I retrieved a jump drive from my pocket and slipped it into the USB port. The drive mounted and I could see the forensic tools.

Opening a terminal shell, I typed a command to change to the E: drive, my mounted jump drive, then typed 'dumpit.exe \N'. This would grab an image of the desktop's memory. While Reba rummaged through a file cabinet, the memory dump finished in just over a couple minutes.

"Find anything?" I said to Reba.

"I found a file on the board members for the school, and it includes Ms. Maja Solomon." Reba took out her cell phone and snapped a few pictures.

"There's probably a separate file with a list of information like her contact, email and all that stuff."

"I'm on it." Reba replaced the one folder and kept looking through the files.

Once the memory image was secure, I instructed the terminal shell to change directories to the E:\KAPE folder on my jump drive. I'd already prepared a Cases folder on the drive and was now ready for KAPE to collect a full triage image, so I typed: 'kape.exe -- tsource C: --tdest E:\Cases\tout --tflush --target !BasicCollection'. This would pull everything from the root of the desktop and write the files directly to my jump drive. 122 seconds to complete, great, I thought. Now to collect any office documents and email folders that may be on the system as well. I typed: 'kape.exe --tsource C: --tdest Y:\Cases\TDD –target OutlookPSTOST,OfficeAutosave,OfficeDiagnostics, OfficeDocumentCache'. This would add any office document cache and email files that it found. Another few seconds passed as KAPE finished this collection. I closed the terminal shell and ejected my drive.

"Got a folder with letters and correspondence between the school and Solomon. Most of the letters are signed by Sargis Petrosyan on behalf of the foundation and Ms. Solomon."

"That will do," I said just as there was a loud thump outside the headmaster's office.

Reba and I froze. I pocketed the drive as I put the desktop back into sleep mode. In the hall outside, we could hear whistling in the tune of "I'm a Lumberjack" from Monty Python. Dorm Dad must be cleaning the floor. Reba carefully closed the file cabinet and tiptoed to the light switch that she flicked off. She pulled her jacket from under the door and felt her way over to me behind the headmaster's desk just as the door flopped open. We dove under the large wooden desk. My heart raced and every hair on my neck stood rigid.

"What..." I started to whisper as Reba's hand clasped over my mouth. Again, I got that angry stare from her.

Dorm Dad's large cleaning broom swept the wood floor in front of the desk and over to the conference table. Back and forth it went. It wouldn't be long before he swept along the side of the desk or recovered the full garbage can beside the desk. We had no hope. At that very moment, as if on cue, Dorm Dad's cell phone rang.

"Oh, what does she want?" He said as he answered the phone. "Hello, my love."

There was a silent pause.

"What do you mean they're not in their rooms?" He said. I could hear my heart thumping in my throat.

"Okay, okay. I'll stop. I'm just cleaning Mr. Hannah's office. I'll be over there right now." The broom handle dropped to the floor, and he walked out of the room. We waited until the outer door shut.

"Time to go," Reba said.

"Go where? You heard him. Sounds like Dorm Mom discovered we're not in our rooms."

Reba stepped to the open door at the hall and snapped a quick look around the corner. "You don't know that. Now, come on."

I followed her out of the admin building. We could just see Dorm Dad climbing the stairs to the dorm building. We followed and made it about halfway when Reba grabbed my arm and pulled me toward the dining commons building. "Better to be caught in here than in the admin building."

The lights were still on in the dining commons, and I could hear a few of the staff working in the kitchen area. Reba went straight to the double metal kitchen doors that led from behind where the food was served. She peeked into the window again. I wanted to ask what she was doing, but new better. She motioned for me to join her and then pressed into the kitchen.

"Hey, what are you guys doing here?" One of the staff asked once they saw us.

"We're hungry," Reba said. "Wanted to see if we could get a sandwich or something to hold us over."

The kitchen worker, a lean woman in her late forties smiled. "Well, honey, I always make a couple of ham sandwiches just in case some kids get hungry for a late-night snack." She crossed over to a large refrigerator, opened it and retrieved a couple of shrink-wrapped sandwiches. I have to admit. At this point, I was a bit hungry.

We walked out of the commons and turned toward the dorm building.

"Hold on you two," the voice of Dorm Mom boomed before us.

"What are you two doing out here?"

"Sorry, Mrs. Fadler," Reba said. "I was real hungry and couldn't fall asleep. I came out here to get something to keep me until morning." She held up her wrapped sandwich. "I ran into Jason out here with the same idea."

I stepped around Reba so Dorm Mom could see me. Half a sandwich in my mouth as I smiled.

"Fine," Fadler said. "Get back to your

rooms. Have you seen Kayleen Masterson while you were on your adventure?"

"Crystal?" I said between bites.

"Yes, Crystal," Fadler said with almost a sigh of anger. Reba and I looked at each other.

"No, ma'am," Reba said.

"Well, when you're on your way to your rooms, if you do see her, tell her to find me now!"

We both nodded and walked past her and up the stairs. What a relief, I thought. It was like I could feel her stare burn into my back as we stepped inside.

"Let's meet after class tomorrow," Reba ran up the left stairs to the women's dorm while I climbed the right set of stairs. Inside my room, I flopped on the bed and got the post-adrenaline shivers. The room felt really cold. I ate the second half of the ham and mayonnaise sandwich, then felt tired. I checked that the drive was still in my pocket.

#

The next morning was anything but a lovely Spring morning. Rain clouds hid the sun and chucked large drops down wetting everything they struck. Gusts blew some of the drops sideways and reminded me of rain squalls back in Bristol. My stupid folding umbrella was hardly enough to keep the top of my head dry, much less the rest of me.

Reba sat in the dining commons by herself at the back of the room. As I brushed off the water from my umbrella and coat, a couple of girls from the soccer team approached her and spoke briefly.

Although it was only Tuesday, if this storm kept up through the week, it would certainly enhance the challenge of the playoff game scheduled for Friday. Once the girls left, Reba went back to reading something on her cell phone.

I set my stuff down on the table and sat across from her. "That was fun last night," Reba said in a soft voice. "Reminded me of old times when we snuck into Lesta's house."

"Yeah," I said. "But Lesta didn't have Dorm Dad and Mom."

"We handled them, didn't we?"

"I guess."

"What did you find in the data?"

"I just ran a couple of parsing modules against the collection but didn't really get much of a chance to review the results yet." I looked at her. "Last night took it out of me, and I just crashed out. You know, one of these days you're going to get caught and there won't be some cell phone call to save you."

Reba nodded. "That was just dumb luck." She leaned closer. "What I can't believe is that it was Crystal that was missing from her room that caused Dorm Mom to sound the alarm."

I looked around and behind me in the room at all the other students. "Have you seen her this morning?"

"No. And no sign of Toby either."

"The plot thickens."

"You know what I say?" Reba grinned, a sparkle in her eyes. "Better them than us."

I gathered my things and slipped on my very wet backpack. "I'm off to math class."

"Aren't you going to eat anything?" Reba asked. "You may need your strength."

"That reminds me," I slipped on my cap and looked back to Reba. "Dad called and said he's going to sign you and me out for lunch. He has to come up to San Mateo to interview someone."

"Cool. It will be good to see detective Palmer again. I'm up for it."

"After math, I'll take a look at the data that's been parsed. I only wish that we could have made it to the data center room to capture some network traffic. I'm still no closer to finding whose been trying to hack into our systems."

"I know," Reba said. "Why not ask Bobby? He seems to do all sorts of tech stuff here. Maybe he has access and would take you in."

"Good idea."

#

Math was easy today. We had a quiz and did a bit of geometry that involved basic algebra equations. My mind wandered back to the network borne attacks on my system and the relentless scanning. It dawned on me that I might have missed something when I set up Sweet Honey as a trap. There were items related to the network activity and the running of Meterpreter against that system that I may have easily missed.

"Mr. Palmer!" the teacher called. "You still with us? What's the answer to this problem?" He pointed at a formula on the board.

"23 point 25," I said.

"Good, you are still with us. I thought your mind was wandering off."

"Still here, sir." Then I remembered that the Meterpreter session would have had an IP address associated with any responses. How could I miss that?

After class, I ran straight back to the dorm building. The rain was relentless, and my shoes were soaked when I got into the building. Squeak, squeak, squeak followed each step along the tile floors up to my door. The thread was still in place. No one had opened my door since I left this morning. I kicked off my shoes and opened my laptop on the desk. It wasn't long before the SweetHoney virtual machine was running inside an isolated sandbox, invisible to the network.

I had to examine 3 packet capture files with CapLoader before I found the one that had the connections from the Meterpreter process. Bingo! CapLoader's host tab listed the machines on the network and identified that it was a Linux system that had the IP address where Meterpreter sent results. I not only had the IP address, but a nice machine ID along with operating system information. I popped open a Linux investigative platform as a separate virtual machine and ran and ARP-scan listing of the local network. This was a massive list but quickly identified the MAC address of the system that was online an had its current IP address. Well, that's a lot more than I had this morning, I thought. So next step was to figure out who among the 64 students on campus used this machine. A task that would require some more thought. Enough chasing Adda Lovelace for now. I plugged in my jump drive and loaded some of the reports and material KAPE had parsed in the modules.

The first step might be searching through the module results for some of the names we knew. But before that, I might as well let Autopsy parse through the files. It was super convenient that raw extracted triage files could be loaded into the Autopsy tool. Because I wasn't loading a full computer system image into the tool, I had the files loaded in no time at all. Now to run a few ingest modules to extract and view data artifacts. I selected the recent activity, email and hash ingest modules. Autopsy began parsing through the files and I watched as email communications were extracted and parsed. Even though the number of files was rather small, the process would take a lot of time, so I was off to the dining commons to just study a bit more of ancient Greek mythology.

5. EXTORTION AMONG "FRIENDS"

The dining commons had a study area that included a few sofas and some work cubicles. I was in the mood for a sofa, so I sat and opened Ovid Book 4, Perseus(1) to read his story about the Gorgon Medusa. I was just getting into Perseus relating his tale about how he single-handedly removed the snake-haired Gorgon's head to the crowd of Cepheus' court when I spied Bobby coming into the commons.

There was something about Bobby's walk and hesitations while heading toward the freshly laid out lunch service. Bobby stopped and turned away from the freshly laid out lunch, sinking his head to his chest.

"Hey, Bobby," I called and waived.

Bobby looked at me and just shook his head as he continued to the exit.

I stood and intercepted him before he reached the door. "Hey, what's up, man?"

"Nothing," Bobby said. "I'm good."

"Come on, sit with me for a bit." I took his arm and moved back toward the sofa. No other students were in that area and we'd be quite alone. We sat. "You're usually all brills. Something's bugging you?"

Bobby looked at me. His eyes were red and looked as though he'd been crying. "No, JP, I can't trouble you with my problems."

"It's no bother, mate. You've always been there for me. Now share."

"I can't. I feel stupid and betrayed."

"Whoa, betrayed? Did someone turn on you? You didn't get slugged by Reba, did you?"

He let out a single chuckle and half a

grin. "Not Reba. She's great."

He sat back and relaxed his shoulders. I was making headway. At that moment, Crystal pranced into the dining commons making her usual commotion. She had no cast, weighing her down and actually bounced around quite well. She shouted to a girl in the center of the room and ran over giving her a tight hug.

"Look," Bobby looked back to me. "The other week I was playing a multi-player tournament game with just a bunch of folks. This girl initiated a personal chat with me. She was all nice and told me about herself. We chatted. Nothing to it."

He sat back and a tear streaked down his cheek.

"Okay, so you chatted. Big deal."

Bobby stared at me with a bit of sorrow and then a frown of anger. "We chatted again the following day and exchanged more information. Then..." He choked back the tears.

I prompted with my hands for more and thought about what Reba might do in this situation, so I rubbed his shoulder, and he sat back, relaxing again.

"We got on the game each evening at about 7. She was always there, it seemed. We'd chat some more and then she asked if we could exchange digits and talk outside the game."

"Bobby, what sort of questions did she ask?"

"You know, my name, what school I went to, how old I was, and what my favorite subjects were."

"Okay..."

"She was real into computers and math, just like me. She has demanding stepparents that make her clean, fix their computers and phones, and work all the time. She only gets free time for a short while every evening. I felt sorry for her."

This is getting much worse. I was reminded of an old Internet saying that no one knows you're a dog online. "What? Did she break up with you?"

Bobby shook his head. "We Facetimed until late last evening. This morning, she sent me a text saying that her father caught her and took her phone. She said she found something about me and my dad online. And that we had to break it off." Bobby stood. "I don't wanna talk anymore. I gotta go."

I stood and grabbed Bobby's shirt sleeve trying to stop him. He walked toward the door, and I was hot on his trail. I felt into my cargo pants pocket and felt the tracker that I kept in my pocket. I needed some way to keep a remote eye on him. If his phone detected the Bluetooth tracker following him, he might toss it out. We reached his dorm room, Bobby was fumbling for his key. I grabbed Bobby's jacket and turned him toward me. I could see that he was seriously crying. As he pulled away, I slipped the tracker into his jacket pocket.

"Bobby, come on, I can help," I said, but

he pulled away from me as he unlocked the door. He stepped inside and turned facing me.

"No offense, JP, but I gotta go." He slammed the door and I heard the lock latch.

I sighed and turned, walking toward my room.

"Jason," a girl's voice called from behind me. I turned looking at a lean girl in a black dress with blonde hair and dark eye makeup. Very goth. "I'm Cordelia. We're in the ancient history class together."

"Yeah, I saw you in the room. You moved and took a seat next to me the other day."

"I'm usually kind of shy, but I just wanted to meet you. You're new, and I wanted to know if you would like a study partner to go through some of the Greek mythologies we're covering?"

"I'm probably good and a bit busy right now."

"But what's up with Bobby? He seems a bit bent."

"I don't really know. Bent? What's bent?"

"You know, frustrated, agitated, just bent out of shape."

"Yeah, I guess you could call it that," I said. "Look, Cordelia, my dad is coming to take Reba and me out to lunch in a bit." I slipped the key into the lock of my door and scanned for the thread that should be in the door. It wasn't there. I opened the door and started inside. "I really have to get ready."

Cordelia pressed her hand on the door and followed me inside. "He's got himself in trouble online, right?"

I froze and looked back at her. I hardly noticed that she was carrying an Alienware laptop. "What do you know?"

"Just that he's a real bright guy. Very techy. From an extremely wealthy family in Hillsboro. And he's a straight 4.0 student here. But," she held a finger up to her mouth as though beckoning me to be quiet, "he plays a lot of online games and not very frosty."

"Frosty?" I frowned.

"Think safe," she said. "Kind of something boys go through at this age. But I just feel that he's been targeted. Maybe a romance scam or something like that."

"You jump to conclusions."

"So, let's check it out." Cordelia stepped over to an empty space on my desk and opened her laptop. "I have access to the firewall logs. Think that might show something?"

"How?"

"I hang around. Listen to people and lurk, especially when they're bragging."

My threat and warning flags climbed higher. Cordelia wasn't just the deadpan sounding drone of a Wednesday Addams, she was dangerous.

"So, you've looked at the logs, what have you found?" I asked trying to keep the subject on track.

Cordelia smiled and tapped her sharp

pointy black painted fingernails on the keyboard. An Edit Pad text editor rose on the screen and showed extracts from the logs. "Four straight days on the Blockers of Doom game site. The amount of traffic for his first day is a lot. Kind of the traffic you'd expect while playing an MMRPG. But near the end of the hour, he switched to a different port on the game, and traffic tapered off. For the next three days at 7 PM sharp, he only connected via the alternate port and interacted for an hour each time. On those days, he wasn't playing the game. He was using it as a chat tool. On day 5 and 6, he only went to Instagram."

"That's a crap load of information derived from firewall logs," I said.

She grinned. "You're a techy type, too. You should know that the school also has an outbound proxy server set up on the firewall. So, yes, I didn't quite just use the firewall logs."

A proxy server might be very helpful in

finding Adda Lovelace, and I wondered if Cordelia and Adda might be one in the same. "It might be nice to see if we could log into this game he was playing." I said, opening a browser and going to download a copy of the game.

"Don't bother, I already have the game on my machine," Cordelia said in her deadpan tone. She launched the game on her machine, and it displayed the login page.

"Since you already have the proxy logs, do you have Bobby's username and password?"

Cordelia returned with a sly look. "Given the game uses an encrypted channel, what makes you think I might have his creds?"

"Just thought I'd ask." At that moment, my cell phone rang. It's my dad, Stafford, the detective from San Jose PD. "Wait." I tapped the answer button. "Hey, dad. Are you on your way?" Dad said he was still at the house but leaving soon. "Can you do me a favor? Grab my other backpack, the dark blue one, and bring it with you." I'm not certain why, but I asked him to bring the pack that held my DJI drones. That would complete the rest of the equipment. Fortunately, after Lesta Andropov smashed my original drone, I was able to replace the DJI system with a much newer and improved version. "Thanks. Yeah, Reba and I will meet you downstairs." Dad said he loved me and would be at school in about 45 minutes and rang off.

"Your dad, huh?" Cordelia said.

"Yep, he's signing Reba and me out to go to lunch with him."

"How nice."

"What about you, where's your family?"

"Florida. They wanted me as far away as possible." Cordelia said as she typed a username for Bobby onto the screen and followed with a 12-digit password that she had clearly memorized. Red flag flying high in the wind now. I thought about calling her Adda, knowing that proxy and firewall logs wouldn't have the full credentials of the user account. Given Adda's use of Meterpreter on the victim machines, she could easily have installed a keyboard logger or worse to capture Bobby's credentials.

"There, we're in. Now what?" She said.

I was a bit gobsmaked at this turn of events but played along. "Is Bobby logged in now?"

She tapped a few keys and selected an item to show local connections from the current account. Only one. "No. I'm the only one in the game."

"Can you return to the game he played last so we're in the correct arena?"

"You know I can." A mouse selection and the screen refreshed showing the last game arena. There were clearly 4 other players in the arena. Cordelia moved Bobby's avatar around a bit and looked through the immediate area. We could see 3 of the other players, but not the fourth.

In that instant, a chat window popped open and a player with the handle 'Valkiree' posted a question, that read: "Why are you online? Aren't you supposed to be going somewhere?"

Cordelia and I looked at each other. I pushed her off the keyboard and took over, typing: "I don't believe you. You have nothing?" There was a pause.

"You creep. Don't push me off my keyboard," Cordelia protested. She grabbed my shoulders trying to wrestle me away, but I pushed her back hard. She fell back a few steps.

"Just sit tight and let's see what happens."

Cordelia round housed a swing with a closed fist connecting solidly with my right shoulder. The pain was sharp as I nearly fell from the chair. I pushed her away once more.

"Now, look!" I said, pointing at the screen. A QR code appeared in the chat screen. My phone was just out of arm's reach, but Cordelia was really quick.

"It's a picture of Bobby, buck-ass

naked," she said.

I stood and looked at Cordelia's phone. It really was a picture of Bobby standing straight with his legs partially spread. The background was blurred but you could make out the outline of a bed and maybe the edge of a desk. No pictures or posters hung on the wall, no lamps in sight, nothing. There was a black bar with yellow writing that read 'censored' over his private parts. Cordelia laughed, not a hardy laugh but more of an A-hah sort of laugh. On the screen another message came in from Valkiree that read: "Log off and go now!" Valkiree closed the chat session.

There's a knock at my door. Reba stepped in just as I was reaching for my cell phone. I really wanted to capture that QR code. "Hi," Reba said. "Hope I'm not interrupting."

"No," I said. "This is Cordelia."

"I was just leaving," Cordelia pocketed her phone. She signed off from the game session and shut the lid of the Alienware, pressed it under her arm and headed for the door. "Thanks, Jason. That was very informative. Let's hang together, later." She flicked a grin at Reba in passing. Reba and I watched as she left.

"What was that all about? New girlfriend?" Reba said.

I frowned, shaking my head. "I'll tell you everything but let me call dad first." I rang dad. He was only a few minutes from the school. "We need to go out front." I grabbed only my tablet PC and jacket as I went to the door. Reba just shrugged and followed.

"I want to hear about Cordelia," Reba said in a sharp tone.

Outside in the courtyard, there were a lot of students and faculty passing between buildings. It was fortunate that Reba and I didn't have any class that afternoon. I related to Reba everything that happened and about the picture of Bobby. We stood by the fountain at the center of the courtyard looking back toward the dorm entrance.

"How did Cordelia know Bobby's password and handle that he used in the game?" Reba said.

"I have a theory but no real proof yet. Remember the other night when I set up the virtual honeypot, SweetHoney, to take the place of your laptop on the network?"

Reba nodded.

"The attacker ran Metasploit and Meterpreter to breech the system and do bad things. These two tools would allow Adda Lovelace to inject malware, like a key logger that could intercept credentials. Even though Cordelia claimed she got them from the firewall proxy logs, the firewall would have been blind to the connection credentials unless the game didn't use transport encryption. Well, the game does use encryption. There would be nothing in the logs that would have had anything like credentials."

"You think Cordelia and Adda Lovelace

might be one in the same?"

I nodded and opened my tablet. "I slipped my tracker into Bobby's jacket outside his room. Hopefully he's still wearing the jacket and didn't find it." I opened the app and scanned for the tracker. It was not an Apple Air Tag but another brand that I modified cutting the small speaker out of the device so it wouldn't beep when some other phone, like Bobby's, might detect that it's being followed. Not a foolproof method for hiding the tracker, but it might buy some time. The signal showed that the tracker was moving closer to the courtyard.

"It's Bobby," Reba said.

Bobby stepped out and down the stairs, staring intently at his phone's display as he walked toward the drive. Reba and I moved around to the opposite side of the fountain as casually as we could. I don't think Bobby ever looked up from his phone and just stood, bouncing nervously and glancing occasionally toward the entrance drive. A small grey

Corolla pulled in that displayed the blueish sign of an Uber car. Bobby waved, and the car stopped in front of him. He got into the back seat of the car, and it pulled around the fountain. Reba and I had just enough time to face the center of the fountain as the car circled behind us. This was all wrong, I thought. At least, the tracker was still on Bobby and transmitting a clean signal as it moved toward the school exit. "Where's dad?" I said, watching as the car disappeared down the long drive.

It wasn't too long before dad's unmarked police car pulled into the courtyard and stopped. Reba and I ran over on the driver's side and jumped into the backseat. Reba positioned my other backpack with the drones in between us as we buckled our seatbelts.

"Hello to you two," dad said very sarcastically. "I'm your chauffer now? You know, I'm supposed to go into the office and sign the two of you out for lunch."

"No time," Reba said.

"Dad, we need to head for Interstate 280 northbound," I said looking at my tablet.

"Why, may I ask?"

I gave him the short version of the story and insisted we needed to follow the tracker.

"Right," dad huffed. "I should know better than to question you two."

"Please, Detective Palmer," Reba added.

He shifted the car into drive and headed toward the freeway. "Do you want the lights and siren, too?"

"Stealth mode, please," I said. The tracker moved swiftly north, up the motorway.

Dad followed and pressed the gas hard as we accelerated in the gutless unmarked car. He was up to 75 miles per hour and seemed to be closing the gap with the tracker.

Ding. A message popped up on my tablet that shared messaging services with my phone. The message was from an unknown phone number. It read: "while you guys are chilling, you might want to look at this."

"What is it?" Reba leaned closer and looked at my tablet. "Unknown caller, but probably Cordelia."

"Whose Cordelia," Dad asked.

"Just drive, dad!" I said. "It's just another part of the problem." I opened the attached MOV file. It's a surveillance video from the other night of Reba and me sneaking into the headmaster's office. "Oh, great," I said to Reba.

"That camera must have been really well hidden," Reba said. "What now?"

Cordelia typed another message that said: "I suppose that you want me to remove this recording?"

"Oh no," I said breathing deeply and thinking what to do. "Dad, he just turned onto the Hillsboro exit and then right at the bottom. Go, go, go."

"This isn't good, JP," Reba whispered. "Tell her to delete it."

"She's got the other photo as well."

"Just tell her. We have no choice."

I typed a message saying that it would be nice if Cordelia deleted the CCTV video. This could easily get us suspended or worse, I thought.

"That goth witch is no good," Reba hissed, grinding her fist into the palm of her hand, then sat back and relaxed.

Cordelia's last message was that the three of us would talk at dinner tonight.

Dad was now on the Hillsboro exit and moving to the traffic light below. "Right at the bottom, then straight," I called. The tracker had stopped at the end of a cul-de-sac. I was still worried that Bobby might find it, so I dropped a pin at the location on the map. Sure enough, in a moment or two, the tracker moved out of the cul-de-sac and back onto the road. On the chance Bobby found it and dumped it in the Uber car, I navigated dad to where the pin had dropped. Dad pulled up in front of a very large, pink provincial home.

French provincial to be exact. It had a large garden in the front and cobbled drive leading to the garages on the side of the house. There was no sign of Bobby.

"Don't park in front of it!" I said to dad. "Pull around to the neighbors."

"I hope the heck you know what you're doing, JP." Dad let the car coast and parked before a neighbor's residence.

"Can you cross-reference the address to see whose house this is?"

Dad sighed and opened the laptop-like automated dispatch system in between the two front seats. He typed in the address, then waited. "Jackson and Amanda Maclean," dad read the result.

"We're at the right place."

"That two-story monster must be at least 10,000 square feet in size. It's huge," Reba said looking over her shoulder out the rear window.

"Yeah, and I bet they have great lawyers as well," dad added.

"Dad," I said. "Run the name Jackson Maclean and see what you might find on him. Who is he and what does he do?"

"Really!?" Dad sighed deeply, then typed away on his system. "This may take a while."

My tablet set aside, I pulled the grey drone and unfolded the propellers. I hoped there was enough battery in it for this mission. There wasn't much wind or bad weather today, so flying shouldn't be much of a problem. Opening the door, I set the drone on the ground then using the control console on my tablet, I launched the device.

"What are you doing?" Dad said. "Don't..."

But the drone was up and I navigated it by the front of the house at just a high enough so the four propellers couldn't be heard from the ground. The new 4K camera gave me a clear feed. I could see in the windows. I circled the drone around the garage side of the house and flew over the top of the house to the back. Turning the drone to look in the windows, I caught sight of a horrible view. I zoomed in. There was Bobby standing on a chair with a rope or something around his neck. "Dad! He's hanging himself." I leant forward showing dad the screen.

"Call 9-1-1, JP." He was half out the door. "Reba, come with me."

Dad and Reba rushed to the front of the house as I recalled the drone. I was really anxious now. It seemed like the drone took a real long time to return. I called emergency services and gave them the location. Once the drone was on the ground, I didn't even bother to fold the propellers back. I threw it in the car and bolted for the house. Upstairs, a maid or housekeeper screamed. I followed the sound.

Dad had his big bear-like arms wrapped around Bobby's torso lifting him to stop the pressure on his neck. Reba stood on a chair with scissors and cut the cord that attached to an open beam in the ceiling. Once on the ground, dad checked vitals and started CPR. All I could do was stand and watch for a moment. Reba had his head and held it as dad performed fast compressions. He'd pause and Reba gave mouth-to-mouth air, then dad started compressions again.

Outside the blare of sirens drew nearer. I just stood along with the housekeeper watching dad and Reba work. Once the shock of all this had settled a bit, I glanced around the room and wondered why Bobby chose this room to try and kill himself. This was a large office space. There was a giant mahogany desk along the far wall, two plush chairs facing the desk, and an active computer monitor on the credenza behind the desk. The broad leather desk chair was turned facing the computer screen. The maid sobbed constantly and spoke what sounded like prayers in Spanish.

Dad paused compressions. Reba gave two quick breaths, then dad pressed his two fingers to Bobby's neck. "There's a pulse!" Dad shouted. They both sat back a bit breathing deeply to catch their breath. "And he's breathing on his own, for now."

I breathed a sigh as a voice shouted from downstairs. Two firemen ran into the room carrying bags of medical equipment.

"We started CPR. No pulse or breathing when we cut him down." Dad again touched Bobby's neck. "He has a pulse and is breathing shallowly on his own."

"We got it," one fireman said as he took dad and Reba's place. The fireman ripped Bobby's shirt open and stuck two sensors from a defibrillator on his chest. The screen immediately beeped and registered the pulse. The other fireman set up an oxygen tank and placed a mask over Bobby's nose and mouth. The first fireman was in communication with the hospital and clearly received instructions to start an IV line.

I turned my attention back to the active computer screen and stepped behind the desk. Assuming the system had a 10-minute timeout when inactive, the screen saver or software lock could start at any time. I took a clean handkerchief out of my pocket, reached over and moved the mouse. As I did, I noticed that there was a USB thumb drive plugged into a port on the side of the monitor. A small tag dangled from the thumb drive that read: 'Just plug me in'.

Nothing on the screen showed that any programs or applications were running, but that didn't mean much. I could hear more boots climbing the stairs in the distance. I wrapped my linen handkerchief around the drive and quickly extracted it, slipping the flash drive into my pocket. In retrospect, this may have been a dumb move by me, but I somehow doubted that the local police would even consider taking the drive as evidence.

"Hey, you, kid!" A uniformed police officer shouted from the entrance. "What are you doing back there?"

"Nothing," I said.

Dad and Reba both looked at me, and

my dad waved his hand motioning me back into the middle of the room. An ambulance crew arrived wheeling a stretcher as the first fireman injected something into the IV line.

"You three and the housekeeper, out! Wait in the hall outside."

We complied as the fire and medical crews did their jobs. Another uniformed police officer arrived and immediately went upstairs.

I dialed Agent Wilson's number on my phone. Voicemail. I left a message explaining what had occurred and that we were probably heading for the local police station.

#

The three of us sat on a bench seat outside the interrogation rooms in the Hillsboro police station. An hour had passed since medics took Bobby to the hospital trauma unit.

"Detective Sergeant Stafford Palmer," a Hillsboro plainclothes officer poked his head out in the hall. Dad went into the room, and the door shut. Reba and I sat quietly. Neither of us played with cell phones or any other technology. We just sat with our arms folded in our laps.

After a half hour or so, Stafford stepped from the interview room and said, "next." Reba and I looked at one another, and I stood. "I'll be staying with you in there since I'm your father and they can't really interview you without me in the room."

I nodded.

"Sit tight, Reba," dad said as he shut the door and we sat across from the Hillsboro detective.

"Right," the detective started. "Jason, you're detective sergeant Stafford Palmer's kid, right?"

I nodded.

"Stafford, now you stay quiet unless you have an objection to voice."

Dad acknowledged with a curt nod.

"Jason Palmer, start from the beginning and don't leave out any details."

I did just that and started the story from

when Bobby and I met earlier this morning in the dining commons. I carefully walked through every step and only left off the part about Cordelia getting the supposed picture of Bobby. At the conclusion, the detective stopped writing, sat back, and chewed the end of his pen.

"Drones. Internet games. Hidden trackers. This sounds pretty farfetched to me. Do you know who might have encouraged the young Mr. Maclean to try and kill himself?"

"No, sir," I said. "But this sounds like a solid sextortion case to me. Some person online baited Bobby and then caused him to do this?"

"Got any evidence?" the Hillsboro detective asked as he scribbled a note.

Now I sat back in the chair and folded my arms.

"Thought so, you got nothing, kid." He turned to Stafford. "I've got half a mind to write up an obstruction of justice case against you and your son, here."

"Hey!" Dad's face was very sober and he frowned. "We saved that kid's life you know."

The detective nodded. "Maybe. We just heard that he's been placed into a medically induced coma. You got to him, but you may not have saved his life. Kids these days..." The door opened hard and Agent Wilson stepped inside, then shut the door.

"Who are you?" The Hillsboro detective said.

Wilson held open her FBI credentials where the detective could see them all. "They all work for me, and we're leaving." Dad and I stood.

The Hillsboro detective slapped his hand on the metal table. "I don't think so, Agent Wilson."

"Speak to your chief then," Wilson said. "For now, you can leave and go talk to him. Ask Rebecca to come into the room on your way out."

"Feds," the Hillsboro detective said

under his breath as he

slapped the folder closed and walked out of

the room. Reba joined us and sat in dad's

chair. She quivered a bit, and I could see that

she was really rattled.

I went through everything for Agent

Wilson and included what Cordelia and I

found when we logged into the game with

Bobby's account. She didn't like it much when

I told her that I didn't have a copy of the

picture.

"We can get the picture," Reba said in a

harsh and angry tone.

Wilson paused, then nodded. "Do it

over the next 24-hours or we'll come in and

get it from her."

"We'll get it. I don't think the formal

route will achieve much. We need more from

her and need her to give it willingly." I said

thinking about the CCTV footage of Reba and

me on our midnight raid at the headmaster's

office.

"Fine," Wilson said. "24-hours. Then we

kick some doors in." Reba and I both nodded.

The Hillsboro detective returned with a much older officer in uniform. The officer had a cluster of 5 gold stars on his epilate and a glistening gold badge. "Chief says we have to take a backseat on this. Agent Wilson, I hope you know what you're doing."

Wilson smiled, then looked to the chief. "We will bring all the resources we need onto this case and keep you informed. If we need assistance, we'll let you know."

"Yes," the chief said. "You will keep us informed. I spoke with your SAIC, and he gave me a commitment."

"SAIC?" I whispered to dad.

"Special Agent in Charge," Dad whispered back.

"We shall," Wilson acknowledged. "For now, I'm going to take them to the San Mateo field office for further work. Oh, and Chief, nothing in the daily police blotter on this as well. It's an active federal investigation and we need to keep the lid on this for now. Have you contacted the parents?"

"Yes. Mr. and Mrs. Maclean are flying back from Denver as we speak. They should be in later this afternoon."

Wilson pulled out a business card and handed it to the chief. "Have them contact me when they return." Wilson stood and beckoned for us to follow. Like dutiful baby ducks, we followed her from the room and station.

As we reached dad's car, I felt the linen wrapped flash drive in my pocket. "Agent Wilson," I said. "One more thing. This was plugged into the desktop computer in that office where Bobby was found." I held it open with the small tag that had 'just plug me in' written in blue ink.

Wilson carefully wrapped the drive back in the linen handkerchief and took it. "You think this might have been plugged in by Bobby Maclean before he did the deed?"

"Good possibility," I said. "It was crazy in there and I figured the locals wouldn't even consider looking at the computer."

"I'll get this to the field lab in San Mateo right away." Wilson pulled her cell phone out of her purse after placing the drive inside. She ordered a field agent to the hospital and a forensic team to the house with a request to fingerprint Bobby Maclean. "You guys head back. And JP, remember 24 hours on that photo from Connie or whatever her name is."

"Cordelia," Reba corrected her.

"Right." Agent Wilson walked toward her car with her cell phone held to her ear.

We got back in the car, and I carefully stowed the drone.

"How'd you know you'd need the drone?" Dad asked after we were all in the car. Reba sat up in front this time, and me in the back.

"I didn't," I said. "I just figured you were coming and could bring it along."

"Good thing." Dad started the car and pulled from the parking lot. "I have half a mind to take you guys back home for the night. This was all quite disturbing. What, seeing a school chum try to end his own life and all."

With that Reba burst into tears, and I followed soon after. Once I composed myself, I said, "You heard Agent Wilson, we've only got 24-hours to get that picture. We need to head back to school."

6. A REVERSE TROJAN HORSE

6:30 PM, no more news on Bobby. Reba and I were at our usual table in the dining commons. Both sober, silent and staring at meatloaf, string beans, and something resembling mashed potatoes but with chunks of brown skin. Reba poked at her food with her fork and only ate a couple bites of the loaf.

Crystal and Toby sat across and down a bit on the long table. Both their trays were piled high with food. It was sick when Crystal scooped up potatoes and meatloaf and then fed Toby. In turn, he did the same. They laughed and nearly spit the food out between giggles. Reba's eyes rolled and she poked a bit harder at the meatloaf. I could tell she wanted to leave. I patted her shoulder, but she pulled away from me.

"When's she going to get here?" Reba said.

As if on demand, Cordelia approached the table. She wore a frilly black skirt with white borders, black torn fishnet tights and shiny black combat boots. She dropped her tray down and sat across from Reba and me.

"Oh my, Toby," Crystal said from the far side of the table. "Looks like Rebecca dear has a new friend."

"Looks to me like the neighborhood has gone to the dogs," Toby stood, picking up his tray. Crystal flicked the back of her hand toward Cordelia then followed Toby. They moved to another table.

"Kinda looks like they really love you, too," Reba said to Cordelia.

I could have sworn Cordelia's eyes were brown when I saw her late this morning. Now they were bright turquoise blue with hardly a hint of the iris.

"Ms. Popular and Mr. Jock aren't my favorite members of the specie," Cordelia said. "Someday they'll be culled from the herd."

"Okay," Reba said. "And us?"

"You two, I don't mind in the least." She pointed a black spike fingernail at me. "He's Mr. Bright-Techy-Guy, and while you...." She pointed the spike nail across at Reba. "While you are the very athletic guardian."

"Thanks. I guess," Reba said.

I bumped my elbow into Reba's ribs. She needed to shut up now. Leaning forward, "Cordelia, we really need something from you..."

"The CCTV, right?" She stabbed her fork into the pile of mash, and it stood rigid. "I took care of it from the school's DVR already. The drive had an unfortunate accident and got reformatted. All videos from that night are magically missing."

"How can we trust you?" Reba asked.

Cordelia swirled her fork around in the potatoes for a bit, stalling for time. I think she already knew where this conversation might be heading. "You can't. I guess you have to trust me."

"Did you keep a copy?"

Cordelia smiled. Her perfect white teeth were bright against her dark black painted lips. "Maybe."

Reba rose and started coming across the table at her, but I pressed Reba's shoulder down.

"Cordelia," I said. "We'll have to trust you for now. There is one more thing that I really need from you."

"What's that?"

"Can I see the picture of Bobby you pulled from the game the other night? Reba hasn't seen it."

She shrugged her shoulders and tapped a few commands on her phone then held it in

the middle of the table toward Reba. I didn't
need to prompt Reba as she snatched the
phone from Cordelia's hand. "Give it back!"
Cordelia lurched across the table at Reba just
as Reba tossed me the phone. Reba grabbed
Cordelia's wrist and twisted hard.

"Ude garami," Reba lashed out in
Vietnamese, then grinned. "Now sit down and
don't make a sound if you want to continue
using this hand."

Cordelia sat back and relaxed, but Reba
held on. I hit the share button on Cordelia's
phone and sent the full image to an
anonymous Proton email address I maintained
for occasional use. After the message went, I
deleted it from her phone. This wasn't a
surefire method to remove the photo from
Cordelia's phone. If her phone was set to use
iCloud, the image could still be in her photo
library. I set the phone back in front of
Cordelia, and Reba relaxed her hold on the
wrist.

Cordelia sat back rubbing and flexing the

wrist. "I'm into rough stuff more than most others." She looked at Reba. "We'll have to grapple sometime when I'm ready." Then looked to me. "That, and the CCTV video are going to cost you something in return."

"Like what?" I asked.

"Like you have to take me to the prom. I think that would be a fair trade."

"Not a fair trade," Reba said.

"After the prom, you can have him back all to your own," Cordelia said.

I patted Reba's shoulder to sit down and signaled her not to make a scene. "I don't know how to dance and would be no fun at all."

"Nerd boys can't dance. Just bounce around on the floor and hug me tight during slow numbers."

"Ooooo," Reba hissed. "Let's go to the gym and see who wins a wrestling match right now."

"Another time, girl." Cordelia dug into the meatloaf and ate. "I'm hungry now."

"Come on, Reba," I said standing and grabbing my tray. "We need to make a phone call. It's time." We both stood and carried our trays toward the kitchen drop.

"That witch is really bad."

"Just be cool. We may need her. She has a lot of access around here."

We passed by the table where Crystal and Toby sat finishing their blue-plate special, as the cafeteria called it.

"Hey bro," Toby called to me and motioned us over. "Lost your appetite sitting with wannabe Wednesday girl, did you?"

"I'm just not into this blue-plate special stuff tonight."

"Bro, Bobby's gone and I need a bit of technology help?"

"What do you mean, gone?" I said. Reba stepped up behind me.

"He's gone. Like, nowhere to be found, bro." Toby said in his usual jock way. "He helps me when I have technology problems with my laptop. Think you can stop by later?

Maybe you know how to deal with it. My laptop display keeps going black. Kind of a rando thing."

"Maybe later. Reba has to call her mum and check in."

"Mommy wants to know you're not up to trouble," Crystal chimed in. Yet another girl baiting Reba.

"Catch you later," I said nudging Reba to continue on our way to dump the trays.

"That girl burns me up as much as the Wednesday Witch," Reba hissed. "I really hate it here but I'm not going to give them the satisfaction of breaking me. And..." Reba set her tray on the return rack. "I don't have to call my mom."

"Code for Wilson," I said. "I'll send you the picture, then you get it to Wilson and give her a call."

#

Back in my dorm room, I packaged the image up and mailed it to Reba. She stood behind me and got the image on her phone then forwarded it to Wilson's mobile and email addresses. It wasn't more than a few minutes before Reba's phone rang. It was Wilson. Reba put her on speaker.

"Thanks, guys," Wilson said. "JP, I think you're right about the entire sextortion situation. I'll get the image into the lab and see what they discover."

"Glad we could help," Reba said.

"There's a bit more," Wilson said. "That thumb drive you collected. It was covered in Bobby's fingerprints. The physical image of the drive that was extracted had a very interesting ISO file on it as well as an autorun program. Seems that it immediately installed a trojan on the system and opened a reverse shell to an IP address in Turkey. Within 10 minutes, someone accessed that connection."

"Did they take anything?" Reba asked.

"Can't tell from the drive by itself. I have a forensic team heading to the house to image that machine. The parents are back, and they're in a real mess over the situation. Mr. Maclean is cooperating, given he's the CEO of a large mining consortium, and his company notified the Street that a news release to their investors was forthcoming. I have a real bad feeling about what might have been taken. We have only a few hours to forensicate the whole thing and get evidence should we want to halt trading on the stock."

"Depending on how stealthy the trojan is," I said. "It may have cleaned up after itself, and you might not get much."

"That's my worry."

"Any news on Bobby?" Reba said.

There was a brief pause as Wilson spoke to some other people in her office. "He's holding his own, for now. The doctors are maintaining him in a medically induced coma. We won't know much until he's stable enough to wake him up."

"That's sad, I hope he pulls through."

"Oh, and before I go, there's one more

thing. The Hillsboro PD guys are still working through their case. I heard they may be getting a search warrant for Bobby's room at the school. Just something for you two to be aware about. Stay out of their way if they show up. That's it. I'll let you know if we find anything on the system." Wilson rang off.

Reba sat on my bed, and I plopped down at the desk. "A coma," Reba said. "That doesn't sound good."

My mum, being a trauma doctor at a hospital had told me about patients that are put into induced comas. "He has a chance," I said. "The coma should let his brain functions recover."

Reba held her hands over her face. "At least we got there and tried. Your dad was the big hero. Without your drone and him, Bobby would be dead."

"Search warrant," I said thinking about Wilson's closing remark.

"What?"

"Search warrant. Wilson said that the

Hillsboro locals would be obtaining a search warrant for Bobby's room." I stood. "We need to have a look around that room before they do."

"And?" Reba said standing.

I pulled my room key from my pocket and looked at its profile, counting the teeth on the key with my free forefinger. "It's just a 4-cylinder Schlage lock, probably set for a master key as well." I rummaged through the drawers of my desk. Where did I stick them? They're here somewhere. I pulled out a plastic tube that held a thin set of tools. "Bingo. Remember Dr. Edmund Locard?"

"Every contact leaves a trace," Reba said.

"Right. Someone had to give Bobby that drive to put in his dad's machine. Whoever did it probably left it in Bobby's room for him to find." We stepped into the hall and I put the thread in my door jam and locked my door. "I figure that there was a reason Wilson gave us the heads-up on the locals coming to serve a search warrant."

"She wants us to do it first."

7. NOT AN UNREASONABLE SEARCH

There's a note on Bobby's door from the headmaster advising that no one should enter this room without authorization or face severe disciplinary action.

"Well, this is a clue," I said. "The police must have called the headmaster and asked him to seal the room as they're coming with a warrant."

I popped the plastic lid from the pick set and the tools flew all over the floor.

"Good grief, JP." Reba bent over and

collected them. "Can you be any more of a klutz?" She handed them back to me. "Have you ever done this before?"

"I practiced on a couple of padlocks."

"Give them to me." Reba grabbed back the tools and fanned them open like a deck of cards. "I need the lever to apply pressure and I like this rake. You hold the rest and keep a lookout."

Reba knelt in front of the door and inserted the short end of the lever into the lock on the side away from the cylinders. With her thumb, she held gentle pressure on the long part of the lever. This would be just enough to get the cylinders to hold position as she raked gently. "Yup. I feel four cylinders. First one is in place. Now the second and third are up. And the fourth." The door bolt slid back and released. Proudly, she stood smiling, reached for the door and opened it. We were in.

"Gloves. I forgot the gloves." I said, exiting the room and returning shortly with two pairs of blue latex gloves. Reba still stood in the same spot when I left and shut the door with her foot. The room was dark with blackout drapes pulled closed. She flicked on her phone's flashlight. "We're going to need more light in here."

I'll get the drapes. I pulled them shut and remembered what Reba did in the headmaster's office. There was a folded blanket at the bottom of Bobby's bed. I took this and stuffed it under the door while Reba set the door lock again and turned on the lights. "Let's do this in an organized fashion," she said.

"I'll start with the desk," I said.

"Yeah, and I'll do the closet." Reba went to the modest wardrobe and worked through the hanging clothes and handful of boxes lining the top shelf.

I opened the desk drawers and looked for anything that might be related to Bobby receiving the flash drive. The drawers had pens, some scratch paper, a half-solved

Rubik's cube, and a few small plastic game figures. Nothing of any note. His laptop was closed and on the desk with the power cord and Ethernet cable plugged in. I lifted the lid. In a moment, I was presented with a login screen that had a thumbnail picture of Bobby with his big, bushy afro and broad smile. More of a taunting smile. I recalled that Cordelia entered a 12-character password into the game when she logged in as Bobby. If I wanted to do a quick forensic collection, I'd need to log into this system. "Let's just hope he isn't using BitLocker and that the storage isn't encrypted." I pulled a CSI thumb drive from my pocket and inserted it into the USB port of the laptop. I then signaled for the laptop to do a hard boot. Fortunately, the default BIOS settings hadn't been altered and the system booted from my thumb drive. This was actually a drive I'd prepared awhile back running the Deft Linux environment. I plugged a T7 drive into another port that was 2TB in size, more than enough to store a captured image from most laptops.

Once the Linux screen was up, I mounted the internal drive from Bobby's laptop as an NTFS drive on Deft environment. I was able to read the drive's root and see files. No BitLocker, nice. The device volume was /dev/sdc as identified by Linux. I ran 'ewfacquire', a Linux tool to acquire and create an EWF compressed disk image of the physical device identified as /dev/sdc1 and wrote it out to my T7 drive. This would take some time to complete, but in the end, I'd have a full physical image of Bobby's laptop ready to analyze.

"Find anything?" Reba stepped up behind me. "Nothing in the closet."

"I'm pulling a full physical image of Bobby's laptop. It's pretty big, and we could be in here for a long while."

"Anything in the desk?" Reba said.

"Junk. And more junk."

"How about under it or in the trash?"

I pulled the black trash can from

beneath the desk and carefully moved a few crumpled pieces of tissue until I saw shreds of hand-torn paper with ink on them. Lifting each piece from the can, I set them on the desk beside the computer. Reba worked this jigsaw and aligned the pieces of paper together. "It's a handwritten note." Reba kept reorganizing the pieces.

"Each alphabetic character is block printed in upper case," Reba said. "But it makes no sense." The reconstructed note read:

'Vram znoy otzu euax vuvy sginotk tuc. Ju oz tuc!'

"It's encrypted," I said. "Or, actually, enciphered... There's no attempt to hide the size of each word or the punctuation. There's a ripped-up envelope in here as well." I set those carefully on the desk above the message then, using my cell phone, I snapped photos of the note and envelope.

"This might be how the thumb drive was delivered to Bobby." Reba snapped a picture with her cell phone as well. "Do you think there's a key?"

"No. It resembles a simple encoding and not encrypted. If there was padding, and the resulting structure appeared in a block of characters, I'd say encrypted with a key. So, if we imagine Bobby getting this envelope and examining the contents, he'd have to have some simple way to figure out the actual message. Now," I looked at Reba, "We have made the women of Bletchley Park proud and figured it out the old-fashioned way."

I put the bits of paper and envelope back into the trash can and mixed it with the other material while Reba killed the lights and folded the blanket. "What about your drive?"

"It's going to run for several hours yet. 512 gig disk will take a few hours to finish. I'll come back and retrieve it later."

"What about the search warrant?"

"Dad told me they're always marked for daytime service unless there's some exigent circumstance. They won't be here until morning at best."

I stood behind Reba as she carefully opened the door, just a crack. "Hall's clear." We stepped out and Reba shut the door behind us. She pulled out the pick tools. "Should I lock it?"

"Probably," I said as Reba set about with the lever and the rake. "Wait. We have to come back. The note should keep others out. Leave it."

I tugged at her. I could just hear someone coming down the hallway. "We go our separate ways, now. It's real close to when Mrs. Fadler will be on patrol looking for students out of their rooms."

Nodding, I agreed. I went back to my room a few doors down. The thread was still on the door, and I was inside in no time. I couldn't believe how tired I was after the day's adventure. Needing sleep, I secured my system and slipped the pick set back into my desk drawer, then plopped back on my bed with only my cell phone. The picture of the enciphered text troubled me. In my mind, I tried a common Rot13 cipher where each letter was offset to mean a letter 13 alphabetic digits away. The first block, Vram, came out as: 'Ienz', garbage. I did a 8-character rotation: Vram came out as: 'Njse'. Still garbage. I set the phone down on my chest and rested my eyes. I fell asleep.

8. DO IT NOW

The next morning, I woke with my cell phone on the floor and still dressed in the same clothes and shoes I had on the prior night.

At breakfast, Reba came skipping in through the dining commons wearing her soccer uniform and stopped in front of my table where I sat with a soggy bowl of cereal in front of me.

"Well, did you figure it out?" Reba said.

"I fell asleep."

"Plug this into your pop's machine now.

Do it now."

"That was the handwritten message?" I said.

"Yup. ROT-6. Yesterday was the 7th and the day before was the 6th. So, rotating 6 characters worked," Reba sat next to me with a cup of tea in her hand. "Big practice today and I'm real excited. Hey, wait. Since you fell asleep, I take it you didn't get the drive out of Bobby's system?"

"Oh damn, that's right. It's still plugged in and running."

"We better get that back before the cops show up," Reba stood still sipping her tea. I abandoned my cereal and followed her back to the dorms.

Reba reached for Bobby's doorknob. It was still unlocked and opened with ease. "Pick set?" She said. "We'll need to lock this when you're done. I'll run back to your room while you extract your drive."

"Right."

The computer was still running with the

Linux terminal shell still displayed on the screen. 'xwfacquire' had finished and displayed information statistics it had just collected. Normally, I'd save the information displayed on the screen to a file and put it with image file on the T7 disk drive. On this occasion, I took a picture with my cell phone of the computer display, shut down the shell and instructed Linux to Power off.

Once down, I unplugged both the flash drive and the T7 storage drive. All drives safely in pockets, I shut the laptop's lid and walked out of the room. Reba inserted the picks. I gave a thumbs up sign and took a post to watch for anyone coming down the hall. Reba knelt and worked the lever and rake until the lock was bolted shut. She replaced the tools into the case and then dutifully wiped the doorknob clean of any fingermarks.

Who do we encounter walking back toward my room? Cordelia. Today, she was modestly dressed in black jeans and a frilly white blouse but still wearing her black military-like combat boots. "Thought I'd find you two together," she said. "Reba dear, looks like rain today so you might get wet on the field."

"The wetter, the better," Reba said.

"Nothing like girls sliding around in the mud," Cordelia said.

Reba grinned. For a moment, I actually thought she didn't know what to say.

"So, Jason," Cordelia said holding up her well-read copy of Ovid. "Thought we could study book 5 together. You said you really like the stories of the Gorgon Medusa." She batted her long eyelashes at me twice.

Now it was me that didn't know how to reply. Reba leaned closer to my ear and said, "Be careful of this witch. I have to go to practice." Then to Cordelia. "It's time I head off to practice. Play nice you two."

"We will," I said in Reba's wake.

Cordelia followed me inside. I slipped the flash drive and T7 from my pocket into the drawer as she was turned away. "You know,

Cordelia, I was planning on doing a bit of system work."

"Come on. We'll go to the community seating area to study there if it makes you more comfortable."

What the heck. I picked up my Ovid book and followed her out of the room. I carefully locked the door on my way. The common area had several easy chairs, a foosball table, and a few sofas. I chose one of the easy chairs and sat. Cordelia moved her chair a bit closer.

"Let's start with Perseus 2," Cordelia said. "I'll begin. The poems should all be read aloud." She read up to the point when Phíneus threatened Perseus, accusing him of stealing his bride-to-be, Andrómeda.

"Andrómeda may have been betrothed to Phíneus," I said, "Until she was bound as an offering to a great sea monster.

Perseus defeated the monster and Cephus and Cassiopía, Andrómeda's father and mother, were delighted at the monster's defeat and hailed Perseus as the newly betrothed."

"But the prior betrothed took exception and created a riot at the wedding dinner," Cordelia said. "Ovid went into great graphic detail of the riot. Many of Perseus' friends were killed even though he was in possession of the ultimate weapon."

"It wasn't until Perseus was about to be defeated that he brought out Medusa's head and turned them all to stone. I find it most interesting and wonder why Perseus didn't produce the head earlier, before many of his friends were slaughtered?"

"Good point," Cordelia said.

"Ah, but maybe this is an example of Ovid writing for his readers at the time. He wrote for Romans, and they were accustomed to great blood lust. If Perseus had turned them to stone at the start, the bloody battle would have been much different, and a lot of the action would not have occurred."

"That's a good observation," Cordelia

said. "Probably not the analysis that our teacher wants though."

At that moment, Toby interrupted us in the study area. "Hey Jason," Toby said in a masterful tone. "I really need your help, now! My stupid Mac won't recognize my finger to log in. I'm really annoyed having to type a password all the time." He held his MacBook out for me to take. Frankly this might be the diversion I needed to step away from Cordelia. I didn't mind studying with her but was suspicious of her intentions.

"Sorry," I said to Cordelia.

She flicked a dismissive wave. Toby and I walked over to one of the study desks in the corner and I had him set the MacBook down. I sat in front of the machine. "So, what's your password?"

"I can type it for you," Toby said.

"Go for it."

Toby leant over my shoulder and typed the characters 'irain5upreme!'. I should have figured he'd use rain as in what falls from the sky rather than reign that describes the activity of a ruler. I opened system settings and behaved like I was moving the mouse for the touchpad settings but selected 'Sharing', instead. The sharing settings came up. None of the remote access settings were ticked and I quickly checked Remote Login then rapidly returned to the main settings menu.

"What are you doing?" Toby said.

"Sorry, it's been awhile since I worked on a MacBook and went the wrong way. Thought it was under General. My bad." I scrolled down the left menu and selected Touch ID & Password. "This is where we want to be." Once I selected the first finger, I told Toby to place his right index finger on the pad. He just touched it and pulled away.

"Watch the screen as it reads your finger," I said. "Again." He touched it and pulled away. "Not enough. Give me your hand or we'll be here way too long." I took his hand in the same manner a policeman might collect fingermarks from a suspect. I tapped his finger on the pad, held it, and moved to the next portion of the fingerprint. Then repeated it until the system reported that the fingermark was fully recognized. "There, done. Now we'll log out and see if it works."

Once the machine rebooted and was back to the login screen, I pointed at the touchpad. "Touch it now but hold your finger gently on the pad."

Toby set his finger on the pad, and the MacBook logged him in. "Oh, man, you're the techy GOAT."

"You're welcome." I shut the laptop and passed it back to him.

Toby smiled, gave me a thumbs up and walked off. I sat for a moment and wondered about what had just happened.

Toby turned and looked back at me. "Hey, if Bobby doesn't ever come back, you'll be my tech-man."

"Only, if I have time," I nodded. What does Toby know about Bobby? I wondered. That was even more baffling. There hasn't been any news releases on campus or discussion about Bobby, yet he seems to know something. I picked up my book and figured I had no more excuse to leave Cordelia sitting by herself. But when I turned, she was nowhere to be seen. Ah, well.

Back at my room, I immediately noticed that the thread was no longer in the door jam. Slowly unlocking the door, I went in, and Reba sat at my desk looking at me.

"Did you expect someone else?" Reba rubbed a bath towel through her hair and was dressed in fresh clothing.

"Cordelia's been on the prowl. She probably has a master key to all the dorm rooms." I set my books down and pulled a second chair beside Reba. "That was a quick practice."

"The field was too muddy and a mess. We did a few laps of the track dribbling and passing the balls, then went inside the gym for the rest," Reba said. "I showered and popped back over here. You were busy with

Toby when I got here."

"I want to take a look at the photo." Opening my computer and my forensic investigative virtual machine, I logged in and then carefully copied the photo image I'd grabbed from Cordelia's phone. I suspected that this image was actually a deep fake done possibly using one of the AI tools. Given this was a photo taken by Cordelia's mobile phone of a computer screen, any metadata would be totally useless. That didn't mean I couldn't find information about the photo itself that might support the conclusion that it was fake.

I opened the image. It was a picture of Bobby standing naked and facing a mirror. The actual image was a reflection of Bobby as if taken by a camera looking at a mirror reflection. A yellow rectangle with the word "censored" covered his private parts. "Let's take a closer look at the image. I'll use a pixel editor to examine the area of contact with the background."

"But it's so blurred," Reba said.

"Even with the blur, we should be able to see transitions between the clear image and the blurred component. If the transitions are inconsistent, that leans toward a manipulated image." Along the line of the throat and neck, he had a protrusive Adam's apple that was fully rendered on the left sphere of the body but absent on the right. More points to suggest a manipulated image. Bobby had naturally curly hair that he wore in a medium-long Afro. Examining the pixels in between the strands of hair showed several inconsistencies against the background. At this point, I sat back and pondered my next action with the image.

"What now?" Reba asked.

"I'd send the picture to my dad and ask him to put it through the tools they have to test if this is a fake image," I said. "I only wish we could have obtained the real image from the site as rendered on Cordelia's system. A photo of a photo doesn't really help, but they may be able to discover something."

"That sounds like a plan."

"But is it?" I said.

"Hey," Reba sat up and stared at me. "You're always the one that says when cyber-bad things happen and victims have to tell a parent or the police. So, just do it."

"You're right." I started by encrypting the image with a key and then sent the encrypted image to my dad along with a request that he run it through the police department systems to test for a deep fake. I then sent a second email with the passkey so he could decrypt the image. "I guess we wait and see what his lab comes back with."

"You think it's fake?" Reba said.

I nodded. "A few indicators suggest it. Kind of like when you use Pixelmator on your phone to alter an image and add someone who wasn't really there. It creates inconsistencies. I really want to know the score the police tool comes back with."

"Oh, and there's this," Reba passed me

an Android phone. When I touched the screen, it powered and logged in. "I found it jammed between the mattress and the frame of the bed in Bobby's room."

I took the phone. "When were you going to tell me about this discovery?" I asked as I fished out a few cables from my lower desk drawer.

Reba punched my shoulder. "Don't be inconsiderate," she said. "There's been a lot happening, and it slipped my mind."

I connected it to the forensic investigative environment. Because the phone still had power and didn't require a passcode to access, I went into system settings and switched on USB debug mode. I used ADB to dump a full physical image of the phone. Since this was running in a terminal shell that remotely connected to the phone, there weren't any meters or information on how long this process would take.

"Um," Reba said. "I kind of forgot something else. It's already late morning and today is the day that the cops are coming to search Bobby's room."

"So, we kind of need to put the phone back where you found it?"

Reba nodded.

"Let's see how long this takes." I tapped the return key a couple times, and it just highlighted that ADB was still chugging away.

After about 20 minutes of foot tapping, and Reba pacing back and forth, ADB finished. I verified that I had the image file and activated a hashing tool to calculate the SHA-1 of it. Ejecting the phone, I then went in and returned the settings to the way they were when she handed it to me.

"Wipe it down," I said tossing the lightweight Samsung phone to her. "Go see if you can put it back and I'll head down in case I need to stall the cops."

Before I went, I launched Autopsy and told it to ingest the Android phone and run the Android analyzer. I also plugged in the drive that I captured the physical image of Bobby's laptop, and Autopsy loaded that image as well into the same case files.

We both walked by Bobby's room and realized the door was still locked with the headmaster's warning sign displayed. I nodded to Reba, and she began picking the lock while I walked closer to the stairs and the community room. After a bit, I jogged down the stairs and out the dorm door.

#

Outside, I took up a position at the fountain in the center of the courtyard. A black Chevy Tahoe pulled in and stopped in front of the administration building. A man and woman wearing suits stepped out. I could tell that the man wore a waist-held firearm from the telltale bulge and the way his jacket fell over his hips. He looked a lot like the detective we met at Bobby's house and later at the station. I didn't recognize the woman at all. They both walked into the administration building. This had to be the cops.

I sent a text to Reba warning that the police were here. No response. When I thought they'd be coming out of the administration building, I headed around the back of their vehicle on an intercept course. They walked by me as they turned toward the dorm building.

"Hold on a second," the male detective said. "Hey kid. You're Jason Palmer, aren't you? I didn't know you went to the same school as Robert Maclean."

"You never asked me," I said. Turning to face the group.

"Detective," the headmaster interrupted. "I really must object. You cannot interview a different student without a parent giving consent or being present." Mr. Hannah motioned for the detective to carry on. "If you need to speak with Mr. Palmer, I can contact his parents to arrange it."

The detective gave a long, deep sigh. "That's alright Headmaster Hannah." Then back to me. "Don't take any long trips. I may want to speak with you later."

"You know where to find me." I turned and walked toward the classroom building. On my way, I texted Reba again saying that she had better be clear of the room. Still no answer.

I sent a '999' to Reba's phone; the UK number for calling emergency services. No response.

Once the two detectives and headmaster disappeared into the dorm building, I looped around the fountain and jogged back toward the dorm building as well. A single word message appeared on my phone 'clear'. Reba was safe. I slowed to a casual walk.

Upstairs, I passed through the community room and walked through the hallway toward my room. Passing Bobby's room on the way, I could hear the detectives along with the voice of Dorm Mom. From outside in the hall, I couldn't make out what they were saying.

I dare not linger or move closer to Bobby's door. I walked on. Reba was back at my computer watching the screen as the Autopsy ingest modules finished running over the Android phone. The ingest modules still ran on the physical image from Bobby's laptop.

As she'd seen me do a few times before, Reba opened the phone's data artifacts for communication accounts. There were several accounts including Facebook, Viber, WhatsApp and Email. Next, she popped open the Autopsy Communications Visualization tool. This tool organized each communication application presenting a browser for the different accounts and number of items contained. From here, she opened the account with the largest number of items, WhatsApp. "You okay if I drive?" Reba said.

"You're doing fine."

"I learned by watching you." Reba navigated through the various WhatsApp communications on the device. There were chat groups with what appeared to be other students and some one-on-one chat and phone calls. Most of the phone numbers were within either the 415, 650, or 510 area codes, which covered several of the San Francisco Bay Area counties. There were several accounts with only 5-digit numbers that contained order acknowledgements or spam messages. Looking at the base Android messaging app, there were several threads. One was identified as a one-on-one thread with someone named Gina. Since on the Internet nobody knows you're a dog, we can't assume that 'Gina' is even a girl. The conversation started at about the time Bobby was playing Blockers of Doom. During the conversation, Gina claimed to be in LA and claimed to have found Bobby through some mutual friend at his school.

"This Gina person seems to have just enough information that maybe she obtained from someone here in the school," Reba said. "Or Gina and someone here are one in the same."

Reba scrolled further through the conversation thread. It's a day later from when the thread started. Gina encourages Bobby to send a photo or two of himself and Gina sends a photo as well.

"Extract that photo and let's have a look at it," I said.

"Got it," Reba said.

I took over the keyboard and transferred the jpg image file to one of my cloud systems where the Faces software ran. "To start with," I loaded the jpg into Faces, "Let's scan and search the Internet for any matches on this photo." I grabbed my tablet PC and logged into one of the cloud servers. Faces had consumed the photo and finished calculating facial geometry to perform the search. Faces usually took hours to complete searching social media and many other visual platforms but, for this photo, Faces had already derived solutions, including images that matched 100%.

"It's a stock photo, Reba," I said.

She sighed, "That figures."

I scrolled through more of the thread until the following date (just three days since the thread discussion started). Gina claimed to have been caught by her big brother. The tone and demeanor of the thread changed, language became intense, and the 'brother' sent Bobby the photo of Bobby wearing no clothes.

"Big Brother says to Bobby using the phone of Gina's that 'the world will know you soon, you perv!'," I read. "And then, Brother says 'Do as you're told. I own you.'" I pointed to the screen. "That was all sent on the 5th,"

"On the 6th, Bobby received the envelope with the encoded message and thumb drive," Reba said.

"Then, on the 7th, Bobby plugged the drive into his dad's computer system and tried to hang himself."

I stood and stepped over to the window and looked down on the courtyard and entrance to the administration building. The black Chevy Tahoe SUV was still parked by the entrance to the admin building. It was already the end of the day's class sessions. Throngs of students walked between the classroom building, the dorm, and the dining commons. I grabbed my cell phone from the desk and called my dad. I'm not certain why I called him instead of Agent Wilson, I was in shock by what we'd discovered.

"Hey, dad," I said once he answered. "Reba and I discovered a bunch of stuff relevant to Bobby's case in his room."

"Don't tell me you searched the room?" Dad said.

"We had a look around." I went on to describe and explain everything we discovered, including the second cell phone. At the end of the call, I asked if he could relay the message to Agent Wilson.

A knock at the door, and the door swung open. Dorm Mom stood there looking at both Reba and me.

"Don't you ever wait for us to answer the door after you knock?" Reba said.

Dorm Mom just frowned. "Missy, it's time for you to go to dinner. Right now! And you," she looked at me, "will accompany me to the headmaster's office."

I was still on the call with my dad. "Don't you tell them anything," dad said then rang off.

I locked my computer screen with a couple of strokes and packed my laptop into my backpack along with a notepad, then Reba and I followed Dorm Mom out of the room. Dorm Mom actually used the master key to lock my door behind us.

9. PLAYING WITH PUTTY

Headmaster Hannah sat behind his desk holding a copy of the search warrant that had been executed. "It's always fun when the police show up with a warrant to search a student's room," he said. "I don't know how, but it seems you were involved in this matter."

I shrugged.

"You can't just shrug this off, Jason Palmer. That police detective clearly knew who you were as we passed by the courtyard fountain. Would you agree with that?"

"Possibly," I said. "He may have confused me with someone else."

"Oh, I think not. He told you specifically not to travel anywhere. Didn't he?"

"Yeah, I think he said something like that."

"So, tell me how you're involved? And where is Mr. Robert Maclean?"

"Robert?" I stalled.

"Bobby, then," he slapped his hand on the desk.

"I don't know where Bobby is right now." I took a deep breath. "Maybe you, sir, should contact Bobby's parents."

Headmaster Hannah reclined back in his chair. "I've done that already. They've informed me that he had been injured and is recovering. Now, I'm asking you once again, how are you involved?"

Don't look nervous. Don't look at the ceiling since the answers aren't there. And don't glance to the right, a tell-tail sign of a lie. "Sir," I held my stare straight at the headmaster. "I don't know how Bobby might have been hurt. I arranged for him to meet my dad, and we were going to lunch together. That's all."

A long pause followed until the headmaster rocked forward in his chair. "Somehow, I don't think that's all."

"I'd like to have my dad here if you want to continue this conversation, sir."

Another pause. This time the headmaster was in careful thought of his next statement. "The next time your father comes on campus, which I believe will be for the soccer playoff game this Friday, I'll arrange for us to get together and continue this conversation."

I started to speak, but he waved the back of his hand at me and pointed to the door. I was dismissed.

Once I walked into the dining commons, I saw Reba sitting along with Crystal and Toby at the back table. As I walked over to get a dinner tray, Dorm Mom approached

Reba and said something to her. Reba got up and followed Dorm Mom out of the dining commons. Guess she was on the way to see the headmaster now. A divide and conquer game to keep me from briefing Reba before she faced the inquisition.

With a serving of sliced brisket, baked beans, slaw and white bread, I walked to the table where Reba had been seated. Crystal was all giggly and kept scratching her face and arms while poking at her food. Toby cracked a joke and shoulder bumped her, stimulating more giggles and laughs.

"Hey, Jason, my tech-man," Toby said. "Any news about Bobby?"

He caught me with a mouthful, so I only shook my head.

"Heard the cops were on campus today going through Bobby's stuff," Toby said. "You must know something. You go and see the headmaster, and then Mrs. Fadler takes Reba away to see the headmaster once you're out. What's up?"

"Nothing's up. I don't know where Bobby is or what happened to him."

"Palmer's hiding something," Crystal sang as though teasing me, then giggled and pointed at my nose. "It's not nice to keep secrets from friends."

I didn't know we were friends, I thought and really wanted to say it to their faces. The brisket and baked beans were real tasty tonight. Some of my favorites, but after being interrogated and then the follow-up quiz by Toby, I lost my appetite. I stood. "I gotta walk this off," I said.

"We'll talk later," Toby said. "By the bye, my fingerprint is working great on the Mac. Thanks."

"Glad to hear it." I walked to the tray drop and was out of the dining commons as fast as I could. I crossed to the fountain at the center of the courtyard and sat on one edge. The cement was very cold, and the evening air had a strong chill. It was going to be a cold one tonight. I texted Reba to meet me in the library.

Since Dorm Mom and Headmaster were fully involved, my room was no longer the best place to meet. Also, I was clearly being watched by Toby, Cordelia and, probably, Crystal. Any of them could be behind the thumb drive delivery to Bobby. The library would be open for another hour or so. It should be long enough for Reba and me to recap where we're at and figure out our next steps.

#

The library was in a large room at the front of the classroom building. Among the racks of books were tables where students could work. Around the far side of the main room, group study rooms lined the wall. Each had a thick glass window that looked onto the main room with a table and chairs that could seat 6. One real nice feature was the sound proofing. These rooms were actually designed as simple sound studios as well. The acoustics were great, and students could actually record podcasts or the like.

I took a position at the far side center of the table so I could see anyone approaching the room. I set up my laptop and opened my journal. I set about writing down all that we found on the Android and what had happened, including making a timeline of the events that led to Bobby hanging himself.

I finished the timeline and entries when Reba appeared outside the room. She glanced around and stepped inside. "I'm really shocked by the limited number of people that actually use the library," Reba said.

I looked quizzically at her. Was she saying this because she thought we might be getting recorded or someone might be listening?

"Look," she waved her hand out at the main area. "There are only about 8 students using this place, and mid-term exams are coming soon."

"I guess there's only a few that want to do really well," I said.

"Entitled. That's what most of these kids are. Entitled."

"Okay   "

"No, I mean it. They're all entitled. Their parents are really rich and powerful. The kids probably think that their futures are already paved in gold."

"Wow," I said. "What's gotten into you?"

She sat down next to me so she could see my computer screen and still face the window. "That little discussion with Mr. Hannah really crawled up my spine. Do you know he even threatened to send me back to public school saying you and me didn't deserve this place?"

"He was aggressive with me as well."

"I didn't tell him crap. He was on a fishing trip, trying to say that because the police knew who you were that they must also know me. I really jumped on him; said he had no right to assume I was involved because he didn't have any proof."

"And..."

"That just pissed him off more. He said you and I were always together, so we had to be involved together. My answer was, 'yeah, we were together having a ham sandwich.'" She sighed deeply and took a small, shrink-wrapped sandwich out of her bag. It was ham and cheese on white bread. One of the late-night sandwiches the kitchen staff made. She took a bite. "Where are we?"

"Right..." I opened the journal and showed her the timeline. "If we consider the timeline from the 4th through the 7th, we have a bunch of things to follow up on." I pointed to the list of questions I thought we needed to work on that included:

Gina's phone number. Could we find a listing for this number online and could we find where it was registered? This might take Agent Wilson to file something with the wireless phone carriers.

Transition from use of WhatsApp to regular Android Messenger. They were doing

WhatsApp messaging once they left the in-game chat. What caused them to transition from there to Android messaging?

The Android phone. Bobby always used Apple iPhone, and I never saw him touch an Android. When did he get the phone and why did he even need the phone?

And the very big question... Who prepared the message and delivered the thumb drive to Bobby on the 6th?

"We need to brainstorm how to answer these questions and where the source of truth might be," I said, running the aLEAPP tool over the Android data collection. It returned a perfect summary report of everything found on the phone.

"I have Gina's phone number that she was using on her side of the conversation. I also have the information from this Android phone."

"Wilson or your dad?" Reba asked. "Who should you send this to?"

"I think Wilson," I said as I wrote a

quick email message about the information and the aLEAPP report asking her to get details on the phones and accounts from the carrier.

Reba opened a notebook and said, "Let's play with the last question. Who are all the people we know that could have produced the Rot-6 message and deliver the thumb drive?"

"Cordelia would have the skill. Toby?" I offered.

"Toby seems so inept when it comes to technology," Reba said. "I think there's another way we should look at this. Who might have the keys to open Bobby's door and place the envelope with the message and thumb drive into his room?"

"I might have a way to answer that," I said. "I have the triage image of the headmaster's computer. Remember, the other night we wanted to find out information about Solomon, the new Board member and philanthropist when I grabbed the image?"

Fortunately, the drive that had the

information from Bobby's system also had the triage capture from the headmaster's machine. I had used KAPE to extract the data quickly, so it was all organized in a tree of folders just as it was found on the file system. I loaded the information, went into the user folder for Hannah and found an administration folder and keys. There was a spreadsheet that included a listing of master dorm building key holders. The list included, Dorm Mom, Dorm Dad, Mr. Hannah, and two keys assigned as spare held in the front office key locker.

"We need to check the key locker in the front office and see if those two keys are there," Reba said after reading the list.

"Why do you think that a key had to be used? You picked that lock just fine."

"True, so add to the list the names of people that we think might be able to pick a Schlage deadbolt lock."

"We're back to Cordelia and possibly Toby," I said.

"I wonder. That could just be a cover. His MacBook was really clean and well organized. Most inept users just save everything to the desktop or documents folder and then can't find anything when they need it. He kept everything well organized in folders."

"I can't think of anyone else that we know. There could be others."

"Well, with Toby, I have remote access to his computer and might be able to find something. But before I do that, let's have a look at the physical image of Bobby's laptop." I opened Autopsy. The ingest modules had finished and everything was organized from recent activity, data analysis, and reporting.

"Communications first," Reba said.

Opening the communications viewer, I saw emails and some other general communications through Gmail, but there were no chat sessions. The recent activity analysis gave me information that Bobby pretty much played video games for no more than 90 minutes each night. This activity stopped dead on the 5th and never started again. Files, program files, run programs, and other elements offered nothing in support of the case. Bobby did some of his homework on the 4th and 5th but then stopped using the computer entirely at around the same time he received the threats and the picture on his Android phone.

"I don't believe that Bobby's system will yield anything," I said. "Seems he only used the Android phone to communicate with Gina and her brother."

"On to Toby's system. See if there's anything interesting," Reba said.

I popped open a Putty session and made an SSH connection to the hostname of Toby's laptop. The school's DNS server resolved the name, and I connected to the IP address assigned to Toby's MacBook. Putty prompted for a username and password. I typed 'toby' followed by 'irain5upreme!'. A moment later, Putty returned a '$' prompt. I was in. Next, I opened a Linux virtual machine that included several forensic acquisition tools. None of which I really planned to use. I just wanted easy shell access. Opening two separate terminal shells, I logged both in via SSH to Toby's machine. Now, I had three independent connections: one from Putty on my PC and two from shells on my Linux investigative virtual machine.

I commanded one shell to create 'tar' archives of the Safari, Chrome, and Mozilla folders beneath Toby's user home and piped the results to a NetCat port on one of my cloud servers. That crunched away and finished without error. The request for Safari went too fast, and I knew that I probably didn't collect anything. As long as he wasn't using some weird browser, I should have most of his browser history, search strings, and cache. Opening another shell, I used SCP to move the tar archives from my cloud server to my local Linux system.

"Back to Autopsy," I said. "Only this time

I'll load the plain files captured from Toby's Mac." That's just what I did. Inflating each archive onto my T7 drive, I instructed Autopsy to load this into the case under the hostname of Toby's system. Because Autopsy only had a few files to work on, the process went quickly and the data analytics and recent activity appeared. I had browser data, except for Safari. "Rats," I said.

"What is it?" Reba looked at the screen.

"Wonderful Apple protects this data from terminal shells. When I opened a remote login to the system, Apple OS saw my session as just a terminal shell. Apple's SIP protects the Safari data folders from terminal shell examination. The stupid thing is that I could type an 'open' command into the shell for the Safari folders and that would pop a Finder window on the console and let me see everything. If we need this data, I'm going to have to do something a bit more covert to get it."

"That may be okay. I really don't think

Toby's our man," Reba said. "His browser history is probably just a bunch of sports crap and porn."

"Geez, Reba," I said. "You're cynical today." I typed a few commands and browsed through the Firefox and Chrome files. Firefox was clearly used more frequently than Chrome. That said, TOR was installed along with Chrome and Firefox. The search strings were still present in history as well as some cache data. Toby searched about use of MDMA, slang terms for hard drugs, and urban dosage instructions. The final search yielded a few dark web sites that included videos of users smoking and hot-railing the crystal meth. These queries were a few weeks old and well prior to the events of the 6th and 7th, but they offered more light on Toby's interests. "I'll filter the data by the week before Bobby's first chat with Gina." The resulting list included Gmail, Firefox searches about soccer and general news from the LA basin.

"Nothing significant," I said. "He's gone into Gmail several times. I have his username. I wonder if the password is the same?"

"Try it."

"No way. At least not yet. If he has multi-factor authentication set up, he'll get notified when I make the attempt."

The lights in the library flashed off and then on twice. Outside the window, we could see other students packing up their books and material to leave. "Guess that's our sign we're done."

"Tomorrow, lunch, in here," Reba said. "Maybe if we sleep on this, we can uncover more. And I'd really like to get back to answering those questions about Madam Solomon and her associates. Something's not right there."

10. FRIENDS WITH BLACK HATS

Reba left early to prepare for the big playoff game this afternoon while I sat next to Cordelia in our ancient history class. I'd been up most of the evening trying to figure out who in the school gave Bobby the thumb drive and note. Toby's laptop didn't yield any real clues that would suggest his further involvement but that didn't remove him from the list of possible suspects. He could have easily used a cell phone to do everything and not his computer. On the other hand, he did use his system to search the dark web and clearly knew how to use TOR.

Cordelia, being very attentive to the lecture, was the next most obvious one on the list. I thought about how I might interrogate her systems.

"...Mr. Palmer!" the instructor called.

"Ah, yes," I stammered back hoping this was the first time he called my name.

"What's your analysis and opinion on Book 5, Perseus 2?"

I glanced at Cordelia who grinned and winked at me. Just what I needed. "Well," I said, "I believe Ovid wrote this mostly to appease his Roman audience at the time."

"Isn't that what all authors do? What about symbolism and any message that Ovid might be conveying?"

"Let me explain. If you consider the riot at the wedding banquet, many of Perseus's associates and friends were killed. The author's words were very descriptive and, I believe, played to his audience's blood lust at the time. At the end, Perseus finally used the

ultimate weapon that he had in his
possession the whole time. He pulled out the
Gorgon Medusa's head and destroyed all
those against him. Ovid made a clear decision
to play to the blood lust of his audience
instead of using Medusa earlier in the conflict
when many of Perseus's friends could have
been saved."

The class was silent. Cordelia grinned
and winked at me again.

"It is," the teacher said, "One of Ovid's
longer and more graphic conflict descriptions.
That's actually a very interesting observation,
Mr. Palmer." He went on to call on some
other students while I gave a sigh of relief.

Class ended as the 11:00 am bell rang.
I was done for the day. The soccer match
would begin in an hour, and I strolled through
the back of the classroom building toward the
gym area. I could see my mum, dad and
Reba's mum, Mrs. Ng, just walking up from
the parking lot toward the athletic field
stands. The latest hip-hop music played from

the public address system, a few students milled around, and Headmaster Hannah stood at the entrance greeting the parents. Our parents stepped up and shook Mr. Hannah's hand as I moved a bit faster to get by my dad's side. They seemed to be exchanging pleasantries and nothing that might be related to the Bobby case. I said good morning to Mr. Hannah and joined the family just as they walked in.

The teams took to the field for warmups. Reba, Crystal, and the other girls ran laps of the half field and passed balls around. Two girls fired shots at the goalie to help her warm up.

My dad climbed the bleacher seats and took a position in the last row with the fullest view of the field. He stood and watched the teams warming up. He held his hands up to shield his face from the midday sun. It was cool, slight breeze from the west, and the waterlogged field still looked soft and muddy as the players ran.

"Reba's number 12, right?" dad asked.

"Yes, that's her," I said.

"She's wearing the captain's arm band."

I could see that she was. Our team had on their home dark blue jerseys with big white numbers and the school's crest emblem on the front right shoulder. The other team had on road white uniforms with red letters and the head of a growling cougar as their team crest. Reba being captain must make Crystal livid. Throughout the entire season, until Reba and I showed up, Crystal had been the captain and star of the team. The coach must have awarded Reba a starting position on the team and given her the captain's armband after the hattrick that got them to the playoffs.

Mum made me move to sit in between her and dad. She looked very proud of me and kissed my cheek. "I've heard such excellent reports from your teachers about your progress." She wrapped me in a big, bear hug.

"I didn't know they were sending reports."

"Private schools do things a bit different, especially when you're new." She hugged me again.

On the field, the teams had left to their respective locker rooms and were awaiting introductions. The cheer squad for the opposing team jumped around and led their stands in various cheers. We didn't have a cheer squad so one parent stood up rallying our stands to chant "go Panthers, go" followed by a group roar. Even my parents and Reba's mom joined in: "Go Panthers, go... Go Panthers Go! ... Roar."

Even though we were seated at the top far side of the bleachers, I could see Dorm Mom down by the fence surrounding the field. She stood close talking to Solomon's man, Sargis Petrosyan. He must have been at the school to attend a board meeting. Why else would he be here? He was dressed in a lightweight, casual suit with a white shirt and bright red tie. He held a black umbrella over his head. At this time of year, there was always a threat of rain. But why would Dorm Mom even know Petrosyan? And what could they be discussing. I took my phone and snapped a few pictures. My timing was perfect as Petrosyan handed something to Dorm Mom. No one else in the stands paid any attention to the two of them, and certainly not Headmaster Hannah. Everyone was busy chatting and getting ready for the opening kick.

The visiting team took the field first while mum and dad applauded politely. Then it was the home team Panthers. Mum and dad stood along with the rest of the parents and spectators in the stands making as much noise as they could. The stands rocked, bouncing me around as the crowd jumped and hollered. I just sat saving and sharing the photo. I zoomed in trying my best to identify what Petrosyan had slipped to Dorm Mom. From the fragment I could see, it looked like an envelope. Now I wondered if this was the same type of envelope we had discovered with the note and thumb drive in Bobby's room?

The two teams lined up facing the home stands as everyone was asked to stand for the playing of the national anthem. I glanced over to see Petrosyan standing alone, facing the American flag. Dorm Mom was nowhere in sight. As the anthem played, I felt my cell phone vibrate for an incoming call. It was Agent Wilson. Dad frowned as I started to answer the phone, but I showed him who was calling, and he nodded.

"Hi," I said. "Give me a sec to get to a better place."

"It's important," Wilson replied.

I pressed passed mum and Mrs. Ng and by a few others and ran down the steps and around to the back of the spectator stands. "I'm here."

"Good," she said firmly. "I want to update you on something and see if you can find out more information."

"Okay."

"The lab says that the drive Robert Maclean plugged into his dad's machine placed a reverse trojan on the system. That trojan opened a reverse SSH connection to a foreign server. I'll send you the IP information after this call. The bad guys used the connection to browse through the system, and they downloaded a document that was to be released by the father's public company. We didn't catch the release information in time, and the bad guys probably cleared a few million dollars option trading on the company stock prior to the release. They cashed out and sent the funds to a US bank. We reached out to the bank to stop any withdrawal but were only able to stop a fraction of the funds from being transferred offshore."

"This really was an extortion job," I said. "Can't you reach through to the receiving bank?"

"We stopped about 300,000 from a third SWIFT wire but about 1.2 million dollars made it to a Brazilian institution. We don't have any direct relationship or authority with Brazilian banks. We've asked our Legat in the embassy in Brazil to see what can be discovered."

"Legat?"

"Sorry, legal attaché. The department has them in every embassy." Wilson sighed. "We hope the Legat can discover where the money went next. If it was transferred again or split into different banks and accounts, we might be able to find a few more leads, but it will take time. Needless to say, this was a very successful sextortion of poor Robert."

"Wow," I said. "Send me whatever you can to my cell, and I'll see if I can find out anymore on this end. Someone had to give Bobby that note and the thumb drive. He didn't produce it by himself. How's Bobby doing?"

"He's holding on. Still in the coma, but the doctors are saying that his chances are looking much better for a recovery. You and your dad were there just in the nick of time."

"Reba was a big factor in that as well. She's just playing in the big State playoff match."

"Hope she does well." Wilson rang off.

I climbed back into the stands. The game was underway as Reba slid into tackle another player but played only the ball and not the player's leg. The ball bounced over to Crystal who jammed it down field. A lanky player made a header, and the ball bounced forward into the opposing team's goalie. Our Pinegrove Panthers were spread wide in an attack formation as their goalie rolled the ball to a defender. That player dribbled the ball forward until Crystal pursued and hammered the player in the back. Whistle. Penalty. A yellow card held at Crystal. The opposing Cougar player rolled around on the ground holding her back. A trainer and coach came in from the sidelines to work on the player. I could see the coach saying something to the referee. Probably complaining that Crystal should have received a red card and kicked out of the game.

"That was an uncalled-for tackle by that girl," dad said. "She was beaten and just needed to run faster to block any pass. Instead, she slammed into the girl's lower back. Bad. Real bad."

"That's Crystal," I said. "She's a real tosser."

Dad looked at me and grinned. He agreed that this was a bad apple. He leaned close to me. "What did Wilson want?"

The field action started again, and the Cougar player was up on her feet running like nothing happened. Crystal kept hounding her as she received the ball again. This time, Crystal cleared the ball directly to Reba. Our number 12 ran down midfield, making a clean pass to one of the other girls.

"Wilson wanted to give me an update on the Bobby matter," I said keeping one eye on the action as Reba received and passed back to the lanky girl who shot it hard and directly on net. The Cougar goalie got a hand on the ball and it bounced over the net for a corner kick.

"And," dad prompted as the team took positions for a set corner play. Reba was in the middle of the group directly in front of the net with Crystal a couple yards to her left. "They have a lot more details on the extortion case. Bobby's doing better."

The corner kick flew high and directly at Reba's position for what would have been a solid header into the net, but Crystal pushed Reba down and took the header. The ball bounced wide and outside. Reba got up, brushed herself off, and spoke sharply to Crystal. Crystal shrugged her off and ran toward the center field before the goalie kick.

This time, the Cougar goalie lobbed a hard, high kick toward the center of the field. The girls fought for the ball, and a Cougar player got it and made a long pass toward the right corner. Another Cougar player made no mistake dribbling the ball twice around one of our defenders and kicking it solidly into the back of our net. The parents and our stands gave a deep sigh as the opposing parents celebrated.

Dad leaned close to me again. "Let's talk after the match," he said.

That's pretty much how the playoff match went after the goal. The ball was back and forth. We'd run the ball down field and turn it over. The Cougar's ran it back on us and turned it over or took a shot. The game ended as a 1 to nothing loss. Our season was over. Dad kept me from standing as mum and Mrs. Ng stood. The moms said they were going to go down and wait for Reba.

"We'll join you in a jiffy," Dad said. The stands were almost empty as we got up and walked to a quiet place. "Spit it out."

I told him what the FBI lab discovered and how Bobby was extorted to put the drive into his father's computer.

"Damn," dad said shaking his head. "And Bobby? Any news."

"Still in a medically induced coma, but the doctors say that he's doing much better. Guess his brain function is better."

"Good. Did Wilson give you an idea on our next move?"

"She's sending some technical details on what they found. Reba and I are trying to figure out who sent Bobby the drive to plug into his father's computer."

I got a stern look from dad. "You two need to be safe and let them deal with this. From what you told me, this sounds like a very organized and nasty outfit that could be extremely dangerous."

"I have to help Bobby. Reba and I will stay out of the field and just report to Agent Wilson."

Dad's face wasn't too happy. He grimaced and said, "Tell me what you have so far."

"Only that a master key or picks were used to leave the message and drive in Bobby's room. There's a handful of possible perps, as you call them."

"And?"

"I'm working on profiling them to see who might have a motive as well as opportunity. I think I understand the capability."

"Let me know," dad said. "I might be able to help if you need it."

I thought for a moment about Petrosyan passing the envelope to Dorm Mom. "There is one thing. There are two people that are a couple of sketchy characters. A lady named Madam Maja Solomon and her chum, Sargis Petrosyan. Would you mind digging around for any information on them that might be relevant?" I said.

"Sure. Send me a text with anything you have."

Reba and several other girls came out of the locker room. Mum and Mrs. Ng gave Reba big hugs even though Reba's hair was a wet mess and she still had mud blotches on her face. The girls weren't allowed to shower in the gym. Some new state law or something. Reba didn't look happy at all and seemed angry.

She kept glancing back at the locker room exit. Mrs. Ng told Reba to go and get cleaned up and that we all would go to dinner.

#

Dinner was anything but a happy event. It took a long while for Reba to calm down. She kept on about how the hit by Crystal took all the momentum out of their game and left them very vulnerable. After the main meal, Reba settled down and enjoyed a desert of tiramisu. We said our goodbyes after dad dropped us back on campus. We decided to stay on campus for the weekend instead of heading home. Dad smiled and gave me a small salute as the three of them drove back to San Jose. Going home for the weekend would have been a nice break, but Reba and I had some work to do.

I briefed Reba on everything, including Dorm Mom.

"So do you think Mrs. Fadler might be involved?" Reba asked. "She has a key to all the dorm rooms. And Petrosyan may have been slipping her a payoff. That would be motive. She also had the best opportunity to know when we're all out. You know how she just opens doors and barges in. It's accepted by all the students. If Bobby had been in the room when she opened the door, she could just make up an excuse and wait for a better time. Lastly, capability. She has a master key to everything."

We headed into the dorm building and down the hall. I stopped as we passed Cordelia's room. I knocked on the door. "What are you doing?" Reba asked.

I knocked again. No answer. "Cordelia knows more and has more access to systems. If I can get some of that access, I might be able to rule out some of the others."

"But that witch?"

"Yeah. The witch you know sometimes can lead you to the devils you don't know." I looked at a small note stuck above the lock on her door. It read: 'don't even think about it' and had a blood red fingerprint as though signing the note.

"See," Reba said. "She's a witch. Who else signs a warning with a blotch of blood."

"It's red but we can't tell if it's blood."

We headed off back to my room. I started by printing out photos of the persons of interest. Toby was the first, Dorm Mom, Cordelia, and Headmaster Hannah.

"Why Cordelia? I agree with the others."

"Simple," I said. "Remember Toby at dinner the other day? He called her his 'Wednesday-girl'."

"That could just be a reference to Wednesday Addams."

I nodded. "Could be. But, for Toby, there may have been a different meaning. He really seems like the type that might two-time his girlfriend, Crystal. Otherwise, she's clear. Cordelia has opportunity and capability. I don't know about motive. I'm going to do some OSINT gathering and build profiles on this group as best I can. In the meantime, I'd really like to talk to Cordelia and keep our cover on this. She could be of real good use if you can dig up something."

Reba smirked. "Oh, I'll find her and drag her back." She left the room almost slamming the door in her wake.

After running a few Google searches as well as Maltego and theHarvester on Toby, I had a clean headshot of Toby and fed this to my Faces application to scan the image into social media sites. I launched the same queries on Cordelia, Dorm Mom (Mrs. Fadler) and Headmaster Hannah. The images I had of the last two required a lot of work and took Faces several hours to process. The only advantage I had was in separating the operations across different systems, each running the Faces application in the cloud.

Data came back from the basic research that I ran on Toby. His real name was Tobias Adams. That was a real coincidence given his reference to Cordelia. His father was a founder of a very successful online company in Silicon Valley and exited with just over a billion dollars after a big IPO. He was now into his next venture, a medical device company. From what I could tell, Toby's dad wasn't a medical doctor and didn't have any real background in health care.

Toby's mom returned much less information, but a public record search suggested that she was involved in a court filing for divorce a year and a half ago. Interesting. Given the family wealth and all the information, I could find money wouldn't really be a motivator for Toby. He probably had opportunity, but the question of capability was problematic. This doesn't mean he couldn't be involved in some influencer capacity but probably wasn't the one to put the drive and note in Bobby's room. He boarded at the school probably to get him out of the way of his parent's lives. Just my hunch. As much as I wanted to find a direct tie, nothing stood out. There were the search strings I found on Toby's laptop that were certainly suspicious of some type of bad activity, but nothing pointing to sextortion.

Cordelia was much harder to find information on. Her name was really Cordelia Kelly. The first name was of Celtic origin, and it meant 'the daughter of the sea'. The family name derived from 'ÓCeallaigh,' meaning 'bright-headed' or 'strife'. Strife. That fit her, a beautiful daughter of the sea in strife. Things got a bit more interesting when I revised a search using the name ÓCeallaigh combined with 'Adda Lovelace'. A very interesting post popped up where she argued about the virtues of the old-time hacker that would break in, steal media, and post pirated items through IRC chat forums. So now I had a weak link between Cordelia and Adda Lovelace only that Cordelia used a portion of the school's shared file server to host pirated media. Based on the initial results, I figured she had opportunity and more than enough capability to place the drive and note in Bobby's room. Motive was the problem.

My searches were still running as my room door swung wide open. Reba had a firm hand lock on Cordelia's left ear as she dragged the girl into the room. Reba kicked the door shut and launched Cordelia onto my bed.

"I'm into the rough stuff as much as the next girl," Cordelia said rubbing her earlobe, then rushed Reba.

Reba popped a gentle forward karate kick solid between Cordelia's chest sending her back onto the bed.

"ENOUGH, you two!" I yelled.

Cordelia lay still just staring at Reba who stepped back into a fighting stance and waved her fingertips for Cordelia to come at her again. "I can make it much worse, you know," Reba said. Her eyes locked on her target as Cordelia slowly sat up, resting on her elbows.

"That's enough." I stood and held my palms at both girls. "Both of you, stop it."

"You won't believe where I found her," Reba said. "She was in Toby's room. The door was open, so I just grabbed her.

Cordelia relaxed, and Reba left her stance taking a couple more steps back. No doubt Reba could cause some severe damage should Cordelia move from the bed again.

"Cordelia," I said, "did you break into Bobby's room before he disappeared?"

Her shoulders rose, chin retracted, as her eyes wide with disbelief stared directly at me. "No."

I nodded as though believing her. She relaxed back, resting once again on her elbows. "But if you wanted to, you could have entered Bobby's or any room in the dorm, right?"

She grinned and stared at Reba. "Just like the two of you." "That's a yes?"

"The locks here are cheap, 4-cylinder

deadbolts. A 6-year-old could pop any of the locks." She stared back at me. "Your muscle dragged me here for an interrogation?"

"No. Not really." I sat back at my desk but watched her closely. "Actually, we kind of need your help."

"You have a real funny way of asking for help." Cordelia said. "What do you want?"

"I noticed a cute little wireless camera stuck on the upper corner of the hallway that looked at Bobby's room door as well as the two doors across the hall."

Now she shrugged.

"How long has that camera been up there and does it connect to you?"

"Maybe," she said.

"And it's been there how long?"

Reba rubbed her right fist into the palm of her hand and took a step closer to Cordelia.

"A week or so," Cordelia said, looking at Reba.

I motioned for Reba to back down for now and stood from my chair. "Show us the footage you have."

Cordelia stood from the bed and gently moved over to my desk and computer keyboard. She logged into a system and opened a video viewer. The video she played was of Reba picking the lock on Bobby's door.

"Not that image." Reba slapped the back of Cordelia's head. I grabbed Reba's hand before she could repeat the slap.

"That's the oldest segment I have. I put the camera up after I saw the headmaster's note on Bobby's door."

I tried pushing her away from my keyboard so I could drive.

Her fingers raced, tapping keys, killing the connection to the machine that had the recorded video.

"No. Before that," I said. "There were earlier videos on the screen. I want before that."

Reba took a couple of steps toward Cordelia. "Let me. I'll make her do it."

"Or," Cordelia said, stopping Reba.

"Maybe I'll hit the keys that will delete all of the videos if you touch me."

I held up my hand to Reba and said, "What's it going to take to see the day before this?"

"We negotiate. Just like before." She grinned her pearly teeth a sharp contrast to her black lipstick.

"What now?"

"Well," Cordelia pondered for a moment and fluttered her eyelids. "You already asked me out to the prom. How about on that night you take me before the prom out for a nice romantic dinner?"

I glanced at Reba. Her face went stone cold. "I like my way better."

Again, I held my hand up to her shaking my head a bit. Any rough stuff and Cordelia could easily wipe everything out. We need this video. "Okay. Show us now and if there's nothing, then all deals are off."

"What about your tough girlfriend? Does she agree, too?"

If Reba's stare could melt steel, it would. "Let's see the video for the 6th."

Cordelia returned a grin. "You're so cute when you're angry."

"Just, get on with it," Reba hissed.

"Maybe you have to come to dinner with us as well. Yes. That's the new deal. Your girl Reba agrees to come to dinner with us, then you and me go to the prom."

"Fine," Reba said, "better to keep an enemy close."

Cordelia smiled sincerely. "See, that wasn't hard." Cordelia turned back to my computer screen, reconnected, and opened the video viewer. Scrolling back to what would be the 6th, she played the video. That was the super rainy day that was just awful. The first image at around 09:45 was Bobby coming out of his room. His arms full of books and notepads, he juggled a bit and locked the door. Cordelia fast forwarded to the next motion event. It was the backside of a large woman using a master key to unlock and enter Bobby's room. The door shut. A few minutes passed, and the woman opened the door and exited the room into the hall. She looked both ways as though checking to see if anyone would see her. Even with the grainy image from the tiny spy camera, it was clearly Mrs. Fadler. She turned to lock the door and then walked off down the hall. We could see a bit of her as she entered another room.

Cordelia stopped the replay. "Is that what you wanted?"

"No, not quite. Keep running the video."

She hit play and the video replay continued. A few other students, including Reba and I walked by the hall. None of the others stopped in front of Bobby's room. Somewhere around the noon hour, Toby appeared and stopped in front of Bobby's door. He knocked on the door and waited. He knocked again and waited longer. Toby tried the doorknob and pressed on the door verifying it was locked, and Bobby wasn't answering. He knocked again. "Toby must have locked himself out of his computer again," Cordelia said.

"Keep it playing," I said.

After Toby walked off, there was a bit of a swarm of students passing through the hall. Clearly the after-lunch rush back from the dining commons and into rooms before the afternoon sessions began.

"Good enough now?" Cordelia said.

"Keep it playing," I said.

The video played on as Bobby appeared later and stepped in front of his door to unlock it. He still carried the stack of books and material. At one point, he dropped something and picked it up from the floor before twisting the key in the lock. I looked over at Reba and tugged on my earlobe then pointed to the bed.

Reba smiled. Her hands flashed forward latching onto Cordelia's left ear tugging her out of my chair to the sound of a loud cry. Cordelia was bent over as Reba pulled her from the desk and computer, and I stepped in. Before any protest could come, Cordelia was propelled back onto my bed. I located the video file name and downloaded it with a quick SCP command back to my system. I was careful to signal that the timestamps of the files had to be maintained.

"That wasn't called for," Cordelia said rubbing her ear once again and sniffling back the tears that streaked her black mascara.

"Sorry," I said. "I need that video file, and I really don't need you screwing it up during the transfer."

"I have a question," Reba stepped up to where Cordelia sat back on the bed. "Why did you place a camera outside Bobby's room?"

"Just some fun," Cordelia said.

"Fun?"

"A bit of a test actually," Cordelia said holding her stare on Reba.

"Test?"

"Yeah. I don't expect the girl muscle to understand a range test."

Reba stared wide-eyed at her and her right hand curled into a fist.

"Look. My room is on the same floor but on the other side of the community area that separates boys from girls. The camera has a tiny battery and is wireless. I put it in a few other places and I wanted to see how far away from my room it could be for me to keep connected and receive the images. It's mount is smooth and will stick above the wallpaper."

Once the download finished, my quick fingers opened another connection to Cordelia's system and closed this one. "Got it."

Reba stepped back motioning to my door. "Get lost, witch."

"I'll see you both Saturday evening," Cordelia said standing and straightening her skirt and blouse. "Choose a restaurant with tablecloths and vegan food. She walked slowly out of the room shutting the door in her wake.

"I really hate her," Reba said with a

gesture behind the now closed door.

"Sometimes you have to do a deal with a black hat," I said. "I need to check and see if this video has been edited or altered."

"How will you do that?"

"First, I'll make a forensic copy. Then I think I'll check the metadata. If it all looks okay, I'll put it in a video editor and see if there are any edits marked on the frames. The tools to do it for real are super expensive, and I'll just check before sending it to Wilson along with the photo of Dorm Mom taking the envelope from Petrosyan. We have a bigger problem."

"The prom?"

"Yup. I don't have clothes, and you might not either." Reba smiled. "I actually do have a few suitable things."

"Guess I'll have to call dad," I picked up my mobile.

"I'll leave you to find the restaurant and settle that problem." Reba patted me on the shoulder and left.

First things first, I opened the video file that I downloaded from Cordelia's system. The images played just as I'd seen them before. I closed the file and opened it again with Wondershare's Filmora. This allowed me to see the image and possibly identify anywhere the file was edited. The video played straight through with no evidence of cuts or scene transitions.

Next, I attached the video along with the still shot of Dorm Mom receiving an envelope from Petrosyan while at the soccer match. I wrote a note to Agent Wilson that it appeared that Mrs. Fadler was the only person to enter Bobby's room, and that I'd seen her receiving an envelope on Friday from Petrosyan.

Although I didn't have direct evidence that Dorm Mom was the person who placed the envelope into Bobby's room before that fateful day, Dorm Mom seemed like the most likely suspect and worth an interview by the FBI.

Now the next problem. I called dad.

"Hey, Jason," dad said. "You're calling and I haven't had any time to check out this Petrosyan fellow."

"I know," I said. "I need some different assistance. You know that Saturday is the prom night and there is a big dance here at school? Well, I kind of need to get something to wear and wonder if you'd be good enough to make a reservation at a restaurant for say 5:30pm before the dance."

"That's my boy," dad said. "Reba the lucky girl?"

"Well, kind of."

"What do you mean?"

"Reba is going as well as another girl named Cordelia."

"Really!" Dad said with proud excitement. "Two girls? That's my boy."

"Dad, dad, it's not what you think."

"It isn't?"

"Can you come to the school early and bring me a coat, shirt and tie? Then, can you drive us to the restaurant and back after dinner?"

"Sure."

"And one more thing," I said. "Can you pay the dinner bill? I'll make it up to you."

A moment of silence on the phone. "I'll check with your mum and let Mrs. Ng know as well. Yeah, I can do this."

11. PROM NIGHT TO REMEMBER

Dad arrived right at 4pm on Saturday. He brought a gray, two-piece suit that mum would make me wear for formal family occasions. I hadn't worn it for a year or more, and the fit was tight as heck. I forewent the necktie and left my collar open.

There was a brief knock at the door. Reba pushed it open just before I arrived to check who was there. She wore a sleek-fitting dress that hugged her figure and came to just above the knees.

"Wow, you look great," I said taking a

step back and holding my phone to snap a picture.

"No snaps," Reba barked. "Remember, I'm not your date tonight. I'm sure the witch will be here shortly."

Sure enough, Cordelia stepped in wearing a frilly white bopeep dress that barely covered her legs with black fishnet tights. Yellow-blonde hair with flowing curls down to her waste. Probably a wig sincer her black hair was not anywhere near that long. Her makeup was done with highlights of pink and the usual black eyeliner. She was not the picture I wanted to let my dad see.

"Come on," Reba said pulling out her phone. "That's a perfect picture. Get next to her, JP."

I shook my head.

"Well, I'll do it," Cordelia said with a wily smirk on her face. She stepped beside me and hugged me close with her arm as Reba snapped the picture.

"That's worthy of the scrapbook," Reba

said.

I rolled my eyes and gave a sheepish grin. This was really uncomfortable. I jumped as Cordelia grabbed my butt cheek and, of course, Reba snapped another picture.

"Perfect."

"We better go," I said. "Dad is in the car downstairs."

Dad made the three of us sit in the back of the car as he drove to the Village Pub in Woodside. Not too far. The mixture of Reba and Cordelia's perfumes clashed as I rode in the middle, and I couldn't help but sneeze. As we pulled up, I was a bit shocked that dad had made the reservation at a pub. Boy, was I mistaken. The chef has a Michelin star. Dad sat at the bar while the three of us dined. We shared an heirloom tomato salad, that really was the perfect starter, and I was able to relax after the photo incident and ride. Cordelia put on a charming attitude and chatted with Reba about soccer and her interests. While Reba succumbed to the charm and spoke pleasantly back. I sort of expected that Cordelia might just select the most expensive thing on the menu given their special was a whole Main lobster but was surprised by her choice of the Ratatouille. Reba had roast sea bass, and I the Cornish game hen. Mine was actually the most expensive item. I could see dad parked at the pub bar having a burger and properly poured pint of Guinness. Cordelia told a couple of silly jokes. "So where did the cybersecurity team go?" She riddled.

I shrugged while Reba thought for a moment and then shook her head.

"They ran some ware."

I giggled while Reba frowned.

"That's really silly," I said.

"Okay, okay," Cordelia said, "you both should get this one: What's a hacker's favorite sport?"

Now I thought for a moment as Reba said, "Phishing."

"Correct!"

We all couldn't help but laugh.

After eating silently, Reba endorsing the quality of the sea bass, we finished and forwent ordering any sweets or desserts. Dad paid for the meal, and we were back in the car. This time, the ride was a bit more animated as Reba joined in the joke telling.

Even dad got into it with, "I got one," he said, "why did the teenager break up with their math teacher?"

"Ah," Cordelia stammered a bit, "math was too hard?"

"Nope. He just couldn't count on them."

Silence.

"Get it? Couldn't count."

A collective groan came from the three of us. Thank goodness we were back at school. We thanked dad for everything, and Cordelia gave him a hug. "I had a fun time at dinner, Mr. Palmer."

#

As with most high schools, the dance was in the gymnasium. Headmaster Hannah greeted us at the door, and Dorm Mom pinned a boutonniere of a blood-red rose on my lapel while Mr. Hannah gave both girls fine white rose-filled wristlets.

"Wasn't expecting that," Reba said admiring the flowers around her wrist.

"That's all fine," I said. "I feel like an undertaker's assistant wearing this red thing."

"Oh," Cordelia said. "An undertaker's assistant. That sounds so different."

We walked through the hall. The main floor was set aside for dancing. The room was filled with students. Everyone with dates, except for Bobby. He's alone in a hospital fighting to survive, I thought.

There was a long buffet table set to one side of the room along the one side with round table seating that looked as though it had been brought in by a rental company. Brightly colored balloons were everywhere. All the tables were covered with red and black linens.

"Let's get something to drink." Cordelia

grabbed both of our hands and dragged us to the punch bowl. Toby stood just beyond the bowl and greeted us all. "I see you have two dates tonight," Toby said. "Nice job. Punch?" He held out the brim-full ladle.

"We'll pass." Cordelia yanked the two of us away from Toby. "He's probably spiked that stuff," she said. "Better stick to bottles of water. Let's go dance." She dragged both Reba and me to the center of the dance floor. I couldn't believe how both Reba and Cordelia were being so civilized. I dreaded that I'd be separating them from each other's throats all night.

The three of us kind of danced together. I was all left footed and couldn't keep any kind of beat with the music. At one point, the DJ yelled: "Put your hands up". Everyone else beat with the music, and mine were the only hands that went up alone in a syncopated rhythm. Reba rolled her eyes looking at me to get with it. Just before the music ended, I finally got the beat with everyone else.

The next song started. I decided to watch Reba and try to mimic her moves on the floor. This went much better. Cordelia danced hard and took a couple of spins. I decided to try a spin as well. Around I went until my shoe caught my pant leg and down I went to my knees. At that moment, my calf cramped. The two girls helped me upright and held me as I limped off the floor. This was so humiliating. I didn't know if my knee or calf hurt more than my total embarrassment. Once seated, I rubbed my calf hard feeling the knot near the top of the large muscle.

"You really need to work out more," Reba said leaning closer to me. Cordelia patted my shoulder.

Toby appeared walking up behind Reba. He tapped her shoulder. "Come on, soccer girl," he said. "Let's dance." He reached for her hand. Reba pulled away then latched onto his wrist.

"It's okay," I said just before she would have twisted him in an unforgiving wrist lock.

She relaxed and grinned back at me, then led him onto the floor.

"I'll keep an eye on them," Cordelia followed them into the heaving crowd of students and dates. Cordelia and Reba seemed to dance together. At one point Reba leaned over to Toby and said something to him. The three danced until the song ended. Toby went toward the far side of the floor, and the girls returned to me.

"Thanks for not hurting him," I said.

"It took every ounce of strength I had not to break every bone in his wrist," Reba replied.

"I had fun," Cordelia said.

"What did you say to him?" I asked.

Reba grinned. One of those sympathetic grins like she was saying oh, you're jealous. "I asked him why he wasn't hanging with Crystal."

"And?" Cordelia prompted.

"Yeah," I said still rubbing my calf that was finally feeling a bit better. "I'd sort of like to know that, too."

"Song ended, and he walked away." Reba grinned.

"She's probably holding court with her other friends."

The prom went on for another hour. I was actually able to dance a bit more, but no spins or aggressive stuff. I just stepped to the beat of the music.

It was nearly midnight when the room went quiet, Headmaster Hannah took the wireless microphone. "How was that?" he yelled.

The students all cheered and chanted more, more.

Hannah pumped his palms toward the crowd. "This was a great prom night. Hopefully you all had a fun time and appreciate what the committee put together. The lights came up in the gym. "One last dance, then all good things have to come to an end."

A slow song started.

"Last dance?" Cordelia asked.

"I've had it," I said. "Let's head back."

We worked our way towards the exit and through the classroom building toward the central courtyard.

As we reached the edge of the drive, I saw Dorm Mom step down the stairs of the dorm building, cradling a blonde girl in her arms that was clearly unconscious. It was Crystal. Dorm Mom didn't see us and turned jogging toward the open backdoors of an ambulance.

"That's Crystal!" Reba said. She took off after them followed closely by Cordelia. I followed but couldn't keep up. I again caught my pant leg and nearly tripped onto my face. Crystal got dropped on the stretcher just as the two girls reached her. One of the ambulance attendants strapped an oxygen mask over Crystal's face while the other one prepped an IV. Dorm Mom, seeing Reba approach, ducked into the shadows around the side of the ambulance. I recovered and ran with a bad limp toward them. My calf flared up with a sharp cramp, and I stopped, rubbing my leg vigorously to relieve the pain. I was no match for Reba or Cordelia even with their heels on. One of the ambulance guys grabbed Reba around the waist, while the other forced the stretcher into the ambulance.

Reba punched the attendant's face with a forearm shiver, but he kept hold. He dragged her toward the side door amidst several blows to his face and neck. He swung back and tossed Reba inside the side door as the other attendant subdued Cordelia with her hair. Her blonde wig snapped off, and he was left with a handful of long blonde locks. With his other hand he grabbed her neck and threw her toward the open side door. I started running as best I could toward the back of the ambulance just as the engine roared with all three girls now inside. I grabbed my phone and snapped pictures of the vehicle. I needed to get a call to dad and Agent Wilson.

Everything went dark.

\#

Oh, what a headache. It was morning. I looked around. Posters of human anatomy and health information covered the walls. A small counter with medical supplies on it stood at the side of the bed I was on. A curled-up stethoscope gave me another clue. I was in the school infirmary in the administration building, down the hall from the headmaster's office. The school nurse stepped into the room carrying a clipboard.

"Ah, you're awake," she said. "Looks like someone slipped you a mickey."

"Where's Reba and Cordelia?" I asked.

She shook her head as she wrapped a blood pressure cuff on me. "Lay still." The automatic cuff filled with air then released pressure, measuring my blood pressure. She took a small handheld device and checked my temperature. "All good."

"What time is it?"

"About 7 AM. You slept hard and didn't

even notice me taking your vitals every few hours."

"Reba. Cordelia." I said. I felt my pockets realizing I had no pants or outer shirt on. "Where's my phone?"

The nurse opened a drawer and held up the pieces of my phone. The screen was smashed, and components hung out of all sides.

"You must've taken quite the fall, Mr. Palmer."

"I need to call my dad." I started to sit up in bed, but the room spun, and I dropped back.

"I've contacted your parents. They'll be here in a bit. Are you hungry? Thirsty?"

I shook my head focusing on the light above me. Pleased the spinning room had stopped turning.

"I really need you to drink some water or juice." The nurse set a plastic glass of water on a small roll up table along with a juice cup. "Now, drink that."

"Yes, ma'am," I said. Picking up the glass of water, I took a sip. It was cool and refreshing, so I downed the whole thing.

The nurse refilled the glass. "Again."

I frowned at her but took the glass and downed it as well.

"Good. Your parents should be here soon. You can explain to them what happened and what you took at the party."

"I didn't take anything," I said. The nurse just flicked a quick smile that said, sure you didn't.

I laid back, my mind going through every permutation of what had happened. Reba was real tough, but those two goons and whoever else was in the ambulance were too much. My damned pant leg and calf. I could've helped. We just so happened to leave the dance a bit early encountering what looked to be a kidnapping.

There was a commotion outside the infirmary. I heard the nurse explaining her prognosis to my mum who said she was a doctor and would make her own evaluation. The door swung open. Mum and dad followed by the nurse.

"Leave us," mum said to the nurse. She stepped back and shut the door. "What happened?"

I explained the story and said that I hadn't had anything since the dinner. Not even water. Dad was immediately on the phone with Agent Wilson reporting what I told them, while mum had me sit up and did a physical examination of my neck and head. "I suppose they think this bump on your head came from a fall."

Each time she touched it, sharp pain caused me to pull away. Mum grabbed the chart and reviewed my vitals from the prior night. "At a minimum, you're concussed and coming with us."

"But Reba," I said.

Dad covered the mic on the phone, "I'm on with Wilson. We'll get this sorted. Were the girls still wearing what they had on at the restaurant?"

"Yeah, but one of the ambulance guys ripped the wig off Cordelia just before tossing her in. She has jet black hair."

Dad related detailed descriptions to Agent Wilson, then hung up. "She's on her way here."

"Well," mum said, "we won't be here when she arrives. I want him home."

"Right," dad said. "I'm going to check around outside. You said that this took place just outside of the dorm stairs?"

I nodded. My neck was real stiff, and I rubbed at it. "Where's your phone?" Dad asked.

I pointed to the mess of smashed electronics on the counter. Dad examined it. "There are wood splinters in the screen. This didn't break when you hit the ground. Someone smashed it with a stick. I bet it was the same stick that gave you that lump on the noggin."

Dad left the room pushing past the

nurse. I heard the nurse talk to him, but he just kept walking. Mum asked where my clothes were. I shrugged. She opened a small closet beyond the bed and pulled out my jacket, shirt, and gray slacks. The pant leg was well ripped. Probably from my other foot stepping on the cuff as I ran.

"This is a mess," she said tossing the trousers and shirt to me. "Put these on. We'll go to your room and change."

I dressed and stood by the bed. Fortunately, the room wasn't spinning. Mum handed me the orange juice and said that I should drink that as well. My blood pressure was a bit low, and she said I was dehydrated.

Once stable on two feet, mum held my shoulder as we walked from the infirmary. The nurse stood with a paper on a clipboard saying that mum needed to sign it since I was being discharged.

"You sign it, honey," mum snapped back. "I don't have any idea how you explained the bump on his head and why you didn't call 9-1-1." The nurse was speechless. Mum led the way holding my arm as we left the administration building.

Dad joined us in my room carrying a large brown paper bag. He opened it. Cordelia's wig. He'd found it in the shrubbery just next to where I said the ambulance was parked when the girls were taken.

"Guess that proves I wasn't dreaming this all up," I said.

Dad nodded. I changed clothes quickly and went over to my open laptop. Seeing the wig gave me a jolt of adrenaline. Now I needed to find the girls. Reba had one of my trackers hidden in the insole of her high heels. If the shoes were still with her, I should be able to find her. I activated the tracking application. No signal from Reba's shoe. It was either destroyed or out of range. That jolt of energy subsided, my shoulders slumped, and I started crying. Mum wrapped her arms around me. "She's not here," I said.

Dad's phone rang. It was Wilson. He spoke quickly to her and hung up. "They found Reba," he said. "She's at Sequoia Hospital ER."

"That's great news," mum said.

"Wilson is on her way and asked if we could join her there."

"Let's go," Mum said. "We can take her home with us as well."

#

Sequoia Hospital sat on the Alameda de las Pulgas in the hills overlooking Redwood City, a short distance from Woodside and the school. Reba was still in the ER. Dad used his police credentials to gain access, and mum actually knew the attending ER physician.

The doc slipped mum Reba's chart, as dad and I went into her small room. Reba was very happy to see us. She had road rash down her left arm that had been treated and a few scrapes on her face.

Mum came into the room. "Nothing's broken, and they're ready to discharge her to her parents."

Dad got back onto his phone and called Mrs. Ng. He said that we were with her in the hospital now and could bring her home if that was approved. They agreed.

"How ya' doin', girl?" I said.

Reba smiled.

Mum came back into the room with the attending physician. They did a review, and mum did a quick examination. "Well, the dress is ruined. And you're in a whole bunch better shape than you should be."

"Her parents will call and send an email authorizing us to drive her home," dad said to the doctor. He responded and said that he'd get the paperwork ready.

As though perfectly timed, Agent Wilson walked into the room along with Agent Reed, whom I hadn't seen for many months. Reed could be a real jerk but was clearly subservient to Wilson. Wilson opened the door and asked Reed to keep everyone out while she got statements. Mum asked if she should leave.

"Nope," Wilson said. "As far as I'm concerned, you're the attending doc now. What happened, Reba?"

The story was harrowing after the ambulance pulled away, and I had been taken out with a head bash.

According to Reba, the battle in the ambulance raged on. Reba punched the guy snapping his nose with blood everywhere, so he had to let her go. The ambulance accelerated, and she was thrown back by the rear doors. Then it swung a hard left turn, and Cordelia was tossed to the same corner landing on Reba. As they stood, Cordelia slipped off one of her heels holding the white satin pump by the toe wielding the stiletto as a weapon while one of the goons filled a syringe. She leapt forward and swung her shoe at him, but he ducked as the blow whizzed by his forehead. He grabbed Cordelia by the back of her dress, pulled her over, and jabbed the needle into her butt. Cordelia staggered back, took a meaningless swing, and lost the shoe before falling. Reba pulled herself up, stepping over Cordelia's motionless body.

"Your turn, honey," one of the attendants said drawing another full dose while the bloodied goon moved toward her. Reba faked with her left and landed a solid blow to the man's throat. He dropped back as the other goon grabbed at Reba from across the gurney where Crystal lay strapped down. Reba ducked back, slapping the man's hand away.

The choking man, who laid half atop Crystal grabbed Reba's leg. And the man with the syringe lunged over Crystal. Reba slapped the man's face and arms away. He nearly lost control of the needle hand. She took his hand in a wristlock then stabbed the choking guy with the needle and drove the plunger down. He fell back and became rubber. Reba shoved the bloodied man off Crystal just as the ambulance swung a left turn, and he fell back against the counter and cabinets. The ambulance broke hard and swerved around something. Reba flew forward by the side door striking the wall with her head against the front bulkhead. She heard a voice from the cab asking what was going on back there. The ambulance slowed, probably getting ready to make another turn. The bloodied goon leapt toward Reba again. She threw a wicked side kick connecting solidly against the man's jaw sending him to the floor.

The ambulance accelerated into a turn and Reba fell over Crystal. The goon on the floor groaned and tried to get up, but she landed a straight thrust between his eyes, and he dropped back, not out, but stunned.

Reba pulled the small tracker from under the insole of her shoe and planted it on Crystal. The ambulance slowed, probably for a traffic light.

"Now, or never," Reba added to her story. "I popped the side door open and jumped out."

"Oh my," mum said.

"Landed a perfect Judo roll. Thank goodness there was no oncoming traffic. The ambulance just drove off. The side door slamming closed as it did."

Mum gave Reba a big hug. "Thank goodness you're okay."

"My dress was ripped. I only had one shoe on that I dumped in the bushes somewhere, and my cell phone was gone. A few minutes later, as I was walking down the sidewalk near an underpass, a couple drove by and saw me. They stopped and drove me here."

"Where's your phone?" I asked.

"Probably lost in the ambulance."

I took out my tablet PC and immediately activated an app to find the cell phone. The signal came from a location in South San Francisco. Wilson got on the phone and ordered other agents and the local police to the location. I searched for the tracker that Reba planted on Crystal. No signal. Either destroyed or out of range.

We left the room while Reba changed into set of blue scrubs the hospital provided. Afterward, mum spoke with the attending physician and arranged for the discharge. Wilson told Agent Reed, who had stood guard outside the room, that they were heading to South San Francisco and she'd brief him on the way. "We have two kidnappings and an attempted abduction. It's going to be a long day," she said as they walked down the hall.

Dad walked in once Wilson and Reed left. "I've been told to keep watch on you guys for the next few days until the FBI gets this stabilized," dad said.

Before we left, I activated a notification flag on the tracker planted on Crystal hoping it would re-emerge.

12. NEW URGENCY, NEW ALLY

I had trouble sleeping even in my own bed, but I did fall asleep in the early afternoon only to wake as my tablet echoed a loud ding. The tracker.

It took me a bit to collect myself after just a few hours' sleep, but I rolled over and tapped the tablet's screen. The map came up and slowly rendered. I tapped the screen a few more times zooming in on the tracker. It moved just beyond the US/Canada border, north of Niagara, traveling along Queen Elizabeth Way toward Toronto.

"Dad!" I shouted and jumped out of bed. "Dad!"

Still wearing my fluffy warm jammies, I burst into my parent's room. They were sound asleep bundled in a big purple comforter.

"Dad, wake up." I shook him. I slapped at him.

He stirred. "Not now, Jason. Fix your own brekkie."

"Dad, wake up. It's the tracker!"

He sat up like an electric jolt hit him. "What?!"

"The tracker. It just showed up." I held the tablet so he could see.

He rubbed his eyes, squinting at the screen. "So where is it?"

"Canada. Heading toward metro Toronto."

He swiveled out of bed. I couldn't believe he was wearing giant pink Hello Kitty pajamas. Mum stirred, so dad grabbed my arm, and we were out the door of the bedroom.

"Really? Hello Kitty."

"Oh, shut up," he snarled. "Phone, where's my phone?"

"On the nightstand?" I said.

He groaned, popped back into the room and returned with the phone. After carefully shutting the door, he said, "Kitchen. Let's let your mum sleep. She had quite the morning." He dialed Wilson's number. "What time is it now?"

"Almost 4 in the afternoon."

"Damn, I feel like I worked a double shift. Wilson, is that you?" Dad said. "Tracker's up in Canada, moving toward Toronto on the Queen Elizabeth motorway. Any chance of an intercept?" A moment later, dad hung up the phone. "She'll get back to us. Asked if we could keep an eye on the tracker."

The tracker crept down the highway. I felt helpless knowing all I could do was watch a little blue dot and report. Nothing more. We didn't know anything about the vehicle they were in or where they might be heading.

Dad's phone rang, an unknown caller ID. He answered, put the speaker on and set the phone on the table.

"Detective Palmer?" A female voice asked. There was the telltale beep that the call was being recorded.

"Here," dad said.

"This is the FBI National Operations Center. Please stay on the line."

"Wilson, 23-1-10 here," Agent Wilson joined the call.

"Confirmed," the operator said. "I have RCMP coming on the line as well. Please stand by. Detective Palmer, are you still with us?"

"Yes, I'm here," dad said.

The operator went on mute.

"We will brief the RCMP shortly," Wilson said. "Is the tracker still moving?"

Dad looked to me.

"Yes," I said. "Just on the outskirts of Toronto. It's moving really slow."

"Probably caught in the evening rush

hour there. Keep on it, JP." We waited for what seemed like an eternity. The tracker barely moved.

"I have the RCMP," the FBI operator came back on. A deep male voice introduced himself from RCMP security operations.

"We have two kidnapped teens," Wilson started, "one has a hidden tracker on that we are monitoring. They were abducted from the San Francisco Bay Area by force approximately 7-hours ago and drugged. We lost comms with the tracker, but it's reappeared heading into Metro Toronto area. JP, location!"

"The tracker," I spoke loudly, "just turned off of the Gardiner Expressway heading north on Bay Street into downtown Toronto."

"We have no vehicle description," Wilson added. She gave the description of the two girls that had been abducted from their high school prom and were both in party dresses and nice clothes. "Our operations center will be forwarding electronic copies of their school photos to you now."

A moment later. "Photos sent," the FBI operator said.

"Got 'em," the RCMP officer confirmed. "Where are they now?"

"They're stopped at Bay and Front Street east," I said and watched the blinking signal on the map. "They've turned east on Front Street."

"Stay on them, please," the RCMP officer said. "I have two TPD uniform units moving into the area. There's a lot of traffic right now and we may not be able to figure out which vehicle they're in."

"Passing Younge Street," I said. "Still moving eastbound on Front." I could hear the RCMP officer speaking to others in the background and across radios. "Picking up speed passing Scott and Berczy Park."

"Ten-four," the RCMP officer said. "The two units are only just arriving from Wellington St. East."

"They've stopped just short of the

intersection of Church and Front."

"If they keep going down Front Street," the RCMP officer said, "we have a chance to identify them. I now have two more units converging on that area."

"They've gone right, I mean southbound on Church Steet. They're picking up speed. Now a left on The Esplanade." He relayed the information to the police units.

"Now, left on George Street. They seem to be doubling back. Could they see your units?"

"Who knows. We don't know what they look like, but they sure know what TPD patrol cars look like."

"We have to risk it," dad said. "Keep on 'em JP. You're the eye- in-the-sky."

"They've turned on some little street from George heading east. They're about a block south off Front Street." I watched closely. I only hoped that tracker had enough juice to stay online. "Now, south on Fredrick Street." I heard commotion from the RCMP side.

"There's been a car collision on Frederick Street that's blocking the road. The TPD unit can't get passed. He's reported that a dark blue BMW sedan just cut off a produce truck, forcing the truck to swerve and hit a city bus. That might be them."

"They're back on The Esplanade heading east again."

"I've got units coming down Berkeley and Princess streets. The units just met on Esplanade. No sign of the BMW. Where are they now?"

"East on Front Street again, from Princess."

"These guys are slippery," the RCMP officer said. "Repositioning units now."

"Trackers turned on Parliament Street, heading south."

The officer spoke on the radio, relaying the location information and the possibility that it was a dark blue BMW, 4-door sedan. "Can we get a direct feed from that tracker?"

"Not in time to catch these guys and rescue the girls," dad said.

"Hey, hey," I said. "The tracker's stopped and seems to have turned off of Parliament Street. Just before the railroad tracks." "Address or coordinates?"

I grabbed the geo-coordinates from the tracker and passed them to the RCMP officer. "Verify that they haven't moved?"

"Just sitting there."

"We have the warehouse location," the RCMP officer said. "We'll set up a perimeter and observe."

"I have a special warrant prepared requesting you to raid the site based on exigent circumstances. That's been sent by our Legat to your offices," Wilson said.

"Stand by. We have confirmed that. Tactical units enroute," the RCMP officer said. "Will advise your FBI operations center after we move." The officer rang off.

"RCMP connection terminated," the FBI operator said.

"Good job, Jason and Detective Palmer," Wilson said. "Now we wait. Center, close the line."

"Thank you all," the FBI operator said prior to the line dropping.

Dad looked at me. "Well, that was exciting." He stood. "Maybe technology can really solve all crimes. The question now is coffee or beer? I don't think I can go back to sleep."

"Go with coffee," I said. "Nothing to celebrate yet." The tracker remained motionless. I wondered if there were any IoT camera devices in or around that building that I might tap into. Opening Shodan and maps on my machine. Entering the geo-coordinates, I got the address of the building. Armed with that, I asked Shodan to list the IoT devices.

Dad returned with a steaming mug of black, instant coffee. It smelled like old socks, I thought. "What ya' doin' now?" he asked.

"Shodan."

"What's that? A game?"

"Hardly. I'm seeing if I can become a real eye-in-the-sky." My system displayed some information but nothing that was interesting. There were commercial IoT cold storage units in the building that might be associated with meat packing. No other IoT devices scanned or reported by Shodan. Nothing that might give me any additional information beyond the temperature in a meat locker.

Reba popped in the front door and joined us in the kitchen. Dad briefed her on where things were at when the unknown caller rang his cell phone once again.

"Palmer," dad said answering the call and activating the speaker phone.

"FBI National Operations Center," a male voice said. "I have Agents Wilson and Baxter on the line."

"Stafford?" Wilson said using my dad's first name.

"Here."

"Do you still have JP there?"

"Yes."

"Any news," I asked.

"RCMP teams are closing the net. We have near satellite images and can see the established perimeter and a mid-perimeter. They're going to hit the site soon."

"You're not going to believe this, but the tracker has just moved." I pointed to the screen. The signal drifted west, north-west between buildings and out onto the street.

"They've hit the site. Looks like gas deployed and tactical teams moving in. Where's that tracker?"

"Moving through the building behind the one they just hit," I said.

"Message from RCMP," FBI operator broke in. "Storage room discovered, housing 12 teenage girls. One is in fancy dress." Dad and Reba high-fived. This could be great news.

"Hold on," I said. "Tracker is on the move. It's crossing behind the target location to a building behind." I couldn't take my eyes off the small flashing dot on the map.

"Operator," Wilson asked, "do we have any confirmation photos yet?"

"Requesting now."

"Send it to Detective Palmer's number once you get it," Wilson ordered. "Let's see if they'll take a quick facial snapshot of the girl in the fancy clothes and see which one we might have. JP, that tracker movement can't be right. RCMP has multiple units positioned at the back of the building."

"I know what I'm seeing. The tracker is still moving diagonally through the building behind the target."

"Ops, relay this to RCMP. Tracker moving again."

Dad's cellphone popped up a message alert. The photo had arrived. It was Cordelia lying back on an ambulance gurney. Her face swollen and bruised from the fight Reba had described. Black eye makeup streaked down her cheeks. Her once frilly, white Bopeep dress was not so white or frilly anymore. Her face and arms were splattered with dirt and grease.

Seeing the photo, the cheers and exhilaration subsided. Reba couldn't hold back tears any longer.

"FBI operations," dad said to the phone. "Confirmed. That's one of the two girls. This is Cordelia." He turned to Reba. "Last name?"

"Kelly," Reba said just before totally breaking down and sobbing.

"Cordelia Kelly," dad relayed to the FBI operator.

"Confirm. We've got one of them." Wilson said. "Operations, please get photos of the other girls and send them to Detective Palmer. Has the RCMP team expanded their search? The other girl has to be there as well."

"Hey!" I said. "The tracker is still on the move. I think it's coming out in a lot a couple buildings behind the one the RCMP raided."

"Understood," the FBI operator said. "Stand by."

"Tracker must be in a car now. They're heading north on Parliament from Mill Street."

"They must have the other girl," dad said. "We're not done yet."

Reba was up and next to dad when his phone went off. Eleven face shots of the other girls with Cordelia. The two of them went through the pictures one by one while I monitored the tracker's movement. Afterwards, Reba shook her head.

"Agent Wilson, none of these are the other girl, Crystal."

"Her full name," Reba said, "is Kayleen Masterson. She just likes going by Crystal."

"Let's focus on the tracker," Wilson said. "JP, what's the location now?"

"Looks like it's stopped at a traffic light. Parliament and Front streets. Wait, now it's moving."

"Keep on it and let me know when it stops."

Reba stood over me now with her hands on my shoulders like she was giving a back massage. Dad leaned closer to watch the marker move across the screen. The tracker worked its way up Bay Street, then left on Bloor. Eventually it took a right on Spadina Avenue then off the road into a lot behind the Madison Avenue Pub, where it stopped.

"They've stopped," dad said. "Looks like they're behind the Madison Avenue Pub off Spadina Street."

After a pause, the FBI operator said, "RCMP has units enroute."

The tracker remained still.

"Patching in RCMP operations," the FBI operator said. "TPD units are on scene," a female voice of an RCMP dispatcher said. "There's nothing moving in the parking lot."

"The tracker is still reporting the same location. It hasn't moved," I whispered to dad.

"JP, tell them what the tracker looks like," dad said.

"Hello," I spoke up. "Have units check for the tracker. The device is housed in a small felt strip 4 inches long and about an eighth of an inch thick."

"Hold, please," the RCMP dispatcher

requested. A few moments of silence followed. "A TPD unit reports locating the tracker. Crime scene investigation unit on the way."

"Damn," I said. "They found the tracker and tossed it." Then to the dispatcher. "Is there any CCTV in that lot?"

"Units will check."

Reba sat back down at the table. "We've lost her."

The RCMP operator advised that detectives would be in touch since this scene was no longer active. The connection with Canada was dropped.

Wilson came on and introduced an Agent Baxter from the Child Sexual Exploitation unit of the FBI. "He'll be covering for me while I travel up to Toronto," Wilson said. "I'm going to escort Cordelia Kelly back. Baxter has been instructed to keep JP and Reba safe as confidential informants."

"Thank you," dad said. "I'm going to keep them safe, too."

"I'm Agent Baxter," a deep male voice introduced himself. "I've seen the information on Mrs. Fadler and put out a nationwide BOLO for her as a person of interest. Is Reba on the line?"

"I'm here," Reba said.

"We recovered your cell phone from a drainage ditch in South San Francisco. They must have discovered it and chucked it out. We don't have the ambulance or the crew. I've put out a notice to all of the hospitals in the area since both of those guys you fought with sounded like they were injured. Nothing yet."

#

After spending the weekend and a day at home, dad dropped us both off at school Tuesday morning. There were three grey cars and a county Sheriff's unit parked around the central courtyard close to the administration building. The bump on the back of my head reminded me of the prior evening. I'd wake up every hour or so and check my mobile to see if there were any messages from Agent Wilson, or anyone for that matter. Nothing. All quiet on the Canadian front. My mind would run scenarios on how to locate and find Crystal. Assuming the RCMP hitting the warehouse in Toronto disrupted the human trafficking options, the people who took Crystal must have some plan. But what? I'd fall back asleep only to wake again when the bump on the back of my head rolled on to the pillow. I remembered how relieved I was when it was finally morning, and I could dress and have breakfast.

Maybe I'd spend my free time figuring out who hit me. Reba rushed off to a chem class, while I was back to ancient history. I was excited and quite pleased to see Cordelia Kelly in her seat next to mine near the back of the class. Her jet-black hair up in a bun, and she wore much lighter makeup than before. She wore a clean tee shirt and jeans, not her usual goth attire. She touched the back of my hand as I passed by her to my usual seat.

The topic today was Persephone and the Seasons. Persephone had been abducted by Hades and taken to the Underworld. Her mother, Demeter, goddess of the harvest, caused a worldwide famine and eternal winter, refusing anything to grow.

Zeus brokered a deal with Hades. Since Persephone had eaten a few pomegranate seeds in the underworld, she would spend part of each year with Hades, then return to her mother. This led to the cycle of life. When Persephone was in the underworld, it would be autumn and winter, a time when crops die. Once she returned, spring would come followed by a bountiful summer harvest.

I felt these stories were very timely given the events with Cordelia. Let's just hope she didn't have to return to the kidnappers each year like Persephone to Hades.

Once class ended, Cordelia and I walked back toward the dorm building. The three grey cars and Sheriff's unit were still parked along the circular courtyard. As we entered the dorm building, a Sheriff's Deputy blocked the door to the Fadler's quarters. Inside, we could hear a male voice talking to Mr. Fadler asking where his wife was. The question was repeated several times. We climbed the stairs and turned toward the girl's side. The door to Crystal's room stood wide open, and Headmaster Hannah stood in the hall outside wringing his hands nervously.

"Nothing to see here," Hannah said as we slowed and passed by the open room. I could see two people dressed in protective clothing inside examining a small box.

"Come on, Palmer, keep moving," Hannah said. "Why are you on this side of the building anyway?"

"Just walking Ms. Kelly back to her room," I said gesturing toward Cordelia. She smiled at Hannah.

"I'm a bit shocked he's still here," Cordelia said as we walked on. "Thought the Board would have done him like an injured horse once the FBI showed up."

Cordelia's room was at the end of the hall on the right. We'd just reached the room when Reba shouted: "Hey, guys, wait up." Reba ran up and hugged Cordelia hard. "I'm so glad you're safe. You fought well and hard. Too bad you didn't bury your heel into that goon's skull."

"Not without trying," Cordelia hugged Reba back.

We went inside the room. There were three computers purring away, each display asleep and awaiting the next command.

"Wow," I said. "This must be the headquarters of Adda Lovelace."

Cordelia flicked a quick grin. "What did I miss once the goon jabbed me with the drugs?"

Reba was quick to brief her on the blow by blow of what happened up until she was ejected from the ambulance. "It was all JP after that." She looked at me.

"We were most fortunate that Reba hid

a tracker on Crystal. By the time we found Reba, you must have been in flight."

"I barely remember landing and being helped off the jet," Cordelia added. "They stuffed me in the trunk of a car and shot me up again."

"That must be about the time the tracker logged in again, and I got the signal. You were already across the northern border heading into Toronto. We got with the FBI and RCMP, then followed you all the way to a big building in the old distillery district of Toronto."

She hugged me again. "Thank God you did. I woke up in a locked room with 11 other girls. It was like out of some weird science fiction film or something. The room was dark with a handful of crummy steel bunk beds. All the girls were dressed in dark, olive-green coveralls. I was messed up as hell and kept falling asleep. I don't really know how long I was in that room with those girls. At one point, I remember waking up and really having to use a toilet. There was a can with a toilet seat on top set in a corner where everyone could watch, but I really had to go. I fell over when I stood, and a girl with a thick Eastern European accent helped me back into the bunk. About then, there was a loud commotion outside. A couple of bangs. Lots of shouting. The steel doors swung open and guys with guns, in combat fatigues, ran in. They had bright flashlights. I had to cover my eyes when they hit me with them. I had no idea where I was or who these guys were. I could have been in Russia for all I knew. They spoke English. I was photographed and taken outside to an ambulance. That's where I found out that I was in Canada. They took me to a hospital, and I remained under guard of uniformed police until Agent Wilson from the FBI showed up. She brought me clothes and took me home, well to here, that is. My parents are God knows where, probably in Ireland somewhere. Wilson said the command center kept trying to reach them. This daughter is just an embarrassment. That's why I'm halfway around the globe." A tear swelled up in her eyes, and Reba hugged her again.

There was a soft knock at the door. Cordelia gave a sniff and stood rigid as she answered it. Mr. Hannah stepped in and pointed at me. "I knew you'd be in here. This is a girl's dorm room. Get out of here. Go to your side or meet up in the common room. Now!"

"I'll catch you guys later," I headed toward my side of the dorm building. Hannah didn't follow. At my room, I was somewhat pleased to see that the strand of hair was still caught in the door jamb where I'd placed it when I left earlier. Inside, I launched my new mobile phone and immediately restored the most recent iCloud backup from my destroyed phone. While this ran, I flipped open my laptop and opened the tracking application. I just had to see if the tracker that was hidden on Crystal was active at all. It wasn't. I knew better. I really wished we'd intercepted her as well as the others.

At home over the weekend, I'd installed the latest update for Microsoft's WSL2 and popped open a terminal session to the installed Ubuntu environment. I still had a few of Cordelia's passwords that she'd used to access the school's CCTV system. I connected to the digital video recorder, then roamed into the folder where videos were cached, and found the two large files dated the evening of the Prom. The playback of the files would take hours. Fortunately, the video streams were timestamped. There was one camera in particular that interested me. It was a bullet camera pointing toward the circular courtyard from the administration building. The ambulance was beyond the camera's field of view given where it was parked, but I should have been well within view.

I forced the playback to Saturday night just before midnight. The screen showed the backside of Fadler, waddling not running, while holding Crystal in front of her. You couldn't recognize Fadler or Crystal in any of the frames. A moment later, Reba ran into view in hot pursuit of Fadler and followed right behind by Cordelia. Then, it was me. I looked beyond clumsy. Once I was in the field of view, I tripped on my pant leg falling forward. Of course, I could just imagine a trial jury bursting into laughter watching this in court. Fortunately, I got up pretty quickly, fixed my shoe and ripped pant leg, then ran forward before stopping. The scene showed me pulling out my phone to capture the fight raging behind the ambulance. At that moment, a darkened figure, a wee-bit taller than me, appeared holding a large stick in two hands. He reared back and struck me across the back of my head, snapping the stick in half. I dropped face first. This explained why my cheek and forehead hurt so much. A moment later, the figure used what remained of the stick, whacking my cell phone several times. Not getting the results from the stick, my attacker ground his heel onto my phone, then ran off into the darkness toward the classroom building where the Prom was just ending.

I disconnected from the school's network, isolating my laptop completely. Copying the video file into a working folder, I loaded Wondershare's Filmora so I could examine each segment of the video. Playing in slow motion, I isolated the scene where the attacker stomped on my cell phone. In doing this, he turned sideways to the camera, giving a reasonable profile. He was about half a head taller than me, lean, and dressed in dark clothes.

The lighting wasn't good, and the camera's night vision recorded off ambient light and UV. In the profile, his facial features were blurred. I couldn't make out much. I commanded Filmora to clip just this section and saved it in a separate file.

The profile shot could be Toby, but I couldn't be certain without a positive ID of the image. I used a couple of tools to deblur and enhance the video images. The handful of free video forensic tools on my investigative platform did the best job they could. The image was just too bad to make it really clear, and I didn't want to use any of the AI tools to fix and fill in the image. The most distinctive feature I had was a clear image of his left ear.

Now, I just needed to locate and compare this ear image with a live ear or some trusted image. I dialed Cordelia's mobile number. She had a whole bunch more access to the school systems than me.

"Are you free?" I asked as she answered. "Cool. Can you come over?"

A few moments later, there was a soft knock at the door.

"Come in," I said.

Both Reba and Cordelia stepped into my room. "Hannah's busy with the cops and didn't see us. What's up?" Cordelia asked.

I demonstrated what I'd derived from the CCTV system and left the still frame of the attacker's left ear up on my screen. "All I really have is a decent ear picture."

"Oh, that's too bad," Reba said.

"Not really. There is a very low probability that two humans have the same ear characteristics. I kind of think Toby might be the attacker or someone like Mr. Fadler, Dorm Mom's husband. So, Cordelia, you have access to a lot of systems here. Do you think you can find left profile pictures of both Mr. Fadler and Toby?"

She grinned really big. "I'd love to see that hammerhead Toby go down. Let me do some digging. The equipment in my room is better. Left side you say? I'll see what I can get."

"I have an idea," Reba said. "What about pictures from the gym? Toby is big time into sports. There might be pics from a practice or some event."

"Good idea." I gave Reba a thumbs up.

#

On the way to dinner that night, Mr. Fadler was in the courtyard sweeping along the curb where the police vehicles had been parked. Reba and I split up passing on either side of Fadler. Reba stopped and addressed him so that I got a clean left profile. Before I snapped the picture, I could see clearly that this wasn't the ear in the image. Fadler had a large dangling earlobe that wasn't anything even close. I shook my head so Reba could see. We just told him to have a nice evening and walked toward the Commons after he gave us a gruff grumble.

That evening during dinner service, Reba and I separated and walked through the Commons. No sign of Toby. We sat at our usual table.

"He's not here," Reba said.

"Let's eat real slow and hang here through the entire dinner service," I said. "It's not like him to miss dinner. One thing for sure, Mr. Fadler's ear lobe didn't match the image at all."

"Could it have been someone else?"

"Maybe, but my money is still on Toby.

Let's hope Cordelia has better luck."

We sat and poked at our food for over an hour. The Commons emptied slowly as the other students finished and went back to their dorms. Just as we were about to give up, Cordelia walked in. Not her usual deadpan stroll we'd seen many times before, but she was bouncing with excitement.

"Well?" Reba asked as Cordelia sat at the table.

"I found both a left and right profile of him that was taken for the school's online news site. I've blown up the ears. Looks like a possible match." She held out her phone and showed the image. I took out my phone and opened the close-up frame I'd recovered from the CCTV. Earlobe correct. Shape of ear matched.

"Looks like a match," I said. "I have a theory. We never saw Crystal at the dance, right? What if she was drugged possibly by Toby. Then he went to the Prom by himself as an alibi?"

"He certainly made his presence known at the prom," Reba said.

"That he did. He seemed to make a point of being seen and heard," I said. "Then Dorm Mom fetched a drugged Crystal and carried her outside to the ambulance when we came out of the event."

"But why did they wait until the prom was almost over?" Reba said. "They had plenty of time to do it earlier."

"Maybe there were too many people around or something simple, like the ambulance was late. Who knows."

"Sounds like a reasonable explanation. Now where is Crystal?" Reba said.

"And where is Toby?" I added. The three of us got up from the table and started back to the dorm.

Reba leaned close to me. "We should chat with Wilson."

"Agreed."

13. TRANSNATIONAL COOPERATION

The next morning came quickly after a fitful night. I just couldn't stop thinking about what Crystal was going through at the hands of her abductors. Reba and I met up in the common area. We decided to skip breakfast and reach out to Wilson.

Agent Wilson expected us to call, and I told her that we had uncovered a bit more information from the school's CCTV system. She didn't want to talk on the phone and arranged to meet us out at Buck's in

Woodside, where we met after the first weekend at school.

An hour later, Reba and I once again borrowed the school bicycles and rode the short mile to the restaurant. This time we were early, beating Wilson. We had no money and could only order two glasses of water, telling the waitress that we were meeting someone. Wilson arrived, dressed in her usual business suit, and came directly to our booth. She looked at the menu, and we all ordered a hot breakfast.

I pulled out my tablet PC and ran the video clip for her. I then showed her the image I'd worked on that gave me the left ear of my attacker and put it side-by-side to the picture of Toby's ear. "I think it's him," I said. Wilson took notes and agreed that this was close to a positive ID and would warrant the FBI bringing him in.

"I have some news to share as well," Wilson leaned forward. "I met with the RCMP and TPD when I went up to get Cordelia. Her story matches the information the detectives gave me. As she recovered from the drug, she was in a large warehouse. There was a dark blue BMW sedan in there. A bald-headed, lean man lifted her chin looking directly at her face and commented that she cleaned up nicely." She flicked to a picture on her cell phone of Sargis Petrosyan. "When I met with her, she picked this fellow out of a photo lineup."

"Petrosyan," Reba said.

Wilson nodded.

"Your tracker," Wilson continued gesturing toward me, "went to a parking lot off Spadina Avenue, behind the Madison Avenue Pub. Since there had been a lot of problems there, the lot was under heavy surveillance. They showed me a clear CCTV video of the BMW pulling in and stopping. A back car window opened and something was thrown out. After a search, they found pieces of your tracker."

"That explains what happened," I said.

"Anyway, the car left the lot, and we had a vehicle license number. Seems the car was a rental out of Pearson International Airport a few days earlier by a lone man from California with a driver's license linked to an apartment building not far from Petrosyan's company offices. Later, a couple were observed driving the car across the US border into Buffalo, New York. A few hours later, a man drove the same car across the border back into Canada. That matches the time when you reported the tracker activity. TPD found the car back at the rental agency. Unfortunately, the car company had already washed and detailed the vehicle and had it back in the lot for the next customer. RCMP crime scene investigators couldn't find any trace evidence in the trunk or finger marks."

"The couple went back to the airport," I said. "They might not even be in Canada anymore."

Wilson nodded. "RCMP is gathering flight manifests and all of the flight plans for any planes departing after the time the vehicle was seen at the Madison Avenue Pub."

We finished our breakfast and returned to school in time for our next classes. Ancient History again for me, and I met up with Cordelia in the room. Just as class began, the public address system sparked to life with an administrative announcement.

Instead of an announcement by Mr. Hannah, it was the voice of Tina Lee, assistant headmistress. She reported that there had been a board meeting and Mr. Hannah had gone onto other opportunities. She'd be standing in for the rest of the term. Lee also announced that due to an incident, there would be a new curfew enforced that all students had to be in their dorm rooms by 9 PM. A private security company would now be patrolling inside the campus during hours of darkness. Any students found outside would face disciplinary action. This would be in place until further notice.

"Go figure," Cordelia leaned over and

whispered.

After class, we couldn't wait to see what more information we could derive about Hannah's demise. This time we went to Cordelia's room. She fired up her large gaming machine and logged into one of the school servers. It didn't take her long to find the written minutes from a board meeting. A decision was taken to remove Mr. Hannah and install Ms. Lee.

"Look at this," Cordelia pointed to the top line of the document. "All board members were present except one."

"Solomon?" I guessed. "She may have a bit more involvement in all this. Afterall, Petrosyan worked for her."

"She wasn't at the warehouse. At least I didn't see her." Cordelia sat back from her computer and swiveled her chair around. "I remember something else from that day," she said softly. "The other girls. A few had obvious drug addictions. A couple were probably destined for massage parlors or even work in salons. Before they took me back into the room with them, I remember Petrosyan remarking that I might do okay in the market and I shouldn't be touched yet."

"The market?" Reba asked. "Touched?"

"That's what he said. I don't know what he was referring to. But maybe that's where they took Crystal. Afterall, she's almost a perfect California blonde beauty."

"A white slave market?" Reba said.

"We shouldn't jump to conclusions, but that's certainly a possibility," I said. "Let me ask, do you have a sense how much time elapsed between him saying this until the police raided the warehouse?"

Cordelia rolled her eyes and thought about this before she answered. "I was pretty out of it still. Time seemed very abstract, and my own anxiety and fear kept creeping in as a distraction. I really couldn't even cry. I was too scared. The other girls were really creepy, too. They were all wearing drab, green coveralls and had no undergarments that I could tell. I was the only one wearing the remains of a white dress." She thought for a moment, then added: "I guess maybe 40 minutes to an hour." Reba hugged her as she whimpered, about to cry again.

At that moment, my cell phone rang. It was Wilson.

14. THE LION'S JAW

I put her on speaker.

"JP," Wilson said. "The RCMP found something on a mobile device and laptop that they seized from the warehouse. Do you remember a few weeks back when I asked you to look at the evidence acquired from that laptop?"

"Yeah," I said.

"Well, the Canadians found two photos that are way too similar to the ones from that auction catalog. Numbers, like item numbers, were added to the bottom of each photo. One of the photos was Cordelia. She was clearly passed out probably from the drugs they injected in her. She was dressed in the same clothes I found her in that she wore to the prom. The background looks like an office sofa that she was laying across. According to the RCMP, they found a different room with the same blue fabric sofa."

"And the other photo?"

"I'm sending it to you now. I think this one might be Kayleen Masterson. Take a look and tell me what you can see."

I opened my tablet and waited a moment. The file arrived attached to an encrypted email message. "Got it." I opened the file as both Reba and Cordelia stood behind me looking at the image.

"That's Crystal," Reba said. "Um, Kayleen Masterson is her real name."

Crystal stood in a classic girl pose with her legs crossed, hands over the front of her white-satin party dress; just like she was about to attend the prom. To Reba, the background was unmistakable. "This was taken here at school in her dorm room."

"Are you sure?" Wilson said.

"Same layout and crap furnishings that are in mine and Cordelia's rooms. Unmistakable."

"Hang on," I said. Tapping out a few simple commands, I exposed the metadata from the JPG photo file. "Geolocation data has been removed, but the picture was snapped by an older iPhone 14 camera."

"Toby has an iPhone 14," Cordelia said.

"That he does," I said. "I think Mr. Tobias Adams, he goes by Toby, is up to his neck in this as well as Mrs. Fadler."

"Is Adams at school today?" Wilson asked.

I looked at Reba and Cordelia. They both shrugged. "We searched around trying to find him, no luck. For now, he's a ghost."

"At this stage, we need to find him and Doris Fadler. Keep your eyes open, and Reba, don't approach either of them if you see them. I'm getting to know how you work. Call me right away."

"I promise, no rough stuff. Not yet at least."

"Good." Beep. The connection dropped.

"Well, she told you," Cordelia punched Reba's shoulder. "But not me."

"Come on guys," I said. "Let's play this clean. They're all eligible to go to the slammer. Let's keep it that way."

Reba and Cordelia said they were going to wander through the campus and check a few more places where Toby might be hiding. As for me, I really wanted to chat with dad.

I reached him at the detective bureau in San Jose. He let me know that the FBI issued a bulletin for Fadler and information for a person of interest named Tobias Adams. A larger nationwide alert listed Sargis Petrosyan on the FBI's most wanted list, offering a $50,000 reward. These alerts would trigger the Department of Homeland Security if any of them tried boarding a commercial flight. They'd be detained and held for the FBI. "The net," dad said, "will tighten around them."

"Let's hope so," I said. "I'm going to do a bit more digging here to see if I can find more leads."

"Be careful, son. That big reward may not be worth it. These people don't play nice." He rang off.

I remembered that I still had the triage evidence I'd gathered with KAPE from Mr. Hannah's desktop computer a few weeks ago. Coupled with the auction catalog I had from the beginning of school, I just might be able to find something useful.

I texted Reba letting her know that I'd be skipping my afternoon math class and following leads. Reba replied that she and Cordelia had gone through most of the campus hunting for Toby but no luck. They'd meet up with me in my room later.

Mounting the drive where KAPE had copied all of the data, I started by running a tool called Hasher against the files and then a Python script to compare the calculated SHA1-base 16 hashes. I had to follow all of the real forensic processes. Afterall, this was a real serious criminal case. Once Hasher calculated all the SHA1 hashes for all the collected files, my Python script ran a comparison against each item listed in KAPEs CopyOut report. In a few minutes, the script finished, confirming that file integrity had been maintained and each evidence file remained unchanged since the original collection.

When I made the collection from Hannah's system, I also collected everything within the User folder. This gave me all the files Hannah, or any other user, had stored to the internal drive. Beneath the Documents folder, Hannah had a folder named 'SchoolAdmin' that contained an HR subfolder. Mrs. Fadler's original job application was there. She listed her home address as Fremont, California. She'd given a Mr. Paul out of Los Angeles as a reference. One thing for sure, I appreciated how organized ex-Headmaster Hannah kept the files on his computer. Every file was named along with a date. He made several separate text files that he saved along with Fadler's application. I opened the one marked as interview notes created just over a year ago. Fadler's answers to his questions made her seem like the best possible residence mom in the whole world. She'd worked not only as a nanny but also had a nursing license in California. If this background was made up, somebody did a fabulous job making her look exceptional. In a file marked as Fadler 6-month performance review, there were numerous notes including statements from students that she was very good. One Tobias Adams had been interviewed for her performance review as well. Toby mentioned how supportive Fadler was to him and his mates.

Back to the reference check. It included that a Mr. Paul had originally hired Fadler as a nanny and then transitioned her to work at a tutoring school that he owned in Long Beach, California. He sold that business, and Fadler was forced to find another placement. The closing remark was that Pinegrove Alpha Academy could not go wrong by retaining Fadler. At the end of the note, Paul's address was listed on Sepulveda Boulevard, Los Angeles. That street name rang a bell, but I couldn't place it. I got up and walked around the room a bit repeating the name Sepulveda.

There was a soft knock on the door, and Reba walked in. "Where's Cordelia?" I asked.

"She ran off to her English lit class."

"Does the name Sepulveda mean anything to you?"

Reba squinted as she thought. "That was the street that was given to rent the BMW in Toronto. Wasn't it?"

I jumped back in my seat. "Numbers. Numbers." The reference check notes were on the screen. "2846?"

"Yeah, that's the address used when the

BMW was rented"

"We have a link," I said pointing to my screen. "Can you believe that Fadler was planted here over a year ago?"

Reba read the material over my shoulder. "This shows real intent. The phases and timing match for when Solomon took a seat on the board."

"Yeah, she probably bought her way onto the board. Do you remember who she interviewed here at school before you and me?"

"Crystal and Toby."

"Yup," I said. "She was probably checking out the prospect after Fadler marked her as a possible."

"And now they have her."

"What about Mr. Fadler?"

"His application and interview notes are here." I opened them and read through everything. He'd been a maintenance engineer at the posh Belaire Country Club. Since he already lived on campus, Hannah was quick to hire him. Everything looks boringly normal."

"Okay," Reba said. "You've probably proved intent, but how might this help us get Crystal back?"

"Never thought I'd hear you say that after all the bad things she's done to you."

Reba slapped my shoulder. "You jerk, I'm bigger than that. She's been kidnapped."

"Sorry, that was rude of me," I said.

"Darn straight it was. Just remember, somebody loves that girl. She was drugged and taken. I wouldn't wish that on anybody."

I nodded and pointed toward my screen where I'd loaded the evidence I'd pulled from the very first machine Wilson had asked for help on. "It may not be much, but I have one more thing to try. Call it a hope and a prayer." I opened the auction catalog from a copy of the case folder I'd presented to Wilson. The auction catalog was named: Mısır Çarşıs Charity Art Auction. I pulled the name and then using Yandex, the Russian search engine, tried to see if there were any relevant hits. No results.

"That magic didn't work," Reba said.

"One more shot." I typed in the international phone number that was printed on the front of the auction catalog into Google. It returned links in Istanbul. "Well, given the name of the auction, this result makes sense."

Reba frowned like she didn't understand.

"The name of the auction. It's also the name of the famous spice bazaar near the Hagia Sophia and Topkapi Palace in the Fatih district of Istanbul. We now have two links to Turkey."

My mobile phone interrupted my train of thought. It was dad. "JP," dad said. "The LAPD organized crime unit reached out to me after my query on Petrosyan. He's Armenian and has links to an Armenian crime family. Turns out LAPD SOC unit has him marked as a possible person of interest. They believe he's an adviser to local Armenian street gangs operating out of South LA."

"I've got you on speaker phone. Reba's here." I gave him the information that I'd derived and that I was still digging for more on the auction catalog.

"Before the fall of the Ottomans," Reba said, "Turkey did everything possible to purge the Armenians. Nowadays, though, many more live there, so this could be a tenuous link as well to Istanbul."

"I had a few run-ins with Armenian gangs back in Bristol," dad said speaking of his prior police assignment. "Real nasty lot, those fellows."

"There's also a strong tie between Petrosyan and Mrs. Fadler." I said. "It appears she was planted at the school over a year ago. Her application lists a Mr. Paul as a reference that uses an address in Petrosyan's building in LA. She might have identified Crystal as a target."

"You say you found some sort of customer service phone number?"

I gave it to him. It was a direct number to country code 90. "Also, the phone number starts with a 4-4-4."

"A call center," dad said.

"Yup. Seems that way."

"Okay, that's a good lead. It's up to me, now. I'll link through my old detective mates in Bristol constabulary and see if we can ring that call center. Maybe I can get a new catalog, if it's available. Send me the number and I'll set up a pivot link."

I texted dad the phone number I found from the original catalog and left the call to let him get on with it.

"It will be really cool if he can get us another catalog," Reba said.

"That's the plan." I went back and played with a few of the file objects extracted from Hannah's computer, then said, "I'm a bit worried about a reasonable cover story for dad though."

Reba frowned, a quizzical look.

"It's a big problem with any illicit

marketplace. Some level of trust has to be established between the seller and buyer of any black-market items. Look at it this way. Thieves and fraudsters are buying from each other. Who can you trust? The cover story has to be solid. Someone in Turkey might even contact a reference before they agree to anything."

"But your dad's a good guy. How can he get a known bad guy to vouch for him?"

My phone rang again. This time I showed Reba the caller ID before I answered. It was Toby!

"Hey," I said answering the call and putting it on speaker.

"You have me on speaker?"

"I'm working and need both hands." Reba knew to stay quiet as a mouse.

"Right, I'm almost back to school. My computer's being a bit wobbly, and I could sure use some techy support."

I sighed and shrugged my shoulders toward Reba. She smiled and pointed down at the phone for me to say something.

"You still there?" Toby barked.

"Yeah, yeah," I said. "Give me a sec. I tapped a couple commands into my computer to run another search. "I'm back. What do you mean wobbly?"

"You know. I'm getting constant messages about my cell phone each time I try to do something on my system. It's driving me nuts."

"Fine. Send me a text when you get back to school, and I'll come over." I tapped the end call button. "You shouldn't meet him on your own."

"I can take care of myself." I stood. "I need you to get with Cordelia and keep her away. If she suspects Toby is back, this could really get ugly before I find the information we need."

"Right," Reba said heading for the door. "Just don't get bonked on the head again. Okay?"

#

A half hour passed, and my phone dinged with a text from Toby. I immediately stood and looked out my dorm window. I saw him climb from a black Mercedes sedan and walk toward the dorm.

As the car pulled away, I tried my best to snap a picture of the car's registration plate. It was fuzzy as heck and totally unreadable.

I grabbed a second tablet computer that I'd built to run UFADE. I may not be able to get a full physical of his phone. I'll settle for a logical and hope that what I need might be there.

Toby's room was immaculate. Everything put away, scrubbed, and not a speck of dust on the floor. In the past, the room always smelt like the cheap, cotton candy perfume Crystal always wore. Now it smelt like bleach. I'm sure the FBI had a fun time searching this room.

Toby passed me his laptop and sure enough, there was a message about his phone not being paired.

"I need your phone," I said showing him the palm of my hand asking for his device.

"It's locked." He handed it to me.

"Fine. Unlock it or give me the passcode. The problem is probably with the phone and not so much the laptop."

Toby thought for a moment. I grinned. He looked so funny when he pondered a problem. "Okay," he said. Toby tapped a four-digit passcode into the phone's home screen and passed me the unlocked device.

I plugged the phone into a dual USB-C cable and the other end into my tablet.

"What's that?" He said trying to reach for the phone.

"No big deal," I said. "This will give me information as to why your phone's screwing your computer up."

He stepped back. "How long will this take?"

Ignoring him. I tapped a couple of setting commands to shut off his iCloud backup and to trust the UFADE device. UFADE made the link and immediately dumped the Apple Unified Log first and then took a full backup of the device.

"Well?" Toby prompted.

"Shouldn't be long. Under an hour."

"Damn, dude. I'm hungry."

"Go down to the Commons and get something to eat. I'll hang here and get it working for you."

"I'm starving." Toby grabbed a jacket and walked out the door. I was alone. I quickly texted Reba to keep Cordelia away from the commons - Toby's heading that way. She acknowledged and said they were actually in my room. Great!

UFADE finished dumping the logical backup of Toby's phone, and I had the full unified log. I disconnected the phone and opened Toby's laptop. It didn't take very long to pair the two devices so that the error messages went away. Toby had shut off bluetooth. Once that was on, the two devices paired and immediately began syncing the photo library from the phone to the laptop. One of the last pictures that sync'd was the shot of Crystal in her prom dress. Her long blonde hair curled and fell over her shoulders. This was the exact picture and pose that looked just like the others that had been in the auction catalog. I couldn't help but snag the picture and transfer it to a jump drive that I brought with me. I'd just finished unplugging the drive when Toby returned.

"You're still here?" He said closing the door behind him.

"Yup all done," I said passing him back his iPhone. "Bluetooth was jinked up, and it took a bit of work. Your phone is sync'ing to your laptop now."

"Cool, thanks bro."

I smiled and packed up my stuff, heading for the door.

"Hey," Toby said just as I opened the door. "Let me know if I can do anything for you in return."

"No problem," I grinned. "You'll get my bill in the morning."

"Right. Whatever."

I was very proud of myself as I headed out the door and back to my room. I'd kept my temper in check. I really wanted to slap him around for clocking me on the back of the head, but I knew that wouldn't have ended well for me. Toby was a real jock and would have bested me easily.

Back in my room, Reba and Cordelia were sitting on my bed.

Ever since her jaunt to Canada, Cordelia looked like a normal girl. No more goth makeup, ripped tights, or frilly emo-girl dresses.

"Well?" Reba said.

"Call Wilson and let her know that Toby's back at school. She may want to pick him up and have a chat with him. As for me, I'm going to mount and check out the unified log from his cell phone."

"He's back?" Cordelia said.

"Yup, and we have this covered," Reba said.

"I just want to scratch his eyes out."

"Wilson will be more than enough for him," Reba patted her on the shoulder. "Let's see what JP gets from the logs."

I'd already passed the logs into my main system and instructed iLEAPP to parse them. In another window, I extracted the EXIF data from the photo of Crystal. The logs had everything I could dream of. The photo was snapped and geolocated to Toby's room. About 15-minutes later, the photo was shared to an LA phone number. The iLEAPP report had a timeline of chat messages between Toby and the LA phone number. One message instructed Toby to give her the hit and tell her that it would make her feel good during the dance.

Health data from the phone showed Toby in his room. Then, about an hour later, his phone moved downstairs and to the dance. About 10 minutes before Reba, Cordelia and I left the dance to discover Fadler carrying Crystal out to the ambulance, Toby's phone went back to his room and then downstairs to the dorm building lobby. "That would be about the time we saw Fadler carrying her out to the ambulance," Reba said.

"Yup. And a moment later, Toby was running out of the dorm building just before I got hit." I sat back in my chair. "You know, Toby's parents have more money than most governments. What the heck is he doing helping kidnappers?"

"Who knows," Cordelia said. "Maybe they had something on him. You know what happened to Bobby. Maybe they had something on him as well."

Reba got off the phone. "Wilson says there's a team on the way to pick him up. She wants anything more that you have."

"Guess I'm not sleeping tonight." I opened a clean notepad and typed out what I'd done and how I obtained the data from Toby's phone and laptop.

"I don't feel like going out or being alone tonight," Cordelia said.

"I'll stay with you. I can sleep on the floor," Reba said and they both left my room.

I worked through my notes and included the unified logs, backup and photo that I'd grabbed from Toby's devices. I'd just put them all on a flash drive when I heard a few cars pull up outside my window. It was dark and well past dinner time. A Sheriff's unit and an unmarked car were outside. The two deputies and plain-clothed officers went into the dorm building. A few minutes later, they emerged with Toby in handcuffs and placed him in the back of the Sheriff's car. There was a knock on my door. One of the plain-clothed officers flashed open his FBI credentials. "You have something for me?"

I passed him the flash drive. "Everything's there." He nodded and left.

15. MEETING AT THE PARA

Wednesday morning, Reba, Cordelia and I headed off for another round of ancient history class. I couldn't help but wonder that Crystal had been gone for almost 5-days, and we were no closer to finding her than when my tracker went dead in Toronto. I hadn't heard back from dad and was beginning to think that we couldn't do anything more.

As the two of us crossed around the courtyard fountain. A small grey Toyota driven by Wilson with my dad in the front seat pulled around and blocked our path. Cordelia waved and smiled at Wilson, then said she'd cover for me at class. She walked around the front of the car as Wilson motioned for Reba and me to get into the back.

"We have a plan, JP," dad said. "Now, it's time to get serious."

Wilson drove the car out of the school, and we rode in silence as she navigated down the hill to a non-descript 6-story office building in San Mateo, off the El Camino Real. We took the elevator to the third floor and entered what looked like any of a few hundred office buildings with lots of cubicles, people working, and most of them carrying guns.

Inside a conference room, there was a man plugging a few cables and a microphone into a bunch of telephone communications equipment. Wilson sloughed her jacket off and sat at the far end of the conference table. "I have to tell you," Wilson said. "I'm kind of nervous about this whole plan."

I sat in a chair across from the guy with the telecom equipment. He introduced himself as Ray, a communications specialist. Ray put a set of headphones on dad that covered his ears and had a boom mic. He looked just like one of the sportscasters on TV.

"It's okay," Dad looked over at Wilson. "Lucky owes me a big debt, and this will work."

Wilson shook her head. "Let's hope."

"JP," dad looked at me. "This started as your idea, and I wanted you here to watch what we do."

"Ready?" Ray said. "Let's do a test. Got a test phone number?" Dad gave him my cell number.

A moment later my mobile rang. The caller ID had the country code for the UK and a local prefix of Bristol, England. I answered.

"Just me, son," dad said.

"It works," I said. "UK prefix and Bristol local number."

"Bingo," dad said. The line went dead. "Let's do this," he looked over at Wilson.

She scribbled a few notes on a pad of

paper, then looked at dad. "We're trusting a bad guy with a reputation in Europe and a rap-sheet a mile long. If he rolls over, this could get really dangerous."

"Lucky owes me big."

"As you've said. What if this gets nasty, and he squeals?"

"I've told you, he won't. I told him we're trying to rescue a girl and that we'd be square if he stood up for me should they call."

"And we trust this Lucky Liam, why?"

"Look, he's a crook. True. He doesn't like crimes against children at all. He draws a line there," dad said. "And I saved his kid's life when an Irish gang tried to put a bullet into him. Lucky won't let me down."

"I really hope you're right." Now Wilson had both palms on the table and glared straight at dad. "They might come after him if this doesn't go well."

"Look, Agent Wilson," dad pressed his palms on the table. "Liam has a reputation as a sledgehammer. Mess with him, get your skull crushed."

I could see that Ray was more and more uncomfortable. He moved toward the door. "Want to settle this and I'll come back?"

"No!" Both dad and Wilson said it at the same time. "Sit down Ray and get ready," Wilson said.

"Call it," dad said as Ray sat behind the audio controls.

"Okay," Ray passed headphones with no microphone to me and Wilson. He put on a set as well. Nodded at dad and pushed a button.

After a couple rings, a girl's voice answered the call in Turkish. "Hello," dad said.

"I speak English," the girl replied.

"My boss asked me to give you a ring to see if he can get a copy of your next art auction catalog. Do you have one?"

"Your name, please," she replied immediately.

Dad looked over at Wilson and smiled. "Talon, Jack Talon."

"One moment, please." The line went quiet for a few seconds that seemed like forever. "Mr. Talon. We don't have you in our database."

"No, you wouldn't," dad said. "My boss is Lucky Liam. He's very interested in some of the pieces you had in a prior auction and would like to acquire a piece or two from the next auction. He heard about it from a business contact in Los Angeles."

There was a pause on the line. Somebody was thinking or typing on a computer. "Mr. Talon, we'll call you back at the number you called us on. It shouldn't take long." The line went dead.

Dad shrugged and looked over at Wilson. "Well, that will either work or was a wasted effort."

"How long should I keep the line available?" The FBI tech asked looking at Wilson.

Her face furled into a deep frown. "You'll keep it set up and open until I say otherwise." I'd never heard Wilson bark like this and figured she must be under some stress with this case. A missing teen that might be at an auction somewhere in Europe or Asia. The case is probably monitored not only by the local special agent in charge, but by the region and national bosses as well. Heck, it could be monitored all the way up to Congressional oversight or even the White House. Wilson's eyes followed the tech as he left the room. After the door shut, her eyes rolled and she looked over to dad. "Alright, Detective Stafford Palmer, what's the plan after we get the catalog?"

Dad nonchalantly shrugged again and said, "We'll cross that bridge when the time comes."

"This won't end well," Wilson said. "Headquarters wants to know our plan."

"Nothing. Zilch, if they don't call back," dad took a sip of tea that came from a very old machine near the front entrance. The black liquid looked like thick mud, and Wilson turned away as he took a long sip. I must admit, it was a bit hard watching him drink the stuff. Wilson had succumbed to tapping her pen on the wooden conference table, Reba and I were heads down and nearly asleep. But dad was still stirring mixing a bit more sugar and drinking it down. He slapped the cup on the table and stood. "I'm off for another. Anybody want one?"

Reba and Wilson shook their heads. "Fine. More for me." He was out the door and walked down the hall. The glass conference room door swung shut, just as a tone erupted from the audio controls and we all startled awake. Wilson pointed at herself and motioned for Reba and me to be still. She slipped on a headphone with a boom mic and pressed a button. "Allo?" Wilson said.

A different voice from before responded to her prompt, asking to speak with Mr. Talon.

Wilson's best English accent sounded more like some strange Australian mutt as she explained that Talon has stepped away and they would get him immediately.

I took that as my signal and ran out of the room and down the hall. Dad stood with the communications tech laughing and joking about how Bristol rugby ran hard over Exeter in the last match.

"Dad," I said breathing deeply as I stopped running. "This is it. Call."

Dad tossed his drink in the sink and together with the communications tech ran toward the room. They arrived in the conference room where Wilson was still connected and on the phone with the call center. Her eyes widened and she made a viscous face at the two of them. The tech quickly wired himself into the call.

"He's just popped back in from tea and is on the line."

"Hello," dad said.

I put on my headset as well.

"You have a very interesting assistant, don't you?" The call center person said.

"Ah, yes," dad said. "Excuse her. She's a

bit of a Sheila. One of Liam's down under acquisitions. Also, a bit of a handful if you know what I mean?"

"The catalog will arrive to your account. This is an exclusive event that you should manage discretely."

"Understood," dad said.

"Bidding instructions shall accompany the catalog. Mr. Liam's representative will need to be at the auction facility. On site."

"I am that representative and I'll be there."

Wilson sat forward, rising up on her fists, and shook her head with an emphatic no. I, too, couldn't believe what I heard on the headset. Dad had just committed to going into the Lion's den directly. Since the auction date wasn't for a week yet, this gave the real bad guys plenty of time to check on dad's story. They could even send a live person to do a background investigation in that amount of time.

The call was terminated, and Wilson

stood exploding, her mouth spewing slurs and all toward dad. She took a long, deep breath. "What compelled you to tell them you were going to be the guy at the auction?"

"Just playin' the role," Dad said.

Wilson fell back into her chair and rubbed her temples with two fingers on either side just like a person sensing a bad migraine about to hit.

A email message landed on the server that I'd set up on the cloud just for this event. After downloading the message and the attached PDF I looked at Wilson. "Hey, hey," I called out. "I have what looks like the catalog that just arrived." The room went silent.

Wilson, dad and Reba stood behind me where they could see my screen. I double clicked on the catalog. The PDF document opened. A single blood-red and black image of roses in full bloom opened and shiny silver letters in some gothic script font read: "23rd Mısır Çarşıs Charity Art Auction" filled the screen.

"This is their 23rd auction?" Reba said.

"That's what it says," I said somehow knowing what she was thinking. How many more children were kidnapped into slavery or worse?

"Scroll through," Wilson said.

I rolled the scrollbar down slowly. On page 6, I saw the picture of Cordelia. She was passed out, and an image of a large, sculpted dragon was photoshopped over her face. Across the picture was stamped with the words "Withdrawn" in red letters. This was repeated in three more languages under it. Clearly, they lost this subject and couldn't sell her off.

"She's lucky, JP," Reba said patting my shoulder. I scrolled two more pages and stopped on a full-page image of Crystal wearing a flowing white sheer gown looking all the roll of a model that would present the gorgeous vase standing on a pedestal next to her.

"That's Crystal or Kaylene Masterson," Reba pointed at the picture. "She looks good in this photo, whereas the snapshot of Cordelia was clearly while she was drugged out of her head."

I activated a zoom feature on a small pointer I retrieved from my bag. The circular image enhanced the photo 20x. I held the marker on her face. Not a blemish or mark. At this magnification, even thick makeup left telltale signs of bruising or abrasions. Nothing. Guiding the magnifier downward, we inspected every pixel in the image. Nothing hinted at any distress.

"What's the opening bid amount?" Wilson asked.

"60,000 Euros," I said. "Detailed instructions are in Turkish." I copied them out and handed it to a GPT translator.

"Translating Turkish to English," the young male voice of GPT said. "Bidders must check-in live in the theatre at the SOHO House Hotel Friday the 23rd of March at 17:00 local time. Registered bidders may inspect the items for the following hour. The auction will be held at 18:30 that same Friday at the SOHO House theater a block from the Para Palace. The owner of all items was listed as Woman of Great Means concerned with the health and welfare of young, orphaned boys and girls."

We sat silently for a moment. I don't think any of us knew quite what to say. "This could be one of the largest child trafficking and exploitation cases in a long while," dad broke the silence. Wilson stood silently with her hands crossed staring at the catalog displayed on my laptop. I turned to look at her, silently asking what was next.

"JP," Wilson said. "Wrap this up and send it to me A-S-A-P. The rest of you wait here." The tech walked over to his equipment.

"Leave it," Wilson added directly to him. "I'll be back." She left the room. I wrapped the auction catalog along with some image collection that I'd done and sent them all to Wilson. Dad and Reba sat back down at the table.

It wasn't long before the large display at the far end of the wall flickered to life and two men seated at their desks came to view. One I knew was the director of the FBI. The other man was unknown to me. Wilson swept into the room. "Good," she said to both men. "This is Director Freedman and Regional Director Samuel." Wilson took her place standing by the large display flanking the men.

"After reviewing the evidence so far, this case will get the Bureau's full attention," Director Freedman said.

"Tech," the Regional Director spoke directly to the communications technician. "Keep the phone lines alive and ready until Quantico can replace you, understood?"

The tech nodded.

"And, Stafford, say your goodbyes to the others. We've scrambled a C-141 Starlifter from Travis into SFO. It will be there within an hour or so. "

"No, sir," Reba said standing hands on hips. "We're going too. JP and me."

Wilson shook her head.

"Out of the question!" The Regional Director said. "No way."

"Nobody knows the evidence better than us," I said. "Also, your DOJ and DOD tech may be known by these bad guys. They've almost been a step ahead the whole time."

"We behave like tourists," Reba interjected. "JP has trackers and all of the tech to properly wire Detective Palmer and Agent Wilson."

"Agent Wilson," Director Freedman said. "Thoughts?"

She stared directly at Reba. "This mission is too dangerous with real international mobsters..."

"We've taken on bigger ones," I interrupted. "Anton and Lesta Andropov were even bigger fish."

Both faces on the screen went silent and sober. They knew who these hoods were and the nature of the international incident both Reba and I spoiled.

"Wilson, will you be responsible for these two?" Freedman asked.

"I will," dad said before Wilson could muster an answer. "I'll be responsible for them, and myself, as well."

Silence. A tension-filled pause.

"Meet that C-141 with your team Agent Wilson," the Regional Director said. "Code assigned: C-471-alpha. You report only to me. An Interpol agent has been assigned and will meet you in Istanbul."

"Yes, sir."

I thought a salute would be appropriate. Reba hit me and dad waved me off. The screens went dead.

"Let's go," Wilson led the way out the door.

#

We landed at RAF Alconbury, just a bit

West of Cambridge UK. The ground never looked so nice to me. The Starlifter, a huge 4-engine jet could carry multiple tanks into combat theaters and had a large passenger section for moving troops. The seats were pretty much the same as on any commercial aircraft. Many crammed together in rows of 5 and six seats. The problem was the bathroom. There wasn't one. Soon after takeoff, I had to pee really bad. A crew member handed me a 5-galon bucket and pointed for me to go behind a curtain. I did my business and left the bucket behind.

Oh, to walk on hard earth again. Once the wheels touched down, Wilson called over to get the transport unit. A white RAF minibus driven by a corporal pulled up to the back of the cooling Starlifter. We walked down the ramp and onto the bus. I was last in wishing I could stop just one more time for a bathroom break as the bus doors hissed closed. We headed down a service road that was between a runway and taxiway. At the end of a runway, two F- 18's wound their engines up, readying for takeoff. I half expected the bus to drive away from the jets, but it stopped.

"Cover your lug 'oles!" The driver shouted.

I immediately plugged my ears and looked at Reba. She looked confused and I raised my eyebrows and motioned to my fingers, plugging my ears. She quickly responded as the afterburners for one of the F-18's roared. The bus shook as the first fighter tore down the runway. The second fighter thundered to life; flames shot from the back of the twin GE 404 turbofans pouring out 17,700 pounds of thrust. The second fighter turned nose straight up and disappeared into the clouds after using only half a runway. Our driver waved an all clear. The bus pulled out once ears were unplugged and silence returned to the field. We drove to the far side of the field to where a black and silver Gulfstream sat. The boarding door was

folded down and two uniformed RAF
policemen stood on either side of the ladder.
Dad and Wilson were first off, approaching the
guards. Reba and I followed. A tall man,
dressed in a black double-breasted suit
emerged from the plane and walked down
the ladder.

"Agent Wilson," he said reaching out to
shake hands.

Wilson didn't move and left him hanging.
His hand dropped. "I'm Patterson, NSA," he
said. "All of the equipment you requested is
onboard. Pilots are both US Air Force dressed
in plain clothes. The Legats have arranged for
your arrival. Flight plan has been filed from
Bristol International Airport."

"Good," Wilson said. "Have the pilots
take us to Bristol before opening the flight
plan."

He nodded, went back up the stairs,
leaned into the cockpit, then returned to us.
He waved notifying the guards to clear out.

With that, the four of us boarded the

luxury, private jet. I ran nonstop for the bathroom at the rear. Returning, I sat in a rear-facing seat across from Reba. The seats were large, first-class style with thick foam seating that you just sank into. A small folding table stood between Reba and me. Dad sat on the other side of the aisle in a seat next to Reba. The engines hadn't started yet, and he was already sweating just with the anticipation of another flight.

Dad glanced at his cell phone and tapped out a couple messages, probably letting mum and Mrs. Ng know where we were and that we were okay. The forward hatch motor whined lifting the stairs and door. It sealed with a slap. A female voice came on the intercom announcing that we should fasten our seatbelts and prepare for departure.

The ride from RAF Alconbury to Bristol International Airport was all of a whopping 25 minutes from wheels up to wheels down. Why Bristol? We needed to open a flight plan supporting our cover.

Dad looked as green as possible from the quick flight. As we taxied right around into the takeoff lineup, dad jumped up and ran to the bathroom. The plane arced into a wide left turn and came to a brief stop before the pilots slammed throttles forward delivering over 7,000 pounds of thrust from the two turbofan engines. The nose lurched skyward as we pressed into an almost vertical takeoff just as the bathroom door swung open, and dad pulled himself out. He was nearly halfway out the door then jumped back in as the plane yawed nose down then banked to port. The bathroom door slammed shut followed by a loud "ouch"! I looked at Wilson. She had a scheming grin on her face as though saying: "got him".

Dad returned to his seat as the plane continued a gentle climb. "I didn't think they'd take off with me in the bog," he said. "The wonders of private jets run by the air force," Wilson said. "They don't care if you make it there in one piece or not."

Dad grumbled and dropped back into his seat. In a few minutes, he was passed out snoring. Wilson motioned for Reba and me to move to the rear of the plane where there was a large sofa and table with two chairs on the opposite side. She pulled out two 3-foot-long black Pelican boxes that she set on the table. The first box was full of trackers the size of cigarette boxes and an audio wire that was basically a wireless microphone. The second box held receivers and recording equipment. The size was nuts and looked like a kit out of the 80's. "This is all you've got?" I said.

"Wow this stuff is old," Reba added. "Does it even have batteries?"

"Okay, you two. Knock it off."

"I thought the NSA would be way more advanced than to pass this crap out."

"They are," Wilson defended. "We can't use the military stuff because it's not permitted when investigating a criminal matter."

I plopped my backpack atop the box with the gear and took out my tablet PC and a single cylindrical device about the size of three quarters stacked together. "This is a bug and a tracker," I said. I reached in the bag and popped open a small plastic container that had two wafer-thin, plastic devices. "And these are just trackers. They're plastic and entirely non-metallic substances so that metal detectors or wands won't detect them."

"If he wears your tech," Reba said, "they'll burn him before he gets through the door."

Wilson sat back. I could tell that she knew Reba was right. "Do you have enough for two people?" Wilson asked.

"In this backpack alone, I have enough to cover 5 people for sound and tracking. I even have a few hidden bodycams that link to one of the trackers to give us visual."

"Done," Wilson slammed the covers of the two boxes closed.

A second cell phone that Wilson carried rang with a gentle chirp. She motioned for me and Reba to go back to our seats. Once we were gone, she folded the satellite antenna up and answered. As I sat facing the back of the plane, I could see her in an animated conversation. She'd glance at us occasionally and then turn away covering her mouth as she spoke. Once done, she folded the antenna down and motioned for the two of us to return. "Turkish National Police will be joining us."

I shrugged.

"Can they be trusted?" Reba asked.

"I doubt it," Wilson said. "Our Legat advised that the leadership of the National Police believe Maja Solomon can do no wrong. She's a wealthy philanthropist that has built several schools on the Asian side of the City."

"Do you think they'll tip her off?"

"We need to take precautions to make certain that can't happen. I'll make an arrangement to drop your dad off when we land. They will guide us to a special parking place for the jet. Your dad needs to be off before we get there."

"I'll get him wired up while he sleeps," I said.

"Do it." Wilson picked up the Iridium phone again. Reba started to stand and follow me. "Reba, stay here."

Dad was out cold. My first plan was to attach a tiny white tracker on his shoulder. The adhesive could withstand even a good shower. Using my tablet, I checked the connection and battery. 100 percent with a solid signal. The second tracker was a small cylinder that was a mere 3 mm thick in the center for its battery. This one would slip nicely under a simple adhesive bandage that I wrapped on his ankle. As I rolled his sock back up over the bandage, I felt dad's paw grab me by the neck. "What are you doing?"

I quickly explained that I was told to wire him up and showed him the two trackers.

"You'll be in Reba's hands once we touch down in Istanbul." Wilson said. "She knows what to do. JP and I will travel separately and meet you at the hotel."

#

A few hours passed. Dad remained asleep while the three of us indulged in a military meal-ready-to-eat. Think canned, chopped chicken with diced veggies, a tin of water and some sort of protein bar that tasted like chocolate dust held together by pressure. Dad didn't wake up or eat anything.

At 16:00 local time, the executive jet touched down on one of the very large runways at the Istanbul airport. We had just turned onto a taxiway when Reba popped her seatbelt and signaled to dad. The copilot came from the cockpit and stood by the door and folding ladder. Wilson and I moved seats to get a better view and strapped back in. The copilot gripped the hatch release waiting for a signal from the captain. The plane turned right, then left in between rows of hangers. "Now!" The pilot yelled.

The copilot yanked the hatch release down and the door unfolded. Reba shoved dad down the stairs. He paused for a second on the last step when she planted a firm kick knocking him from the ladder. On the bottom step, looking back at Wilson and I, she gave a salute and leapt to the moving ground. The copilot quickly raised the hatch and stairs, then gave the all-clear signal to the captain. The jet accelerated on the taxiway and turned around another hanger returning to the main taxiway. Wilson and I jumped to the side window in time to see Reba and dad running off toward one of the hangers.

"Let's hope Lisa's not late," Wilson said as we returned to our seats.

I opened the tracker display and had both Reba and dad on the screen between two of the hangers. In a few moments, they were moving rapidly behind the hangers as we continued taxiing toward the VIP holding area. I could see that Reba and dad were clear of the airport and heading down the motorway toward downtown Istanbul.

As the plane came to a stop, Wilson and I were met by two Turkish National Police officers and a team from the local consulate. One of the police officers drove the SUV that Wilson and I sat in.

The other officer followed in a rather plain sedan. As we pulled to a stop, the Para Palace stood before us in its neoclassical majesty. The hotel was built in the late 19th century to house passengers from the Orient Express and was the first hotel built to European standards in Istanbul. A smartly dressed woman stepped forward after recognizing the two national police officers. She introduced herself to Wilson as the hotel's acting General Manager and passed Wilson a key packet. We were on the third floor in the room next to the Agatha Christie Suite, where the famous author penned Hercule Poirot's adventure, The Orient Express. The room was exceptional with two beds, a sitting area, and a third roll-away bed placed probably for me. Once we were alone, I opened the tablet activating the tracking application. Wilson signaled me not to speak. Clearly, she perceived that the room was bugged probably by the national police.

There was a soft tap on the door. Wilson answered. A lean, muscular blonde woman stood outside looking both ways down the hall. She wore an elegant dress highlighting her figure. Silently, she signaled for Wilson and me to follow her. I grabbed my bag and tablet PC and walked two doors down. We were in another room much like ours but with a single king bed. Reba sat on the edge dangling her legs over the side.

"Hey, guys," Reba said.

"I see dad is in one of the corner rooms," I said pointing at the tablet display.

Wilson nodded. "Everything in position?" She asked the blonde woman. "Reba and JP meet Lisa Vandermeer."

"Hi," I said.

"Sarah, I never knew you to work with kids," Lisa motioned to me and Reba.

"They're kind of different," Wilson said. "Lisa is one of the best and most trusted Interpol agents I've had the pleasure to work alongside of. "

"Cool," I said.

"A real trick getting Detective Palmer and Reba off the plane that was," Lisa said.

"I'd much rather their identities stay out of the Turkish National Police field of view until the evening of the auction."

"Agreed," Lisa said. "The Turkish Police have made it clear that they believe our prime suspect is a saint and clean as could be."

"We have to go with what the evidence tells us." Wilson pointed to me. "I want JP to fix you up with a tracker. Just in case you both get separated."

I prepared one of the small 3 mm thick disks that fit inside a bandage strip. Lisa planned to wear a revealing evening gown to the auction and needed the tracker placed high on her thigh. Nervous as heck. I'd never touched a woman this high up on the leg. My hands shook as I peeled the adhesive off of the bandage and positioned the tracker disk in the center. Now I was sweating as well once Lisa pulled her dress up giving me a full view of her black high-waisted panties. She laughed as I quivered getting closer to putting the band aid on.

"Oh, good grief," Reba jumped up off the bed. "Give it to me." She grabbed the bandage, pulled Lisa's panties aside, and pasted the tracker just beneath the elastic. "Done." Reba stepped back.

"Lisa, here," Wilson continued, "will be with Stafford, I should say Mr. Talon, the whole time. She's going in as his personal assistant."

"And distraction," Lisa added putting one leg up on a chair and straightening her hosiery. I couldn't take my eyes off her and felt the beads of sweat forming on my forehead again.

"Agent Vandermeer has that part down," Reba said looking at me.

The three women laughed. I felt that unmistakable heat flood through my cheeks. This was so embarrassing.

#

Friday morning was the day of the auction. Wilson, Reba and I had breakfast in the hotel restaurant. Once we finished, we walked the few blocks up Belyoz alleyway from the Para to the busy Istikial Avenue and the Church of Saint Anthony of Padua, a large neo-gothic church nestled along a warm courtyard. Dad and Lisa stood by a statue of Pope John the 23rd just outside the church. Dad wore a smart suit, bright red necktie, starched white shirt and long black overcoat. She wore a fitted grey business suit with her blonde hair tied back in a bun and her perfect features highlighted by dark red lip gloss.

Wilson walked casually over to them and set a fat leather valise down, propped equal distance between herself and Lisa. Reba tapped me on the shoulder and pointed toward a bench at the front of the courtyard looking at the statue and grand entrance to the church. We walked over to the cement bench and sat. She took out her cell phone and began playing with it just like any teenage girl. I pulled out my tablet PC activating the tracking software. Afterall the darkened screen with the bottom half being a map and the upper two quadrants signal graphs illustrating gain, frequency, battery, and any other metric I chose, it looked like I was just being a teen geek playing an advanced game. I verified that the trackers concealed on both dad and Lisa broadcast strong signals and had full charges. Now it was time for a bit of an electronic concealment trick.

Assuming the bad guys wired radio detection capabilities in the auction site for devices broadcasting over open channels, I activated frequency hopping on all of my devices hidden on dad and Lisa. They'd now hop channels 30 times a second, and only my receiver knew the timing sequence

Reba watched over my shoulder as the graphs on my screen jumped and bounced. The tracker beacons appeared on a map along the lower half of the screen. The map zoomed into the church's courtyard identifying the trackers' exact position just outside the church.

"What is that?" Reba said pointing to the map and screen.

"An insurance policy," I said. Reba frowned. "I've activated a countermeasure. The devices dad and Lisa are wearing are synchronized to my tablet and laptop. I can read the signals from the trackers, but no one else will detect them."

"What about video and voice feeds?"

"Video is a problem. It only works if Lisa wears a big ugly and obvious broach with the camera. I think voice is a more important part and doable." I took out two black, elastomer cards that were just a wee-longer than a credit card but a couple millimeters thick. "They're sensitive radio transmitters with omni-directional stereo microphones on the edges," I said handing Reba one of the cards. "You take this one to Lisa and tell her to put it somewhere. I'll give mine to dad."

Not a moment later, the three adults stepped over to the bench where Reba and I sat. Now Lisa carried the brown leather valise. Wilson walked off leaving Dad in front of me, and Lisa over by Reba. "Dad, slip this beneath your belt buckle," I handed him the small rubber card.

"Like this?" He tucked it under the buckle of this belt.

"Yup. That will do." I tapped a few commands and paired the voice capture device to the app on my tablet and then activated frequency hopping on a slightly different timing scale. Even though none of us were speaking, the noise of people moving around the courtyard in front of the church was enough for the devices to capture and register sounds on my tablet.

Wilson glanced at us and I gave her a thumbs up. She immediately walked out of the courtyard, back to Istikial Avenue. Reba and I jumped up and followed. Wilson walked briskly down the center of the pedestrian mall that was the avenue while Reba kept close pace next to her. I nearly ran at a gentle trot trying to catch up with either of them. The women cut right down Belyoz Alley, disappearing from my sight. I ran harder. As I turned down the alley, I realized Wilson and Reba were standing back against the wall just beyond the alley entrance.

"Keep moving back to the hotel," Wilson said harshly as I slowed. I upped the pace moving quicker. Then a block later, slowed to a stroll. My heart pounded in my chest, and I panted catching my breath. I stepped onto the sidewalk on Meşrutiyet street where the Para Palace was located. I waited. No sign of the girls. I walked the block to the Para and went into the lobby where I sat just beyond the front reception. I took out my tablet and looked at the tracker locations. Dad and Lisa were still walking down Istikial Avenue, not far from where we left them. Reba's tracker crossed into the hotel. She walked next to Wilson. The two of them came into the lobby, walked right by me, not paying me even a glance. They were in the elevator and off to the 3rd floor. I waited for a bit, stowed my tablet in my backpack and followed into the next elevator up. In the room, Reba and Wilson sat on the two twin beds.

"All clear out there?" Wilson asked after I shut the door.

"Ah, yeah."

"Good. We have a few hours before your dad and Lisa need to make an appearance at the auction site. I'm going to take a nap. You two make yourselves scarce. But don't wander far from the hotel."

Reba jumped up, and we left Wilson behind in the darkened room.

\#

With Wilson down for a power nap, Reba and I walked to check out where the actual auction would take place this evening. I grabbed a shopping bag and stuffed a few technology items in it along with a new sweater. On inspection, this might look just like my shopping.

Although when we first planned this operation, we thought the auction would take place in the Para Palace's main ballroom. But it was actually being held in the Soho House, a building originally constructed as the Palazzo Corpi in 1882. The property had been bought by the US Government in 1907, then occupied between 1937 to 2003 by the Consul General of the US in Turkey. As we approached the building on the street side, Reba held her hand out stopping me.

"This place is just amazing," she said. "Do you realize that this was the first diplomatic premises owned by the US government in Europe?"

"Really?" I said as she snapped a picture and we walked toward the modest entrance.

"It's actually still owned by the US but leased to Soho House and Company."

"So, it's a hotel now?"

"Kind of," Reba said. "More than a hotel, a social club."

We stopped and admired the massive neoclassical building. Although only two stories atop a basement level, this structure was truly magnificent standing with very high ceilings along the great entry and halls.

"Let's check it out," Reba pulled me. We approached the valet and a security guard at the front entrance. The guard held up his hand stopping us.

"We're meeting Madam Solomon in the restaurant," Reba said.

The guard immediately straightened and held open the large metal door. "Through the Great Hall on the left," he said as we passed by.

"How did...?" I said.

"Just a lucky guess," Reba said as we passed by a second door and into the Great Hall. The frescoes depicted scenes from Roman and Greek mythology.

"Check that out," I said pointing toward a poster mounted on an easel announcing the auction. The easel stood in front of double doors along the right side of the great hall.

The unmistakable hyena laugh of Crystal's echoed through the hall. I felt the tingle of the hairs on my neck flair as we both moved to study a picture across the Great Hall. It was Crystal accompanied by three men wearing grey suits and looking quite nasty. She spoke to one of the men and laughed again. A grating high-pitched, rapid series of staccato "hee, hee, hee" sounds that piqued with a hiccup after each. It echoed so unmistakably through the Great Hall, making me wonder if a laugh could identify someone just like a fingerprint. I glanced over my shoulder watching as the group disappeared into the restaurant.

"Guess we're not going over there," I said.

"We never were," Reba said. "Let's see if we can find anything in the hall?"

She started off toward the door adjacent to the poster announcing the fifth annual charity art auction tonight. But I pulled her back.

"How about we check out whatever surveillance there is in the facility? I saw that the valet stand had a monitor with images from 6 cameras around the front perimeter of the building. Don't look up, but at both of the far corners of this Great Hall there are analog cameras pointing down from the roof. We kind of need to find the security control room and see if we can access this system."

"Okay," she said, "but for now, we will just snoop a bit in this place."

Reba grabbed the handle of the left side door that was labeled "theater" and pulled it open. We walked through a deep red-velvet corridor and into a theater that would rival any of the old Las Vegas showrooms. A stage was being set up along the front wall and several tech-type people scurried along it doing their jobs.

"Hey, you two," a voice called out from the side of the stage to us. "You can't be in here."

"We were just looking to see if there's a movie tonight," Reba said.

"Out!" The voice shouted.

I snapped a couple of pictures of the stage using the down volume button on my phone as best I could. Reba tugged my shoulder and we left the room.

"That was close," I said once we were back in the Great Hall.

"No, it wasn't." Reba grinned. "We're just stupid teenagers. They won't think anything of us. We can go places others can't because everyone thinks we're stupid."

We climbed downstairs after finding a side door in the Great Hall. It took us into the basement of the old consulate building and the dingy corridors of an area frequented by staff members only.

There were halls that led to all four corners of the building, including two elevators to the upper floors. By one of the elevators, there was a door marked 'Security Centre'. I stopped Reba as she reached for the doorknob and waved her back. In my other hand, I extracted an ultra-slim, 5.5-millimeter endoscope camera on the end of a snake tube. I L-shaped the bottom six inches of the tube and slid it beneath the closed door. The USB-C connection went into my mobile, and the screen showed a mouse-level view of the other side. "It's a hall with two doors at the end. One of the doors has a quarter glass panel in it. The other looks solid." I said.

Reba curtly nodded and pulled the door open. We were in. She stood just inside and carefully let the door shut behind us. Approaching the far door with the small glass panel in it, I could see two uniformed security guards seated inside. They faced a wall full of independent video monitors, most of which gave them static views from cameras covering entry points. A couple of the lower monitors had joysticks in front of them. One guard politely used the joystick to alter the view of a camera covering an outside patio and bar area.

I stepped back from the door looking at Reba and held up my flexible camera cord. "Let's see what's behind this other door." I stepped over to the door on the side of the hall that was shut and had no glass. Slipping my camera cord under the door gave me the mouse's view of the room. It was lined with a couple of racks of computer systems, each box with flashing green or yellow lights. "This is promising," I said.

"Any cameras inside?" Reba whispered. She still had eyes on the security control room in case one of the guards got up. I extracted the tiny camera and made a few adjustments to the tip, then reinserted it.

"Nothing obvious that I can see," I said. "There could still be a camera facing the door from inside one of the racks."

"Well," Reba rubbed her chin. "We'll have to risk it. That was clearly Crystal back in the hall with those men. We need to take a few chances." She pushed at the door. It was locked.

"Great," I said.

"Hold on." She held up her finger and extracted my lock pick set from her back pocket. "I've been practicing since our last case and have gotten pretty good."

"Are those mine?"

"You didn't miss them." She inserted the lever into the bottom half of the lock and started to rake with a tool in her other hand.

I moved to watch the guards. They sat working at their screens and occasionally making notes in a book. It didn't take Reba long to have the lever twist open the doorknob.

"Ta-dah," Reba said proudly opening the door and holding it for me to pass.

"Hey. It was barely more than a bathroom door lock," I said. "I think it took you way too long to get through it."

Reba rolled her eyes.

Inside the small server closet, I took a couple of pictures of the equipment. A single 24-port network switch was at the top of the rack and a network cable connected from there into a wire that dropped from the ceiling. There were two large analog DVR boxes with about forty coax cables coming in from the back wall behind the rack. Each of these was a feed from an analog camera.

I had a modified Linksys TP-Link WRT tap with me and decided I'd better install this. The device would connect in between an Ethernet cable and capture all traffic passing the connection. What I really wanted was to mount the tap so I could intercept all the camera feeds. Since both DVRs were hybrid devices converting the analog camera feeds to digital and then connecting to the switch, I needed to find a choke point where I could get the feeds from all the cameras. Correctly placed, I should be able to intercept the feeds from both DVRs leaving nothing to chance. This was a cold-war era analog to digital system that could have some significant challenges. Placing the tap was only one part of the problem. Software would be the next. Both DVRs were connected to ports on the switch. I really needed to tap the main feed from the switch that ran up through the ceiling along with 6 other Ethernet cables. My problem was which one since there were 6 cables running to the ceiling.

"I've got six wires and one tap with me," I said to Reba as we both stood behind the rack looking up at the wires. "Do you see the 6 or so wires that run from the switch into the ceiling tiles above?"

She nodded.

"It's a one in six probability that I pick

the correct wire to tap." I rubbed my finger over the first serval plugged in connectors that ran from switch ports labeled 0 to 5. "I figure one of these is the actual feed that goes into the rest of the network and outbound network. The others are probably connected to workstations driving those monitors in the security center."

"That's not very good odds," she said. "Hmmm. If you were the IT guy hooking this all up, where would you have plugged in the main feed?"

I patted my fingertip on the wire plugged into port 0.

"Then, pick that one," Reba said.

The WRT was a small 3 x 3" box that had a folding 120-volt connector. At the bottom of the rack, an APC power distribution unit was mounted. This device would convert and keep 120v-power clean for the devices. This was most convenient. I connected a single extension cord to an open US-style power port on the APC and threaded it up toward the switch. I then connected the TP-link and watched as the small LED on the side indicated the device was booting. A few years ago, I modified and flashed my own Linux OS onto this device that would operate the network captures as well as open a reverse shell to a cloud server. Assuming the hotel's firewall didn't have any real outbound filters, by the time the light on the TP-Link turned solid green, the shell connection should be established to my cloud server.

"Now for the tricky part," I said as I connected an Ethernet jumper to the tap. "I need to quickly plug this into the switch and TP- Link. As I unplug the wire in switch port 0, you plug this jumper from the TP-Link into the same port."

Reba held the black jumper wire, and I readied to unplug the wire in port 0. "Ready," Reba said.

"Go."

I unplugged the wire and snapped it into one of the TP-Link ports while Reba quickly plugged the jumper into that port. I held my breath watching all the little yellow lights come back on both the switch and the tap. The link lights immediately began flashing back to normal. The green lights twinkled as packets traveled. With a bit of tape, I packed the TP-Link out of sight and behind a bundle of wires on the rack. We both stood looking at one another in the silence of the room. The brief interruption would have been momentary and probably didn't change any of the operations in the security center. "We're clear," I said.

"Let's get out of here," Reba said heading toward the door. I packed my stuff away in the shopping bag and followed.

We made a quiet exit from the security center, back up the stairs into the Great Hall, and strolled out of the building. Outside, we thanked the security guard and valet then walked back to our hotel.

In the room, Wilson was still asleep on one of the queen beds as Reba and I snuck back in. I opened my laptop and logged into my cloud server. The reverse shell connection was open, and I logged into the tap. It was working perfectly. The remote SSH connection showed the network traffic being captured. I'd configured the system to allow me to pivot from my connection to the other systems on the internal network of the SOHO house security network. I extracted a portion of the PCAP files and ran them through Zeek, a tool that would quickly analyze the network packets identifying the hosts and types of connections. There were two connections generating a lot of traffic. These had to be the hybrid DVRs. Now I just needed a way to connect with a viewer.

Cordelia, back at school, would possibly know what tools I should use to connect directly to the DVRs through my tap. It was nearly midnight back in California, and I hoped Cordelia would still be up. I tapped out a message asking if she was still up. I gave a bit of a sigh and looked at Reba.

"What?" Reba whispered.

"I need to find a viewer. Did you snap a picture of the DVRs?"

She nodded and quickly showed me the image of one of the rack-mounted devices.

Cordelia answered my text. "Reba," I said, "send Cordelia the picture of the device."

Reba was quick sending the image as a text, and I followed asking her what sort of viewing software to use. I added that I had an SSH tunnel to the network.

Wilson stirred in the bed rolling over and then snapping upright. She looked around seeing both Reba and me at the computer. Wilson smiled, got up and went to the bathroom. A moment later the response came from Cordelia. She had identified a piece of software I could download and use to open the connection to the DVR. She asked for credentials to my cloud server just in case I had trouble. I provided it. Before I finished downloading and installing the tool, Cordelia came back and said she had images from 30 cameras on her screen. I ran the software connecting back through my SSH tunnel to the network and I had a screen with tiled camera displays on my laptop as well. Reba gave me a thumbs up. I set up the display to show the cameras in the theater and the Great Hall. There was a bit of a lag given the number of hops that the network traffic had to make, but we could clearly see what was going on.

Wilson emerged from the bathroom still fluffing her long black hair and had changed into a pair of jeans and black, Metallica world tour tee shirt. "What are you two up to?" She asked, walking up behind me and looking at the video images on my screen.

"We took a bit of a field trip," Reba said.

"What's on the screen?"

"We kind of installed a tap in the SOHO House security network and have access to all the hotel's camera systems," I said. "That's the theater where the auction will be held tonight."

"I would say that was a dangerous move

if you'd been caught."

"We weren't," Reba said.

"That's the Great Hall outside the theater where guests will arrive," I pointed at the screen. "The other two pictures are live from the cameras in the theater. One looks at the guests. This one at the stage. And I think this is the backstage wings."

"Nice."

We could see staff arranging plush chairs and a podium on the stage.

"We saw Crystal when we were there," Reba said.

"Did she see you?" Wilson said.

"Naw. She was laughing with that unmistakable hyena laugh and being escorted by three men into the restaurant."

"We went the other way," I added.

"Well, good. At least we know we're in the right place." Wilson pointed back to my laptop screen. "I'd be really pissed off that you guys did this, but I'll just say good job. Now, pack up your stuff. We're moving over to Lisa's room that is adjacent to the suite where your dad is."

#

Lisa's room was identical to ours. The three of us entered, and I started setting up my system on the desk. Lisa was dressed in a grey pant suit.

My laptop system reconnected and had the camera feeds back on the screen. People were moving around in the Great Hall, and the theater feed showed less activity. The stage had been set up and was cleared.

"That's cute," Lisa said looking at my laptop screen.

"We should be able to see everything going on inside the auction," I said while setting up my tablet PC next to my laptop. "With this, we can follow the trackers and hear everything from the microphones tucked in dad's belt."

"National police called," Lisa said turning to Wilson. "They'll put two detectives up here. Because there's some type of protest planned to happen out front of the SOHO House where the auction will be taking place, they'll have a lot of uniformed police out there as well. They're using this excuse to prep a tactical team to hit the auction site when we say so."

"Two detectives, here?" Wilson said.

"Think of them as controllers."

"Not observers?"

"The National Police inspector said this was their case and they were in control."

A phone ring erupted from my tablet. The sound was from dad's room. He answered the burner phone. "Fine," we heard dad say. "My secretary will obtain the funds. We can bring them over in the next few hours." A pause, then, "right. At least an hour before the auction."

We all looked at one another as the house phone by Lisa's bed chirped. She answered, listened and then said, "On my way.

Ten minutes. Meet me in the bar." Lisa

hung up the phone. "Thank goodness I planned for this contingency," she said picking up a duffle and flopping it on the bed. "Seems the auction people want a good-faith deposit before accepting bids from us." She unzipped the bag. That was more money than I'd ever seen. The bag was full of 100-pound notes wrapped in packets of 4,000 pounds each. They were sealed in plastic pouches. Lisa counted out three packets that she stuck in another brown leather valise. "They want 10,000 as a faithful deposit, but we'll give them 12 in three packets. Seems this is their standard procedure."

"How much do you have in there?" I asked.

"An even 100 thousand pounds, sweetie. Pulling 12, the rest of which I'll stash in the room. No touchy while I'm gone." Lisa crammed the remaining packets into the hotel room safe, then grabbed the valise.

"I have one more tracker here," I said holding it up. "I can hide it in the valise." I waved the credit card sized sleeves that held a tracker.

"No way," Lisa responded. "I guarantee you they will search this thing thoroughly. We know each note. Even though they're random, we have their serial numbers in our system. Anyone passing them will be in jail before you can say: so schnell du kannst."

So what? I thought.

"As fast as you can," Wilson said reading my thoughts.

Lisa snapped her forefinger like a toy gun at Wilson then turned and walked out of the room.

"Be safe," Wilson called as the door swung shut.

Reba glanced at Wilson, then looked back at me raising her eyebrows.

"Okay," I broke the silence. Let's see what we can monitor." I opened my laptop as both Wilson and Reba took positions on either side of me. My system showed the map and two glowing dots from dad and Lisa's trackers. They were together, still in the hotel. Probably down in the lobby. I set up my La Salle portable display on a stand next to my laptop and connected the HDMI cable and USB power. The monitor came to life extending my laptop's display. A bunch more keystrokes and I had the tunnels open to my cloud system and the SOHO hotel's DVR through my tap in the security network.

Camera images illuminated the second display. I chose the camera looking down at the length of the great hall. We could see people milling through the hall. A few examined the tapestries draped down the side walls while others moved with purpose to the front desk or restaurant entrance.

Reba drew Wilson's attention to the restaurant entrance. "That's where we saw Crystal this morning being escorted by three men."

"Mood? What was it?" Wilson asked.

Reba and I looked at one another. "Jovial, I'd say," Reba said.

I nodded agreement. "She walked as though she was leading them."

"Hmmm," Wilson thought for a moment. "Stockholm Syndrome possibly. She may have already suffered programming. And you're sure she didn't see you?"

"Look at the size of this hall," I said pointing at the display. "You can't see where we were because we were just to the left of the entrance by a large statue."

"We turned away once we saw her," Reba said.

"Let's hope we're not compromised," Wilson said. "Is that them?" She pointed to the camera scene as my dad and Lisa walked into view.

"Yes," I pointed to the other screen where the trackers reported their location in the SOHO Hotel. We watched as the two figures moved to the center of the great hall and stopped. They chatted together until a man approached them both.

"I wish we could hear them," Wilson

said.

I hit a couple of switches on the display and delayed voices appeared. The microphone and transmitter on dad's tracker broadcast everything via the frequency hopping and distance. Voices were delayed, but we eventually had it all.

"This way," the man said to dad and Lisa.

They followed him to the entrance of the theater and went inside. I switched to the theater camera, and they appeared walking through the rows of seats and up to the stage. They climbed up and walked to the backstage area, behind the dark crimson curtains.

I switched cameras again, toggling through all of the camera feeds. None were positioned to see the backstage area. We had audio from the microphone only.

"You brought the deposit?" the man said.

"Yes," Lisa said.

"Set it here while we count it."

We heard a light thud. Probably the valise being set on a table.

"You don't have to search for it," Lisa said. "12 thousand pounds in the main compartment."

No response from the man. Lisa was right that the man searched the entire valise.

"I'll take a receipt for that," my dad said.

"Not a problem," the man replied. "Nadya, will make one out to your bidder number. If you don't see anything you like, the money will be immediately returned."

"Fair enough."

Silence followed for a while. My heart raced as my mind envisioned all sorts of the bad things that could happen. We had no idea how many people were backstage or what was actually happening. They could grab the funds, decide to take both Lisa and dad and be done with them.

"Cheers, then," dad said breaking the silence. I took a deep breath.

Moments later, Lisa and dad appeared

from the backstage area and walked by themselves back through the center of the theater.

"We need a camera in the backstage. The hotel security only has a camera looking at the exit and rear door for the stage. Nothing else."

"I don't think you have time to plant one," Wilson said.

"I could ..." Reba said but was cut off by a wave of Wilson's hand.

"Too risky. You two have done enough. Now it's up to us."

16. EXTRACTION

Friday evening, we met up in Lisa's room and even dad was there. His outfit was a clean grey suit, white shirt, and tie. He had a large overcoat that he carried on his arm. Lisa looked like anything but an Interpol agent. In the role of his secretary, she wore a long gown with a near waste-high slit up the side highlighting her long nylon covered legs down to her white stiletto heels.

I checked that the tracker on dad was well hidden behind his belt buckle, its tiny microphones poking just above the waist. I fumbled a bit with the device and checked the output on the tracker application. "This is going to be dangerous," I said as I tucked the device a bit lower in his belt and pants. "Be safe in there. Mum will never let me live it down if anything happens to you."

"I'll be fine, son."

I turned to Lisa. "Now your tracker?" I asked examining her sleek dress and outfit. "Where is it?"

Lisa grinned and shook her head. "You're cute, you know that."

"Okay, I just want to make certain it's hidden."

She smiled again. "It's somewhere you won't be able to go and check it."

"Ah," I stepped back.

Reba laughed along with Wilson. "JP, women have places to hide things no men should go looking."

"Okay, then," I stammered a bit. "Guess we're ready."

"We should go," Lisa said. She led and dad followed her out the door.

I tested my laptop and the applications. I had full view of the video displays from the SOHO Hotel. As before, I had the full screen display on the great hall, leading to the theater entrance. I'd pre-selected a camera view for the theater and knew exactly which one I'd put on the screen.

We watched as the tracker signals moved out front of the Para Palace, turning right and heading the two blocks to the SOHO Hotel.

At that moment, there was a light knock on the door. Wilson answered and two suited men entered showing their credentials as they passed.

"What's this?" The older detective gestured toward Reba and me. "Children?"

"Specialists," Wilson replied.

The man gave a smirk. "We're here to monitor this situation and control our units."

"I've been briefed," Wilson said. "Let me

know if you plan to make a move."

"Sure." The two men sat at the end of the bed where they had a view of my computer screens. Reba and I sat in chairs while Wilson stood over us.

"They're inside," Reba said pointing to the screen. The image showed Lisa and dad walking casually through the great hall toward the theater entrance.

"Iyi akşamlar," a woman's voice addressed dad in Turkish. "English, please, love," dad said.

"Certainly. Good evening. Mr. Talon, I presume."

"That's right."

"Your bidding placard. Hold it up to lodge a bid."

"Cheers."

Dad passed the placard to Lisa and walked by the woman. An arrogant move, befitting a mobster, I was proud of dad's acting. But technology is what would make this all happen tonight. Not play acting.

A moment later, Lisa and dad appeared on the theater camera. They walked down the center aisle and occupied the first two chairs of the second row. I switched to a feed of a second camera that gave a full-stage view in the theater and split the viewing screen to show both the full theater and the stage only side by side.

"Please," one of the Turkish officers said, "may I ask which are your people?"

Wilson pointed to the two people seated in the second row. "The two people we followed into the Theater. That should be obvious."

The officer grinned. More of a smirk. "Thank you," he said.

A nicely dressed man, carrying a gavel, stepped up behind the podium on the left side of the stage. The gavel slapped down and the sound echoed on my speakers. "On behalf of our hostess most wonderful, I welcome you all to tonight's auction. All profits above the base value of the art object shall be contributed to helping house and educate orphan children. So be generous."

The first item, a painting was displayed on center stage. And a young girl stands next to the painting pointing at it with her arms. She's dressed in a modest white dress that highlighted the wheat-skin tone and long black hair. She looked all of 16 years old. The bidding concluded at nearly 12,000 Euros. The girl and painting were escorted into the backstage area by two men.

"I think those are the same men we saw earlier with Crystal," Reba said.

"Good to know," Wilson made a note.

The auction proceeded. With each item, a kid accompanied the art object. One of the men backstage led them onto the stage, positioned the item and pointed to where the kid should stand. The men dropped back to the side stage and watched the proceedings.

Some of the girls walked slowly, taking deliberate steps, as though they might be intoxicated or on drugs. A few of them drifted or shuffled their feet with each step. One boy dressed in a white cotton safari suit almost turned his ankle as he took a misstep near the art object. The escort grabbed him hard on the arm as the boy's face looked at the locked hand above his elbow, pain in his eyes. Several of the kids escorting art were Asian boys and girls.

The bidding was brisk, and we watched as several items were sold for less than 20,000 Euros each. A few of the art objects were handled by men wearing white lab coats and clean cotton gloves.

Before the next item, Madam Maja Solomon stepped onto the stage to a standing ovation and applause. Once the room quieted, she spoke softly, praising the audience for how wonderfully they were supporting her foundation. While she spoke, the two white coated workers placed a gorgeous landscape painting on the easel, and a dark-haired woman of Solomon's own stature wearing a fitted evening gown covered in sparkling rhinestones, presented the picture. Dad grabbed the placard from Lisa and bid on this item a couple of times.

"That's not Crystal," Reba said. "What's he doing?"

Wilson barked in a radio connected to an earbud in Lisa's ear, but Lisa never moved or spoke to dad.

Dad held his hand up in a position between him and Lisa, knowing our camera could see it and gave the Blah-Blah gesture. Four fingers strait, thumb below, and repeatedly snapped the fingers down toward the thumb.

Wilson let out an audible growl in the room. Fortunately, dad didn't win.

"Maybe he was just helping his cover," I said.

Wilson let out a rumbling growl to that.

The very next item was described as an intact Greek vase that was most likely used as a wine vessel. The vase was from the first century AD and required two men in lab coats to lift and place the large ornate vessel on the stand. Even with the resolution of the stage camera, I could make out the carving of Perseus holding the head of the gorgon Medusa before him. A blonde girl wearing a black satin gown complete with white gloves above her elbows, high heels and golden hair extensions down to her waist took a slow spin before standing next to the vase.

"That's her!" Reba exclaimed sitting up in her chair. Both the Turkish police officers stood behind us. Everyone watched the screen as Wilson relayed the message to Lisa.

The auctioneer read a card describing the vase and its lineage. He paused, losing his train of thought as he glanced over at Crystal. Probably boosted her ego, I thought. The auctioneer shook his head once and returned reading the card. He opened the bidding at 60,000 Euros. A Saudi Sheik poked his placard in the air, raising the stake to 65,000. An African man stood raising his placard high in the air, raising the bid to 70,000 Euros. The Saudi responded with 72,000 right away.

The African stayed standing and locked eyes on the Saudi. The contest was on, but dad wasn't involved yet. The African motioned to one of the staff standing on the left side of the stage. The African approached the stage acting as though he was inspecting the object. His stare wandered to Crystal, inspecting her from neck to toe. She returned with a bright smile and actually turned a bit so he could really see her.

The African went back to his seat and waved his hand that he was no longer interested.

"Not enough meat on those bones," Reba smirked. Wilson slapped the back of her head for the comment.

The Auctioneer called 72,000 once and then a second. Dad raised his placard, bidding 73,000. The Saudi's head snapped around to take in dad's face. We could only see the back of dad's head, so we didn't know what sort of expression he was making. I imagined that he was Daniel Craig as James Bond, giving his opponent a challenge. The Saudi raised the stakes to 80,000.

At that moment, the older of the two Turkish National Police officers in the room said, "enough of this." He barked a command into his radio.

"What are you doing?" Wilson shouted, confronting the officer. "The scene is not stable."

"This is a Turkish matter now."

Three Turkish commando units of 8-men each burst through the Great Hall and into the theater. Chaos ensued. Everyone in the theater stood and their hands were cuffed or bound with black plastic flexicuffs. One commando unit made it to the stage and grabbed one of the men from the side.

Wilson and the two Turkish police officers ran out of the room, leaving Reba and me alone.

"What now?" Reba asked.

"I actually don't know," I said. I scanned through the rest of the security cameras looking for any motion at all. No sign of Madam Solomon or Crystal. The police began marching the kids and models from the backstage area, and they even had Petrosyan in cuffs. No Crystal.

"This is really bad. We don't have trackers or any technology that will help."

"So, come on," Reba said. "We do this the old-fashioned way."

I grabbed my backpack with a tablet and a few other tech items, and we ran hard out of the Para Palace and down the street. Aside from the protest outside on the street, there were tons of police vehicles near the SoHo House Hotel. Reba and I were stopped by a police officer in riot gear from going into the hotel. He held us back and barked in Turkish, which neither of us could understand.

"We don't speak Turkish!" Reba shouted.

"You..." The officer said. "Now... Leave!"

He pointed back toward the Para.

"But our parents..." Reba said. "Leave!"

"This way," Reba said, pulling me back the way we came. The crowd of protesters were marching down the street carrying signs and ringing cow bells making even more noise. There were several hundred people in the street and the sidewalk area seemed reserved for press and media. We just dodged around news cameramen and reporters focused on the protest marching down the street. The road went down a gentle hill to a main thoroughfare that ran behind the back walls of the SoHo House Hotel. We ran fast down the hill. At the bottom, Reba stopped and I pulled up beside her huffing and puffing like a man with a lung disease.

"You're pathetic," Reba looked at me. "That was downhill. Come on." She walked quickly off to follow the back wall of the hotel. There were no entrances back here, so she kept moving. I followed along at a jog. When she moved quickly walking, I had to jog to keep up.

We stopped maybe 20 yards from the next intersection. "There are always escape tunnels that lead from consulate buildings, aren't there?" Reba said. She hadn't even broken a sweat, while I was bent over, hands on knees, panting away.

Across the next intersection, there was a hair salon and a kabob shop. The door to the salon swung open, and Maja Solomon, followed by one of the guys that had been onstage, dragged Crystal behind them onto the street. We ducked for cover against a stone wall and a small planter.

Sirens wailed as two police vans approached the intersection and swung up toward the protest and the front of the SoHo House Hotel. Maja walked briskly away from the intersection and down the street, stepping into another store.

"See if you can ring Wilson and let her know what we're seeing." Reba ordered.

I grabbed my cell phone and dialed the

number. After a few rings, it went straight to voice mail. "Wilson," I yelled into my phone. "We found them out back. Call me. J. P."

"What a mess," Reba said. "This may be up to us now."

A white Mercedes sedan passed us and the intersection stopped just outside the store where Maja and Crystal had gone inside.

Maja, holding Crystal by the wrist, stepped from the store and climbed in the back of the Mercedes E-class saloon car. The car started to pull into a very busy street and had to stop. Another police unit screamed by and pulled through the intersection climbing the hill up to the front of the SoHo Hotel. Two police motorcycle units followed. The Mercedes nudged a bit forward and honked the horn at a motorist that blocked them. That motorist gestured back with two fingers and slipped forward to block the Mercedes a bit more.

"Come on Wilson," I said. "We need wheels."

"I may have that covered," Reba pointed at a food delivery guy parking his scooter by the side of an apartment building next to the shop Maja exited. Reba pulled me along across the intersection toward the scooter that idled outside the building. Reba jumped on and balanced the scooter off its kickstand.

"Come on." She patted the seat behind her just in front of the orange box that has goodness knows whose food in it.

"Do you know how to drive one of these?" I jumped onto the seat.

"How hard can it be?" She revved the engine and let the clutch out. We were away. A bit wobbly, but away, nonetheless. Reba cut in front and in between cars crossing the 4-lane thoroughfare behind the SoHo House Hotel and the shop at the end of the escape tunnel. She cut through lanes of traffic. Ahead was the Mercedes sitting at a red traffic light. Reba navigated through a couple of cars and even used her hands to shove us forward off a few other cars. The traffic light changed to green, and the Mercedes lurched off the line. We were still a couple of cars behind as Reba twisted the throttle all the way. The scooter's motor whined.

"Shift gears," I yelled. "What?"

"Shift gears!"

"You want to drive?"

"Use this. Pull the clutch and twist one notch."

Reba did it and the motor settled as the scooter went faster. Instead of being passed by a wall of cars, we were actually passing them. The Mercedes was just ahead turning right onto another boulevard heading toward the waterfront.

The traffic light changed. Cars stopped blocking our exit to follow behind the Mercedes. Reba shifted down and took us up onto the sidewalk and followed around to the right down the same street. There were fewer cars on this street, and Reba accelerated down the road. She actually shifted to yet another gear, and we raced even faster down the road. As the road bent to the left, we could just see the taillights of the Mercedes ahead of us. We were unobstructed to our target. Reba revved the engine faster and put on more speed.

As we approached, the Mercedes's brake lights came on and slowed hard. "Hey, hey, brake!" I shouted.

Reba hit the scooter's brakes, and we slowed as the Mercedes swung right into a street that led a bit closer to the waterfront. This was the cruise terminal in Istanbul. A large shopping mall ran for a few blocks along the waterfront where cruise ships docked during the high tourist season. Right now, it was cold, rainy and wet. So, cruise ships were elsewhere in the Mediterranean. We couldn't follow down the side street that the Mercedes took, but we could see the sedan swing along an access road that went behind many of the stores beside the Galataport wharf. Supply trucks and tour buses would use that road when ships were in port.

Reba jumped the curb by one of the shopping center entrances and parked the scooter beside the building. I climbed off as she set the kickstand down and followed. The scooter fell over on its side as we stepped away and looked at one another. Reba shrugged and walked to the entrance of the shopping mall surrounding the Galataport. We passed through a security checkpoint and then ran toward the wharf.

Although cruise ships were not in port, a large yacht rest moored about 300 yards from where we stood. We ran toward the ship. Two crewmen winched a gangplank away from the side of the yacht. Other dock workers stood beside each of the lines holding the yacht to the dock. They all wore brightly colored vests. We ran harder as the dock hands released the yacht. The vessel sounded three sharp horn blasts signaling to any other boats in the area that engines were in reverse as the yacht pulled away. As we drew adjacent to the yacht, I could see Solomon and Crystal standing in a large parlor room on the vessel. Solomon raised a glass of champaign in a toast.

Reba grabbed her phone and snapped a photograph of the yacht and the two women in the large room.

The yacht sounded two more long blasts of its horn, pivoting the nose of the vessel to the dark waters of the Bosphorus. The yacht engines thrust forward as it slowly moved into the waters.

"Now what?" Reba shouted.

My phone rang, a call from Wilson. I answered explaining where we were and sharing my location with friend Wilson. Wilson advised that she was on the way with help, and we should sit tight.

Reba followed up, sending photos of the yacht and pictures of Solomon and Crystal on board.

The yacht cruised to the center of the Bosphorus, its bow turning toward the Black

Sea. The vessel was about a half mile out, still cruising slowly and keeping toward the right side of the channel. A Guiana-flagged tanker passed by the other direction, blocking our view as it lumbered toward the Mediterranean. Once it cleared, I could still see the yacht.

Sirens wailed down as three police cars pulled up behind the empty Mercedes left abandoned on a wharf access road. Wilson, Lisa and dad climbed out and rushed over to us. Reba pointed to the lights of the now distant boat out in the Bosphorus. "That's them," she said. "We saw them both on board."

"I wish I'd been close enough to put a tracker on that thing," I said.

"Not a problem, JP. Your tech has done its job up to now," Wilson said. The older Turkish National Police detective that had called the raid was on his radio. In a moment, two high-speed police boats raced past, their blue lights flashing, horns and sirens screaming. They cruised directly toward the yacht.

A third police vessel settled its twin engines and stopped alongside the wharf. Wilson, dad and the detective climbed down a ladder boarding the vessel. Reba jumped on the vertical ladder and slid holding the rail with her hands and feet and landed on the deck of the police boat while I carefully stepped down one rung at a time.

"These kids can't be here!" The officer complained.

Lisa, the Interpol Officer, slid down the ladder the same way Reba had done and landed cleanly with her high heels on the deck. "They're agents of Interpol," Lisa said snapping a quick wink to Reba.

"On you, be it then," the Turkish officer said. He then shouted orders to the boat's crew and the engines whined to maximum power sending the boat to a quick 30+ knots and us grabbing whatever we could to keep from getting flung off the back.

We slowed, approaching the yacht. The two other police boats were attached at the side of the yacht with armed police making their way through the yacht. As our boat neared the side of the yacht, 4 well equipped commando police officers stood near rope ladders ready to join their companions. Our boat touched the side of the yacht, and the commandos were off. They scampered up the ropes and were on the main deck. A hand signaled that all was clear.

"These kids stay here!" The Turkish detective shouted as he grabbed one of the rope ladders.

"Agreed," Wilson shouted back and then pointed her finger directly at us. "Sit. Stay! I mean it."

"Yes, ma'am," Reba and I said together.

"Do as she says guys," dad added as he hoisted his big body onto the rope ladder and up to the side of the main deck. We were left on the police boat as the engines shifted to reverse and pulled gently away from the yacht. Reba and I worked our way to the flying bridge of the police boat as its driver welcomed us.

The Bosphorus felt quite rough when the boat you're on was motionless and all you do is rock back and forth in the chop. We were back 50 or so feet off the yacht that loomed large before us. The radio cracked that the yacht was secure and they would offload prisoners.

The other two police boats took turns taking people on board. I could see the unmistakable dress of Madam Solomon as she climbed down to the police vessel and was clapped in handcuffs. I thought she actually stared directly at Reba and me from the other boat, sending a chill down my spine. I'd really made a new enemy.

In a moment, it was our turn. Dad, the detective, Lisa, and Wilson descended the ladder. They also had Crystal with them. Reba ran to Crystal. Crystal lashed out and slashed her palm against Reba's face dropping Reba to the deck. Wilson grabbed Crystal who then sobbed and cried aloud.

17. EPILOG - BACK AGAIN

I reclined in my chase, folding my journal shut as the last rays of sunlight sank into the Caribbean. This was by far one of the most emotional cases I'd ever worked.

Crystal's resistance to the rescue was a testament to their programming. Solomon and her thugs wasted no time brainwashing Crystal while they had her. From the moment she was taken on the yacht, Crystal adamantly claimed that she was there of her free will.

We took her back to the US on a military transport, and she cried through most of trip.

At one point, Crystal told of how frightened she was at first. She had been raped by multiple men, and her life was in real danger until Maja Solomon saved her. Crystal was dressed well, given the finest quarters and food, and treated like a visiting dignitary. Once she asked if she could go home, they threatened to take her out to a massage parlor and make her work.

Feeling lost, confused, without a passport, and hopeless, she surrendered. She was lavishly dressed, entertained in public, taken to theater, and told that a new passport and identity would be forthcoming.

It never came. She learned that she would be a model for an auction and instructed what she needed to do. She met some of the other girls and boys. They were not allowed to talk to one another. They all stayed at a big, luxury compound somewhere in the city.

On the plane, Reba sat next to her and consoled her. I remember how tender she was with Crystal, and Crystal really appreciated it. Little did she know what Reba and I went through to find and rescue her.

Somewhere over the mid-Atlantic, Wilson was called to the communications room. She looked entirely deflated as she returned. "What's up?" I asked.

"Solomon was taken to the marine police station on the Asian side. She was to be secured there before being transferred to the National Police headquarters. The detectives and investigators interviewed the other kids recovered from the SoHo raid. Solomon was in custody for maybe 3 hours before a suspected Russian extraction team hit the police station. Two officers were injured and Solomon escaped with the team."

"All of the other subjects arrested on the yacht," Wilson continued, "were assassinated by the extraction team. They were lined up and each shot in the back of the head."

"They didn't want them talking," dad

said.

Wilson sank into one of the aisle seats on the transport. "No. I thought we had the kingpin when we took down Solomon. I fear that someone else might be pulling the strings."

"One more thing," Wilson said. "The body of Mrs. Fadler was found in a ditch by the side of the highway running between Niagara and Toronto."

The biggest fish the FBI had was Petrosyan. They'd also had Toby for what that was worth. The goons and staff at the auction were clueless as to what was going on.

"This is far from over." I remember Wilson announcing on the plane. Even though all the money was recovered, Wilson stated that Interpol was beyond pissed off about the events in Turkey. The fact that the Turkish National Police housed Solomon in a marine substation and a "possible" Russian sponsored extraction team was able to release her and silence the other witnesses and subjects had them fuming.

After several weeks locked in a special Federal unit, Crystal returned to school. Reba was actually happy to see her. Believe it or not... Cordelia, Crystal and Reba became close friends for the rest of the term. Toby never returned. To make matters even better, Bobby returned concluding his long recovery. He had been in a unit to relearn how to walk as his motor skills were the absolute last to recover. He was really happy to find Reba and me. We helped him set up his dorm room right across from mine. Bobby became a part of our Fantastic 5 as we worked to bring him up to speed on the lessons he had missed. And believe it or not, Cordelia continued dressing like a normal kid, aside from the new nose ring she wore. The little witch had totally changed. Each weekend, our parents would visit the school, and the Fantastic 5 was always treated to something special.

Just as the skies darkened to nearly

black, the outline of a slender diver rose from the water, slipped off a pair of fins, and walked onto the beach stopping just in front of my cottage.

I took cover and peered out the window at the top of my door. My shoulder ached from the remnants of my injury that put me here originally. The diver still had on a partial wetsuit and diving hood. The diver peeled off the hood and stepped up to face the door of my cottage. I yanked the door open and jumped out telling the figure to freeze. The long flowing black mane that fell from under the hood threw me for a loop. Her deep black eyes looked right through me. It was Reba. Tears welled in my eyes as I stepped forward.

There was that grin as she raised her hand stopping me. "JP," she said, "you're far from being out of danger."

END – Jason will be back

DIGITAL SAFETY: What to do if you are targeted

If you or someone you know is being threatened with the release
of intimate images, the most important thing to know is:
This is not your fault, and you are not alone. The person
threatening you is a criminal, and there are ways to stop them.

STOP Communication Immediately:
Do not negotiate, do not plead, and do not pay. Paying or sending more
images never makes the threat go away; it only proves to the attacker
that their tactics work.

DO NOT Delete Anything:
It's tempting to hit delete to make it "disappear," but you need evidence.
Take screenshots of the threats, the username, their profile URL,
and any payment demands.

Block, Don't Delete, the Account:
Once you have your screenshots, block the attacker on all platforms.
Deactivating your own account temporarily is better than deleting it,
as it preserves data for law enforcement if needed.

Use "Hash" Technology:
There are tools (i.e. StopNCII.org) that can "fingerprint" your images and
alert social media platforms to block them from being uploaded or
shared, often before they even go live.

Tell a Trusted Adult:
This is the hardest step but the most effective. Whether it's a parent,
a teacher, or a counselor, bringing a "grown-up" into the situation
shifts the power balance back to you.

If you are in immediate danger, please contact your local emergency services (911 in the US, 999 in the UK).

NORTH AMERICA

NCMEC "Take It Down" (USA/Global): A free service to help people under 18 remove or stop the sharing of their explicit images. Website: TakeItDown.ncmec.org

CyberTipline (USA): To report the online exploitation of children. Website: MissingKids.org/CyberTipline | Phone: 1-800-843-5678

NeedHelpNow.ca (Canada): Guidance for youth to regain control of images and report incidents. Website: NeedHelpNow.ca

UNITED KINGDOM & EUROPE

CEOP Safety Centre (UK): The National Crime Agency's command for reporting online grooming or abuse. Website: ceop.police.uk

Childline (UK): Free, confidential support for anyone under 19. Phone: 0800 1111 | Website: childline.org.uk

AUSTRALIA & NEW ZEALAND

eSafety Commissioner (Australia): Australia's independent regulator for online safety. You can report image-based abuse directly here. Website: esafety.gov.au

Kids Helpline (Australia): 24/7 support for young people. Phone: 1800 55 1800

GLOBAL TOOLS

StopNCII.org: A tool for individuals over 18 (if the images were taken when you were an adult) to prevent the non-consensual sharing of intimate images on participating platforms like Facebook and Instagram.

To whomever is reading this.

We closed the door on the Dark Web, but in the digital world, every time you shut down one threat, another one boots up.

While I'm trying to get back to a "normal" life, I've started noticing things that don't add up. Glitches in the system that feel too... human. I'm picking up a trail that leads to something far more sophisticated than a simple hacker. This time, the enemy isn't just behind a keyboard; it might be the keyboard itself.

I'm starting to realize that when the intelligence is artificial, the danger is very real.

I'm diving into the deep end of the algorithm to find out who or what is pulling the strings. I'm going to need you ready for what's coming next.

Stay safe, stay skeptical, and remember:
Don't believe everything you see.

I'll see you in Book Three.

Happy reading,

Jason Palmer

From the Creators of The Digital Detective

The Digital Detective series is proud to be a project of Cloud 10 Studios, a creative house dedicated to telling stories that matter. Whether we are navigating the dangerous corners of the dark web or bringing holiday magic to life, our mission is to create content that inspires, educates, and entertains.

Support Our Next Big Adventure!

While Jason Palmer fights digital crime, another hero is preparing for his big-screen debut. We are in production on an animated project:

The Greatest Gift

Starring Christmasaur™

Step inside the branches of the world's most magical Christmas tree and meet Christmasaur, a dinosaur ornament on an epic journey to discover the true meaning of the holidays. Featuring a world-class team of animators and creators, this is a story for the whole family.

How you can help:

Visit the World at
www.christmasaur.com

Watch & Share:
Check out our
latest trailers and
sneak peeks on
YouTube: @Christmasaur

Learn more about our studio at:
www.cloud10studios.com

www.ingramcontent.com/pod-product-compliance
Lightning Source LLC
Chambersburg PA
CBHW071725150726
47998CB00005B/1511